AN EXPENSIVE
PLACE TO DIE

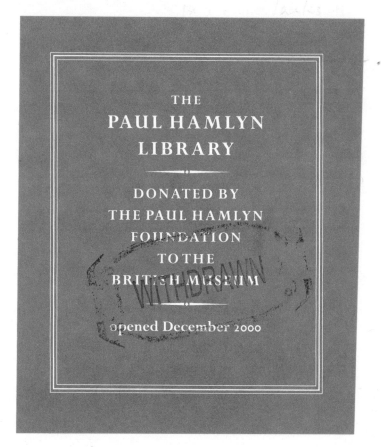

Len Deighton

AN EXPENSIVE
PLACE TO DIE

JONATHAN CAPE
Thirty Bedford Square London

FIRST PUBLISHED 1967

© COPYRIGHT 1967
VICO PATENTVERWERTUNGS-
UND VERMÖGENSVERWALTUNGS-G.M.B.H.

PRINTED IN GREAT BRITAIN
BY EBENEZER BAYLIS AND SON, LIMITED
THE TRINITY PRESS, WORCESTER, AND LONDON
ON PAPER MADE BY JOHN DICKINSON AND CO. LTD
BOUND BY A. W. BAIN AND CO. LTD, LONDON

*'Do not disturb the President of the Republic
except in the case of world war.'*
Instructions for night duty officers
at the Élysée Palace

---

*'You should never beat a woman,
not even with a flower.'*
The Prophet Mohammed

---

*'Dying in Paris is a terribly expensive
business for a foreigner.'*
Oscar Wilde

AN EXPENSIVE
PLACE TO DIE

1

The birds flew around for nothing but the hell of it. It was that sort of day: a trailer for the coming summer. Some birds flew in neat disciplined formations, some in ragged mobs, and higher, much higher, flew the loner who didn't like corporate decisions.

I turned away from the window. My visitor from the Embassy was still complaining.

'Paris lives in the past,' said the courier scornfully. 'Manet is at the opera and Degas at the ballet. Escoffier cooks while Eiffel builds, lyrics by Dumas, music by Offenbach. Oo-là-là our Paree is gay, monsieur, and our private rooms discreet, our coaches call at three, monsieur, and Schlieffen has no plans.'

'They're not all like that,' I said. Some birds hovered near the window deciding whether to eat the seed I'd scattered on the window-sill.

'All the ones I meet are,' said the courier. He too stopped looking across the humpty-backed rooftops, and as he turned away from the window he noticed a patch of white plaster on his sleeve. He brushed it petulantly as though Paris was trying to get at him. He pulled at his waistcoat—a natty affair with wide lapels—and then picked at the seat of the chair before sitting down. Now that he'd moved away from the window the birds returned, and began fighting over the seed that I had put there.

I pushed the coffee pot to him. 'Real coffee,' he said. 'The French seem to drink only instant coffee nowadays.' Thus reassured of my decorum he unlocked the briefcase that rested upon his knees. It was a large black case and contained reams of reports. One of them he passed across to me.

'Read it while I'm here. I can't leave it.'

'It's secret?'

'No, our document copier has gone wrong and it's the only one I have.'

I read it. It was a 'stage report' of no importance. I passed it back. 'It's a lot of rubbish,' I said. 'I'm sorry you have to come all the way over here with this sort of junk.'

He shrugged. 'It gets me out of the office. Anyway it wouldn't do to have people like you in and out of the Embassy all the time.' He was new, this courier. They all started like him. Tough, beady-eyed young men anxious to prove how efficient they can be. Anxious too to demonstrate that Paris could have no attraction for them. A near-by clock chimed 2 p.m. and that disturbed the birds.

'Romantic,' he said. 'I don't know what's romantic about Paris except couples kissing on the street because the city's so overcrowded that they have nowhere else to go.' He finished his coffee. 'It's terribly good coffee,' he said. 'Dining out tonight?'

'Yes,' I said.

'With your artist friend Byrd?'

I gave him the sort of glance that Englishmen reserve for other Englishmen. He twitched with embarrassment, 'Look here,' he said, 'don't think for a moment ... I mean ... we don't have you ... that is ... '

'Don't start handing out indemnities,' I said. 'Of course I am under surveillance.'

'I remembered your saying that you always had dinner with Byrd the artist on Mondays. I noticed the Skira art book set aside on the table. I guessed you were returning it to him.'

'All good stuff,' I said. 'You should be doing my job.'

He smiled and shook his head. 'How I'd hate that,' he

said. 'Dealing with the French all day; it's bad enough having to mix with them in the evening.'

'The French are all right,' I said.

'Did you keep the envelopes? I've brought the iodine in pot iodide.' I gave him all the envelopes that had come through the post during the previous week and he took his little bottle and painted the flaps carefully.

'Resealed with starch paste. Every damn letter. Someone here, must be. The landlady. Every damned letter. That's too thorough to be just nosiness. *Prenez garde.*' He put the envelopes, which had brown stains from the chemical reaction, into his case. 'Don't want to leave them around.'

'No,' I said. I yawned.

'I don't know what you do all day,' he said. 'Whatever do you find to do?'

'I do nothing all day except make coffee for people who wonder what I do all day.'

'Yes, well thanks for lunch. The old bitch does a good lunch even if she does steam your mail open.' He poured both of us more coffee. 'There's a new job for you.' He added the right amount of sugar, handed it to me and looked up. 'A man named Datt who comes here to Le Petit Légionnaire. The one that was sitting opposite us at lunch today.' There was a silence. I said,

'What do you want to know about him?'

'Nothing,' said the courier. 'We don't want to know anything about him, we want to give him a caseful of data.'

'Write his address on it and take it to the post office.'

He gave a pained little grimace. 'It's got to sound right when he gets it.'

'What is it?'

'It's a history of nuclear fall-out, starting from New Mexico right up to the last test. There are reports from the

Hiroshima hospital for bomb victims and various stuff about its effect upon cells and plant-life. It's too complex for me but you can read it through if your mind works that way.'

'What's the catch?'

'No catch.'

'What I need to know is how difficult it is to detect the phoney parts. One minute in the hands of an expert? Three months in the hands of a committee? I need to know how long the fuse is, if I'm the one that's planting the bomb.'

'There is no cause to believe it's anything other than genuine.' He pressed the lock on the case as though to test his claim.

'Well that's nice,' I said. 'Who does Datt send it to?'

'Not my part of the script, old boy. I'm just the errand boy, you know. I give the case to you, you give it to Datt, making sure he doesn't know where it came from. Pretend you are working for C.I.A. if you like. You are a clean new boy, it should be straightforward.'

He drummed his fingers to indicate that he must leave.

'What am I expected to do with your bundle of papers—leave it on his plate one lunchtime?'

'Don't fret, that's being taken care of. Datt will know that you have the documents, he'll contact you and ask for them. Your job is just to let him have them ... reluctantly.'

'Was I planted in this place six months ago just to do this job?'

He shrugged, and put the leather case on the table.

'Is it that important?' I asked. He walked to the door without replying. He opened the door suddenly and seemed disappointed that there was no one crouching outside.

'Terribly good coffee,' he said. 'But then it always is.'

From downstairs I could hear the pop music on the radio. It stopped. There was a fanfare and a jingle advertising shampoo.

'This is your floating favourite, Radio Janine,' said the announcer. It was a wonderful day to be working on one of the pirate radio ships: the sun warm, and three miles of calm blue sea that entitled you to duty-free cigarettes and whisky. I added it to the long list of jobs that were better than mine. I heard the lower door slam as the courier left. Then I washed up the coffee cups, gave Joe some fresh water and cuttlefish bone for his beak, picked up the documents and went downstairs for a drink.

2

Le Petit Légionnaire ('*cuisine faite par le patron*') was a plastic-trimmed barn glittering with mirrors, bottles and pin-tables. The regular lunchtime customers were local businessmen, clerks from a near-by hotel, two German girls who worked for a translation agency, a couple of musicians who slept late every day, two artists and the man named Datt to whom I was to offer the nuclear fall-out findings. The food was good. It was cooked by my landlord who was known throughout the neighbourhood as *la voix* — a disembodied voice that bellowed up the lift shaft without the aid of a loudspeaker system. *La voix* — so the stories went — once had his own restaurant in Boul. Mich. which during the war was a meeting place for members of the Front National.* He almost got a certificate signed by General Eisenhower but when his political past became clearer to the Americans he got his restaurant declared out of bounds and searched by the M.P.s every week for a year instead.

La voix did not like orders for *steck bien cuit, charcuterie* as a main dish or half-portions of anything at all. Regular customers got larger meals. Regular customers also got linen napkins but were expected to make them last all the week. But now lunch was over. From the back of the café I could hear the shrill voice of my landlady and the soft voice of Monsieur Datt who was saying, 'You might be making a mistake, you'll pay one hundred and ten thousand francs in Avenue Henri Martin and never see it come back.'

* Politically mixed but communist-dominated underground anti-Nazi organization.

'I'll take a chance on that,' said my landlord. 'Have a little more cognac.'

M. Datt spoke again. It was a low careful voice that measured each word carefully, 'Be content, my friend. Don't search for the sudden flashy gain that will cripple your neighbour. Enjoy the smaller rewards that build imperceptibly towards success.'

I stopped eavesdropping and moved on past the bar to my usual table outside. The light haze that so often prefaces a very hot Paris day had disappeared. Now it was a scorcher. The sky was the colour of well-washed *bleu de travail*. Across it were tiny wisps of cirrus. The heat bit deep into the concrete of the city and outside the grocers' fruit and vegetables were piled beautifully in their wooden racks, adding their aroma to the scent of a summer day. The waiter with the withered hand sank a secret cold lager, and old men sat outside on the *terrasse* warming their cold bones. Dogs cocked their legs jauntily and young girls wore loose cotton dresses and very little make-up and fastened their hair with elastic bands.

A young man propped his *moto* carefully against the wall of the public baths across the road. He reached an aerosol can of red paint from the pannier, shook it and wrote '*lisez l'Humanite nouvelle*' across the wall with a gentle hiss of compressed air. He glanced over his shoulder, then added a large hammer and sickle. He went back to his *moto* and sat astride it surveying the sign. A thick red dribble ran down from the capital H. He went back to the wall and dabbed at the excess paint with a piece of rag. He looked around, but no one shouted to him, so he carefully added the accent to the *e* before wrapping the can into the rag and stowing it away. He kicked the starter, there was a puff of light-blue smoke and the sudden burp of the two-stroke motor as he roared away towards the Boulevard.

I sat down and waved to old Jean for my usual Suze. The pin-tables glittered with pop-art-style illuminations and click-clicked and buzzed as the perfect metal spheres touched the contacts and made the numbers spin. The mirrored interior lied about the dimensions of the café and portrayed the sunlit street deep in its dark interior. I opened the case of documents, smoked, read, drank and watched the life of the *quartier*. I read ninety-three pages and almost understood by the time the rush-hour traffic began to thicken. I hid the documents in my room. It was time to visit Byrd.

*   *   *

I lived in the seventeenth arrondissement. The modernization project that had swept up the Avenue Neuilly and was extending the smart side of Paris to the west had by-passed the dingy Quartier des Ternes. I walked as far as the Avenue de la Grande Armée. The Arc was astraddle the Étoile and the traffic was desperate to get there. Thousands of red lights twinkled like bloodshot stars in the warm mist of the exhaust fumes. It was a fine Paris evening, Gauloises and garlic sat lightly on the air, and the cars and people were moving with the subdued hysteria that the French call *élan*.

I remembered my conversation with the man from the British Embassy. He seemed upset today, I thought complacently. I didn't mind upsetting him. Didn't mind upsetting all of them, come to that. No cause to believe it's anything other than genuine. I snorted loudly enough to attract attention. What a fool London must think I am. And that stuff about Byrd. How did they know I'd be dining with him tonight? Byrd, I thought, art books from Skira, what a lot of cock. I hardly knew Byrd, even though he was English and did lunch in Le Petit Légionnaire.

16

Last Monday I had dined with him but I'd told no one that I was dining with him again tonight. I'm a professional. I wouldn't tell my mother where I keep the fuse wire.

3

The light was just beginning to go as I walked through the street market to Byrd's place. The building was grey and peeling, but so were all the others in the street. So, in fact, were almost all the others in Paris. I pressed the latch. Inside the dark entrance a twenty-five watt bulb threw a glimmer of light across several dozen tiny hutches with mail slots. Some of the hutches were marked with grimy business cards, others had names scrawled across them in ball-point writing. Down the hall there were thick ropes of wiring connected to twenty or more wooden boxes. Tracing a wiring fault would have proved a remarkable problem. Through a door at the far end there was a courtyard. It was cobbled, grey and shiny with water that dripped from somewhere overhead. It was a desolate yard of a type that I had always associated with the British prison system. The concierge was standing in the court-yard as though daring me to complain about it. If mutiny came, then that courtyard would be its starting place. At the top of a narrow creaking staircase was Byrd's studio. It was chaos. Not the sort of chaos that results from an explosion, but the kind that takes years to achieve. Spend five years hiding things, losing things and propping broken things up, then give it two years for the dust to settle thickly and you've got Byrd's studio. The only really clean thing was the gigantic window through which a sunset warmed the whole place with rosy light. There were books everywhere, and bowls of hardened plaster, buckets of dirty water, easels carrying large half-completed canvases. On the battered sofa were the two posh English Sunday papers still pristine and unread. A huge enamel-topped table that Byrd used as a palette was sticky with patches of colour, and across one wall was a fifteen-foot-high hardboard construction upon which Byrd was painting a mural. I walked straight in — the door was always open.

'You're dead,' called Byrd loudly. He was high on a ladder working on a figure near the top of the fifteen-foot-high painting.

'I keep forgetting I'm dead,' said the model. She was nude and stretched awkwardly across a box.

'Just keep your right foot still,' Byrd called to her. 'You can move your arms.'

The nude girl stretched her arms with a grateful moan of pleasure.

'Is that okay?' she asked.

'You've moved the knee a little, it's tricky ... Oh well, perhaps we'll call that a day.' He stopped painting. 'Get dressed, Annie.' She was a tall girl of about twenty-five. Dark, good-looking, but not beautiful. 'Can I have a shower?' she asked.

'The water's not too warm I'm afraid,' said Byrd, 'but try it, it may have improved.'

The girl pulled a threadbare man's dressing-gown around her shoulders and slid her feet into a pair of silk slippers. Byrd climbed very slowly down from the ladder on which he was perched. There was a smell of linseed oil and turpentine. He rubbed at the handful of brushes with a rag. The large painting was nearly completed. It was difficult to put a name to the style; perhaps Kokoschka or Soutine came nearest to it but this was more polished, though less alive, than either. Byrd tapped the scaffolding against which the ladder was propped.

'I built that. Not bad, eh? Couldn't get one like it anywhere in Paris, not anywhere. Are you a do-it-yourself man?'

'I'm a let-someone-else-do-it man.'

'Really,' said Byrd and nodded gravely. 'Eight o'clock already, is it?'

'Nearly half past,' I said.

'I need a pipe of tobacco.' He threw the brushes into a floral-patterned chamber-pot in which stood another hundred. 'Sherry?' He untied the strings that prevented his trouser bottoms smudging the huge painting, and looked back towards the mural, hardly able to drag himself away from it. 'The light started to go an hour back. I'll have to repaint that section tomorrow.' He took the glass from an oil lamp, lit the wick carefully and adjusted the flame. 'A fine light these oil lamps give. A fine silky light.' He poured two glasses of dry sherry, removed a huge Shetland sweater and eased himself into a battered chair. In the neck of his check-patterned shirt he arranged a silk scarf, then began to sift through his tobacco pouch as though he'd lost something in there.

It was hard to guess Byrd's age except that he was in the middle fifties. He had plenty of hair and it was showing no sign of grey. His skin was fair and so tight across his face that you could see the muscles that ran from cheekbone to jaw. His ears were tiny and set high, his eyes were bright, active and black, and he stared at you when he spoke to prove how earnest he was. Had I not known that he was a regular naval officer until taking up painting eight years ago I might have guessed him to be a mechanic who had bought his own garage. When he had carefully primed his pipe he lit it with slow care. It wasn't until then that he spoke again.

'Go to England at all?'

'Not often,' I said.

'Nor me. I need more baccy; next time you go you might bear that in mind.'

'Yes,' I said.

'This brand,' he held a packet for me to see. 'Don't seem to have it here in France. Only stuff I like.'

He had a stiff, quarter-deck manner that kept his elbows at his waist and his chin in his neck. He used words like 'roadster' that revealed how long it was since he had lived in England.

'I'm going to ask you to leave early tonight,' he said. 'Heavy day tomorrow.' He called to the model, 'Early start tomorrow, Annie.'

'Very well,' she called back.

'We'll call dinner off if you like,' I offered.

'No need to do that. Looking forward to it to tell the truth.' Byrd scratched the side of his nose.

'Do you know Monsieur Datt?' I asked. 'He lunches at the Petit Légionnaire. Big-built man with white hair.'

'No,' he said. He sniffed. He knew every nuance of the sniff. This one was light in weight and almost inaudible. I dropped the subject of the man from the Avenue Foch.

Byrd had asked another painter to join us for dinner. He arrived about nine thirty. Jean-Paul Pascal was a handsome muscular young man with a narrow pelvis who easily adapted himself to the cowboy look that the French admire. His tall rangy figure contrasted sharply with the stocky blunt rigidity of Byrd. His skin was tanned, his teeth perfect. He was expensively dressed in a light-blue suit and a tie with designs embroidered on it. He removed his dark glasses and put them in his pocket.

'An English friend of Monsieur Byrd,' Jean-Paul repeated as he took my hand and shook it. 'Enchanted.' His handshake was gentle and diffident as though he was ashamed to look so much like a film star.

'Jean-Paul speaks no English,' said Byrd.

'It is too complicated,' said Jean-Paul. 'I speak a little but I do not understand what you say in reply.'

'Precisely,' said Byrd. 'That's the whole idea of English.

Foreigners can communicate information to us but Englishmen can still talk together without an outsider being able to comprehend.' His face was stern, then he smiled primly. 'Jean-Paul's a good fellow just the same: a painter.' He turned to him. 'Busy day, Jean?'

'Busy, but I didn't get much done.'

'Must keep at it, my boy. You'll never be a great painter unless you learn to apply yourself.'

'Oh but one must find oneself. Proceed at one's own speed,' said Jean-Paul.

'Your speed is too slow,' Byrd pronounced, and handed Jean-Paul a glass of sherry without having asked him what he wanted. Jean turned to me, anxious to explain his apparent laziness. 'It is difficult to begin a painting— it's a statement—once the mark is made one has to relate all later brush-strokes to it.'

'Nonsense,' said Byrd. 'Simplest thing in the world to begin, tricky though pleasurable to proceed with, but difficult—damned difficult—to end.'

'Like a love affair,' I said. Jean laughed. Byrd flushed and scratched the side of his nose.

'Ah. Work and women don't mix. Womanizing and loose living is attractive at the time but middle age finds women left sans beauty, and men sans skills; result misery. Ask your friend Monsieur Datt about that.'

'Are you a friend of Datt?' Jean-Paul asked.

'I hardly know him,' I said. 'I was asking Byrd about him.'

'Don't ask too many questions,' said Jean. 'He is a man of great influence; Count of Périgord it is said, an ancient family, a powerful man. A dangerous man. He is a doctor and a psychiatrist. They say he uses LSD a great deal. His clinic is as expensive as any in Paris, but he gives the most scandalous parties there too.'

'What's that?' said Byrd. 'Explain.'

'One hears stories,' said Jean. He smiled in embarrassment and wanted to say no more, but Byrd made an impatient movement with his hand, so he continued. 'Stories of gambling parties, of highly placed men who have got into financial trouble and found themselves … ' he paused ' … in the bath.'

'Does that mean dead?'

'It means "in trouble", idiom,' explained Byrd to me in English.

'One or two important men took their own lives,' said Jean. 'Some said they were in debt.'

'Damned fools,' said Byrd. 'That's the sort of fellows in charge of things today, no stamina, no fibre; and that fellow Datt is a party to it, eh? Just as I thought. Oh well, chaps won't be told today. Experience better bought than taught they say. One more sherry and we'll go to dinner. What say to La Coupole? It's one of the few places still open where we don't have to reserve.'

Annie the model reappeared in a simple green shirtwaist dress. She kissed Jean-Paul in a familiar way and said good evening to each of us.

'Early in the morning,' Byrd said as he paid her. She nodded and smiled.

'An attractive girl,' Jean-Paul said after she had gone.

'Yes,' I said.

'Poor child,' said Byrd. 'It's a hard town for a young girl without money.'

I'd noticed her expensive crocodile handbag and Charles Jourdan shoes, but I didn't comment.

'Want to go to an art show opening Friday? Free champagne.' Jean-Paul produced half a dozen gold-printed invitations, gave one to me and put one on Byrd's easel.

'Yes, we'll go to that,' said Byrd; he was pleased to be organizing us. 'Are you in your fine motor, Jean?' Byrd asked.

Jean nodded.

Jean's car was a white Mercedes convertible. We drove down the Champs with the roof down. We wined and dined well and Jean-Paul plagued us with questions like do the Americans drink Coca-Cola because it's good for their livers.

It was nearly one a.m. when Jean dropped Byrd at the studio. He insisted upon driving me back to my room over Le Petit Légionnaire. 'I am especially glad you came tonight,' he said. 'Byrd thinks that he is the only serious painter in Paris, but there are many of us who work equally hard in our own way.'

'Being in the navy', I said, 'is probably not the best of training for a painter.'

'There is no training for a painter. No more than there is training for life. A man makes as profound a statement as he is able. Byrd is a sincere man with a thirst for knowledge of painting and an aptitude for its skills. Already his work is attracting serious interest here in Paris and a reputation in Paris will carry you anywhere in the world.'

I sat there for a moment nodding, then I opened the door of the Mercedes and got out. 'Thanks for the ride.'

Jean-Paul leaned across the seat, offered me his card and shook my hand. 'Phone me,' he said, and—without letting go of my hand—added, 'If you want to go to the house in the Avenue Foch I can arrange that too. I'm not sure I can recommend it, but if you have money to lose I'll introduce you. I am a close friend of the Count; last week I took the Prince of Besacoron there—he is another very good friend of mine.'

'Thanks,' I said, taking the card. He stabbed the accelerator and the motor growled. He winked and said, 'But no recriminations afterward.'

'No,' I agreed. The Mercedes slid forward.

I watched the white car turn on to the Avenue with enough momentum to make the tyres howl. The Petit Légionnaire was closed. I let myself in by the side entrance. Datt and my landlord were still sitting at the same table as they had been that afternoon. They were still playing Monopoly. Datt was reading from his Community Chest card, '*Allez en prison. Avancez tout droit en prison. Ne passez pas par la case "Départ". Ne recevez pas Frs. 20.000.*' My landlord laughed, so did M. Datt.

'What will your patients say?' said my landlord.

'They are very understanding,' said Datt; he seemed to take the whole game seriously. Perhaps he got more out of it that way.

I tiptoed upstairs. I could see right across Paris. Through the dark city the red neon arteries of the tourist industry flowed from Pigalle through Montmartre to Boul. Mich., Paris's great self-inflicted wound.

Joe chirped. I read Jean's card. ' "Jean-Paul Pascal, artist painter". And good friend to princes,' I said. Joe nodded.

4

Two nights later I was invited to join the Monopoly game. I bought hotels in rue Lecourbe and paid rent at the Gare du Nord. Old Datt pedantically handled the toy money and told us why we went broke.

When only Datt remained solvent he pushed back his chair and nodded sagely as he replaced the pieces of wood and paper in the box. If you were buying old men, then Datt would have come in a box marked White, Large and Bald. Behind his tinted spectacles his eyes were moist, and his lips soft and dark like a girl's, or perhaps they only seemed dark against the clear white skin of his face. His head was a shiny dome and his white hair soft and wispy like mist around a mountain top. He didn't smile much, but he was a genial man, although a little fussy in his mannerisms as people of either sex become when they live alone.

Madame Tastevin had, upon her insolvency, departed to the kitchen to prepare supper.

I offered my cigarettes to Datt and to my landlord. Tastevin took one, but Datt declined with a theatrical gesture. 'There seems no sense in it,' he proclaimed, and again did that movement of the hand that looked like he was blessing a multitude at Benares. His voice was an upper-class voice, not because of his vocabulary or because he got his conjugations right but because he sang his words in the style of the Comédie Française, stressing a word musically and then dropping the rest of the sentence like a half-smoked Gauloise. 'No sense in it,' he repeated.

'Pleasure,' said Tastevin, puffing away. 'Not sense.' His voice was like a rusty lawn-mower.

'The pursuit of pleasure', said Datt, 'is a pitfall-studded route.' He removed the rimless spectacles and looked up at me blinking.

'You speak from experience?' I asked.

'I've done everything', said Datt. 'Some things twice. I've lived in eight different countries in four continents. I've been a beggar and I've been a thief. I've been happy and sad, rich and poor, master and manservant.'

'And the secret of happiness', mocked Tastevin, 'is to refrain from smoking?'

'The secret of happiness', Datt corrected, 'is to refrain from wishing to.'

'If that's the way you feel,' said Tastevin, 'why do you come to my restaurant almost every day?'

At that moment Madame Tastevin came in with a tray holding a coffee jug and plates of cold chicken and terrine of hare.

'There's your reason for not smoking,' said Datt. 'I would never let tobacco mar the taste of the food here.' Madame Tastevin purred with delight. 'I sometimes think my life is too perfect. I enjoy my work and never wish to do less of it, and I eat your wonderful food. What a perfect life.'

'That's self-indulgent,' said Tastevin.

'Perhaps it is—so what? Isn't your life self-indulgent? You could make far more money working in one of the three-star restaurants but you spend your life running this small one—one might almost say for your friends.'

'I suppose that's true,' said Tastevin. 'I enjoy cooking, and my customers appreciate my work I think.'

'Quite so. You are a sensible man. It's madness to go every day to work at something you do not enjoy.'

'But suppose', asked Madame Tastevin, 'that such a

27

job brought us a lot of money that would enable him to retire and then do as he wishes?'

'Madame,' said Datt. His voice took on that portentous, melodious quality that narrators on arty French films employ. 'Madame Tastevin,' he said again, 'there is a cave in Kashmir—Amarnath cave—the most sacred spot on earth to a worshipper of the Hindu god Siva. The pilgrims who journey there are old; sometimes sick too. Many of them die on the high passes, their tiny tents swept away by the sudden rainstorms. Their relatives do not weep. To them this does not matter; even the arrival— which must always be on a night of full moon—is not more vital than the journey. Many know they will never arrive. It is the journey that is holy, and so it is to Existentialists: life is more important than death. Whatever they do, men are too anxious to get to the end. The sex act, eating a fine meal, playing golf, there is a temptation to rush, gobble or run. That is foolish, for one should move at a relaxed pace through life doing the work one enjoys instead of chasing ambition helter-skelter, pursuing one's ultimate death.'

Tastevin nodded sagely and I stopped gobbling the cold chicken. Datt tucked a napkin in his collar and savoured a little terrine, pursing his lips and remarking on the salt content. When he had finished he turned to me. 'You have a telephone, I believe,' he said, and without waiting for my reply was already on his feet moving towards the door.

'By all means use it,' I told him and by a burst of speed was able to get upstairs before him. Joey blinked in the sudden electric light. Datt dialled a number and said 'Hello, I am at the Petit Légionnaire and I am ready for the car in about five minutes.' He hung up. Datt came over to where I was standing with Joey. 'It's my belief', said Datt, 'that you are making inquiries about me.'

I didn't answer.

'It would be a fruitless task.'

'Why?'

'Because no matter what you discover it will not harm me.'

'The art of Zen in clandestine behaviour?'

Datt smiled. 'The art of Zen in having influential friends,' he said.

I didn't answer him. I pushed open the shutters and there was Paris. Warm streets, a policeman, two lovers, four cats, fifty dented *deux-chevaux* cars and a pavement full of garbage bins. The life of Paris centres on its streets; its inhabitants sit at the windows gazing down upon people as they buy, sell, thieve, drive, fight, eat, chat, posture, cheat or merely stand looking, upon the streets of Paris. Its violence too centres upon the streets and outside the public baths the previous night M. Picard, who owned the laundry, was robbed and knifed. He died twitching his own blood into ugly splashes that could still be seen upon the torn election posters flapping from the ancient shutters.

A black Daimler came down the road and stopped with a tiny squeak.

'Thank you for the use of your telephone,' said Datt. At the door he turned. 'Next week I should like to talk with you again,' he said. 'You must tell me what you are curious about.'

'Any time,' I agreed. 'Tomorrow if you wish.'

Datt shook his head. 'Next week will be soon enough.'

'As you wish.'

'Yes,' said Datt. He walked out without saying good night.

After Datt left Joey took a brief swing. I checked that the documents were still in their hiding-place. Perhaps I should have given them to Datt a few minutes before, but

I looked forward to seeing him again next week. 'It seems to me, Joe,' I said, 'that we are the only people in town who don't have powerful friends.' I put the cover on him before he could answer.

5

Faubourg St Honoré, seven thirty p.m. Friday. The tiny art gallery was bursting at the seams. Champagne, free champagne, was spilling over high suede boots and broken sandals. I had spent twenty-five minutes prising triangular pieces of smoked salmon away from circular pieces of toast, which is not a rewarding experience for a fully grown human male. Byrd was talking to Jean-Paul and rapping at one of the abstract panels. I edged towards them, but a young woman with green eye-shadow grabbed my arm. 'Where's the artist?' she asked. 'Someone's interested in "Creature who fears the machine" and I don't know if it's one hundred thousand francs or fifty.' I turned to her but she had grabbed someone else already. Most of my champagne was lost by the time I got to Byrd and Jean-Paul.

'There's some terrible people here,' said Jean-Paul.

'As long as they don't start playing that dashed rock-and-roll music again,' said Byrd.

'Were they doing that?' I asked.

Byrd nodded. 'Can't stand it. Sorry and all that, but can't stand it.'

The woman with green eye-shadow waved across a sea of shoulders, then cupped her mouth and yelled to me, 'They have broken one of the gold chairs,' she said. 'Does it matter?'

I couldn't stand her being so worried. 'Don't worry,' I called. She nodded and smiled in relief.

'What's going on?' said Jean-Paul. 'Do you own this gallery?'

'Give me time,' I said, 'and maybe I'll give you a one-man show.'

Jean-Paul smiled to show that he knew it was a joke, but Byrd looked up suddenly. 'Look here, Jean-Paul,' he said severely, 'a one-man show would be fatal for you right now. You are in no way prepared. You need time, my boy, time. Walk before you run.' Byrd turned to me. 'Walk before you run, that's right, isn't it?'

'No,' I said. 'Any mother will tell you that most kids can run before they can walk; it's walking that's difficult.'

Jean-Paul winked at me and said, 'I must decline, but thank you anyway.'

Byrd said, 'He's not ready. You gallery chappies will just have to wait. Don't rush these young artists. It's not fair. Not fair to them.'

I was just going to straighten things out when a short thickset Frenchman with a Légion d'Honneur in his buttonhole came up and began to talk to Byrd.

'Let me introduce you,' said Byrd. He wouldn't tolerate informality. 'This is Chief Inspector Loiseau. Policeman. I went through a lot of the war with his brother.'

We shook hands, and then Loiseau shook hands with Jean-Paul, although neither of them showed a great deal of enthusiasm for the ritual.

The French, more particularly the men, have developed a characteristic mouth that enables them to deal with their language. The English use their pointed and dexterous tongues, and their mouths become pinched and close. The French use their lips and a Frenchman's mouth becomes loose and his lips jut forward. The cheeks sink a little to help this and a French face takes on a lean look, back-sloping like an old-fashioned coal-scuttle. Loiseau had just such a face.

'What's a policeman doing at an art show?' asked Byrd.

'We policemen are not uncultured oafs,' said Loiseau

with a smile. 'In our off-duty hours we have even been known to drink alcohol.'

'You are never off duty,' said Byrd. 'What is it? Expecting someone to make off with the champagne buckets?' Loiseau smile slyly. A waiter nearly passed us with a tray of champagne.

'One might ask what you are doing here?' said Loiseau to Byrd. 'I wouldn't think this was your sort of art.' He tapped one of the large panels. It was a highly finished nude, contorted in pose, the skin shiny as though made from polished plastic. In the background there were strange pieces of surrealism, most of them with obvious Freudian connotations.

'The snake and the egg are well drawn,' said Byrd. 'The girl's a damn poor show though.'

'The foot is out of drawing,' said Jean-Paul. 'It's not well observed.'

'A girl that could do that would have to be a cripple,' said Byrd.

Still more people crowded into the room and we were being pushed closer and closer to the wall.

Loiseau smiled. 'But a *poule* that could get into that position would earn a fortune on the rue Godot de Mauroy,' said the Chief Inspector.

Loiseau spoke just like any police officer. You can easily recognize them by their speech, to which a lifetime of giving evidence imparts a special clarity. The facts are arranged before the conclusions just like a written report, and certain important words—bus route numbers and road names—are given emphasis so that even young constables can remember them.

Byrd turned back to Jean-Paul: he was anxious to discuss the painting. 'You've got to hand it to him though, the *trompe l'œil* technique is superb, the tiny brushwork. Look at the way the Coca-Cola bottle is done.'

'He's copied that from a photo,' said Jean-Paul. Byrd bent down for a close look.

'Damn me! The rotten little swine!' said Byrd. 'It *is* a bloody photo. It's stuck on. Look at that ' He picked at the corner of the bottle and then appealed to the people around him. 'Look at that, it's been cut from a coloured advert.' He applied himself to other parts of the painting. 'The typewriter too, and the girl ... '

'Stop picking at that nipple,' said the woman with green eye-shadow. 'If you touch the paintings once more you'll be asked to leave.' She turned to me. 'How can you stand there and let them do it? If the artist saw them he'd go mad.'

'Gone mad already,' said Byrd curtly. 'Thinking chaps are going to pay money for bits cut out of picture books.'

'It's quite legitimate,' said Jean-Paul. 'It's an *objet trouvé* ... '

'Rot,' said Byrd. 'An *objet trouvé* is a piece of driftwood or a fine stone—it's something in which an artist has found and seen otherwise unnoticed beauty. How can an advert be found? How can you find an advert—the damned things are pushed under your noses every way you look, more's the pity.'

'But the artist must have freedom to ... '

'Artist?' snorted Byrd. 'Damned fraud. Damned rotten little swine.'

A man in evening dress with three ballpoint pens in his breast pocket turned round. 'I haven't noticed you decline any champagne,' he said to Byrd. He used the intimate *tu*. Although it was a common form of address among the young arty set, his use of it to Byrd was offensive.

'What I had,' interrupted Jean-Paul—he paused before delivering the insult—'was Sauternes with Alka Seltzer.'

The man in the dinner suit leaned across to grab at him, but Chief Inspector Loiseau interposed himself and got a slight blow on the arm.

34

'A thousand apologies, Chief Inspector,' said the man in the dinner suit.

'Nothing,' said Loiseau. 'I should have looked where I was going.'

Jean-Paul was pushing Byrd towards the door, but they were moving very slowly. The man in the dinner suit leaned across to the woman with the green eye-shadow and said loudly, 'They mean no harm, they are drunk, but make sure they leave immediately.' He looked back towards Loiseau to see if his profound understanding of human nature was registering. '*He's* with them,' the woman said, nodding at me. 'I thought he was from the insurance company when he first came.' I heard Byrd say, 'I will not take it back; he's a rotten little swine.'

'Perhaps,' said dinner-jacket tactfully, 'you would be kind enough to make sure that your friends come to no harm in the street.'

I said, 'If they get out of here in one piece they can take their own chances in the street.'

'Since you can't take a hint,' said dinner-jacket, 'let me make it clear … '

'He's with me,' said Loiseau.

The man shied. 'Chief Inspector,' said dinner-jacket, 'I am desolated.'

'We are leaving anyway,' said Loiseau nodding to me. Dinner-jacket smiled and turned back to the woman with green eye-shadow.

'You go where you like,' I said. 'I'm staying right here.'

Dinner-jacket swivelled back like a glove puppet.

Loiseau put a hand on my arm. 'I thought you wanted to talk about getting your *carte de séjour* from the Prefecture.'

'I'm having no trouble getting my *carte de séjour*,' I said.

'Exactly,' said Loiseau and moved through the crowd towards the door. I followed.

Near the entrance there was a table containing a book of newspaper clippings and catalogues. The woman with green eye-shadow called to us. She offered Loiseau her hand and then reached out to me. She held the wrist limp as women do when they half expect a man to kiss the back of their hand. 'Please sign the visitors' book,' she said.

Loiseau bent over the book and wrote in neat neurotic writing 'Claude Loiseau'; under comments he wrote 'stimulating'. The woman swivelled the book to me. I wrote my name and under comments I wrote what I always write when I don't know what to say—'uncompromising'.

The woman nodded. 'And your address,' she said.

I was about to point out that no one else had written their address in the book, but when a shapely young woman asks for my address I'm not the man to be secretive. I wrote it: 'c/o Petit Légionnaire, rue St Ferdinand, 17ième.'

'The woman smiled to Loiseau in a familiar way. She said, 'I know the Chief Inspector's address: Criminal Investigation Department, Sûreté Nationale, rue des Saussaies.'*

*   *   *

* France has a particularly complex police system. The Sûreté Nationale is the police system for all France that operates directly for the Minister of the Interior in the Ministry at rue des Saussaies. At Quai des Orfèvres there is the Prefecture which does the same job for Paris. There is also the Gendarmerie—recognized by their khaki coats in summer—who police the whole of France under the orders of the Army Ministry and are, in effect, soldiers. As well as this there are special groups—Gardes Mobiles and C.R.S. (Compagnie Républicaine de Sécurité) companies—which are highly mobile and have violent striking power. Loiseau worked for the first-named, the Sûreté Nationale, who as well as all standard police work also attend to counter-espionage, economic espionage (unions and potential strikes etc.), frontier policing and gaming. The sixty C.R.S. units are also controlled by one of the directorates (Public Security) of the Sûreté Nationale.

Loiseau's office had that cramped, melancholy atmosphere that policemen relish. There were two small silver pots for the shooting team that Loiseau had led to victory in 1959 and several group photos—one showed Loiseau in army uniform standing in front of a tank. Loiseau brought a large M 1950 automatic from his waist and put it into a drawer. 'I'm going to get something smaller,' he said. 'This is ruining my suits.' He locked the drawer carefully and then went through the other drawers of his desk, riffling through the contents and slamming them closed until he laid a dossier on his blotter.

'This is your dossier,' said Loiseau. He held up a print of the photo that appears on my *carte de séjour*. ' "Occupation," ' he read, ' "travel agency director".' He looked up at me and I nodded. 'That's a good job?'

'It suits me,' I said.

'It would suit me,' said Loiseau. 'Eight hundred new francs each week and you spend most of your time amusing yourself.'

'There's a revived interest in leisure,' I said.

'I hadn't noticed any decline among the people who work for me.' He pushed his Gauloises towards me. We lit up and looked at each other. Loiseau was about fifty years old. Short muscular body with big shoulders. His face was pitted with tiny scars and part of his left ear was missing. His hair was pure white and very short. He had plenty of energy but not so much that he was prepared to waste any. He hung his jacket on his chair back and rolled up his shirtsleeves very neatly. He didn't look like a policeman now, more like a paratroop colonel planning a coup.

'You are making inquiries about Monsieur Datt's clinic on the Avenue Foch.'

'Everyone keeps telling me that.'

'Who for?'

I said, 'I don't know about that place, and I don't want to know about it.'

'I'm treating you like an adult,' said Loiseau. 'If you prefer to be treated like a spotty-faced j.v. then we can do that too.'

'What's the question again?'

'I'd like to know who you are working for. However, it would take a couple of hours in the hen cage to get that out of you. So for the time being I'll tell you this: I am interested in that house and I don't want you to even come downwind of it. Stay well away. Tell whoever you are working for that the house in Avenue Foch is going to remain a little secret of Chief Inspector Loiseau.' He paused, wondering how much more to tell me. 'There are powerful interests involved. Violent groups are engaged in a struggle for criminal power.'

'Why do you tell me that?'

'I thought that you should know.' He gave a Gallic shrug.

'Why?'

'Don't you understand? These men are dangerous.'

'Then why aren't you dragging them into your office instead of me?'

'Oh, they are too clever for us. Also they have well-placed friends who protect them. It's only when the friends fail that they resort to ... coercion, blackmail, killing even. But always skilfully.'

'They say it's better to know the judge than to know the law.'

'Who says that?'

'I heard it somewhere.'

'You're an eavesdropper,' said Loiseau.

'I am,' I said. 'And a damned good one.'

'It sounds as though you like it,' said Loiseau grimly.

'It's my favourite indoor sport. Dynamic and yet

38

sedentary; a game of skill with an element of chance. No season, no special equipment ... '

'Don't be so clever,' he said sadly. 'This is a political matter. Do you know what that means?'

'No. I don't know what that means.'

'It means that you might well spend one morning next week being lifted out of some quiet backwater of the St Martin canal and travelling down to the Medico-Legal Institute* where the boys in butchers' aprons and rubber boots live. They'll take an inventory of what they find in your pockets, send your clothes to the Poor Law Administration Office, put a numbered armband on you, freeze you to eight degrees centigrade and put you in a rack with two other foolish lads. The superintendent will phone me and I'll have to go along and identify you. I'll hate doing that because at this time of year there are clouds of flies as large as bats and a smell that reaches to Austerlitz Station.' He paused. 'And we won't even investigate the affair. Be sure you understand.'

I said, 'I understand all right. I've become an expert at recognizing threats no matter how veiled they are. But before you give a couple of cops tape measures and labels and maps of the St Martin canal, make sure you choose men that your department doesn't find indispensable.'

'Alas, you have misunderstood,' said Loiseau's mouth, but his eyes didn't say that. He stared. 'We'll leave it like that, but ... '

'Just leave it like that,' I interrupted. 'You tell your cops to carry the capes with the lead-shot hems and I'll wear my water-wings.'

Loiseau allowed his face to become as friendly as it could become.

'I don't know where you fit in to Monsieur Datt's clinic,

* An old building on a prison site adjacent to Mazas Square near Austerlitz Station. It is used as a mortuary.

but until I do know I'll be watching you very closely. If it's a political affair, then let the political departments request information. There's no point in us being at each other's throat. Agreed?'

'Agreed.'

'In the next few days you might be in contact with people who claim to be acting for me. Don't believe them. Anything you want to know, come back to me directly. I'm 22.22.* If you can't reach me here then this office will know where I am. Tell the operator that "*Un sourire est différent d'un rire*".'

'Agreed,' I said. The French still use those silly code words that are impossible to use if you are being overheard.

'One last thing,' said Loiseau. 'I can see that no advice, however well meant, can register with you, so let me add that, should you tackle these men and come off best ... ' he looked up to be sure that I was listening, ' ... then I will personally guarantee that you'll *manger les haricots* for five years.'

'Charged with ... ?'

'Giving Chief Inspector Loiseau trouble beyond his normal duties.'

'You might be going further than your authority permits,' I said, trying to give the impression that I too might have important friends.

Loiseau smiled. 'Of course I am. I have gained my present powerful position by always taking ten per cent more authority than I am given.' He lifted the phone and jangled the receiver rest so that its bell tinkled in the outer office. It must have been a prearranged signal because his assistant came quickly. Loiseau nodded to indicate the meeting was over.

'Goodbye,' he said. 'It was good to see you again.'

* Senior police officers in France are assigned their own private lines.

'Again?'

'NATO conference on falsification of cargo manifests, held in Bonn, April 1956. You represented B.A.O.R., if I remember rightly.'

'You talk in endless riddles,' I said. 'I've never been in Bonn.'

'You are a glib fellow,' said Loiseau. 'Another ten minutes and you'd convince me *I*'d never been there.' He turned to the assistant who was waiting to conduct me downstairs. 'Count the fire extinguishers after he's left,' said Loiseau. 'And on no account shake hands with him; you might find yourself being thrown into the Faubourg St Honoré.'

Loiseau's assistant took me down to the door. He was a spotty-faced boy with circular metal-framed spectacles that bit deep into his features like pennies that had grown into the trunk of a tree. 'Goodbye,' I said as I left him, and gave him a brief smile. He looked through me, nodding to the policeman on sentry who eased the machine gun on his shoulder. Abandoning the *entente cordiale* I walked towards the Faubourg St Honoré looking for a taxi. From the gratings in the road there came the sound of a Métro train, its clatter muffled by four huddled *clochards* anxious for the warmth of the sour subterranean air. One of them came half-awake, troubled by a bad dream. He yelled and then mumbled.

On the corner an E-type was parked. As I turned the corner the headlights flashed and it moved towards me. I stood well back as the door swung open. A woman's voice said, 'Jump in.'

'Not right now,' I said.

6

Maria Chauvet was thirty-two years old. She had kept her looks, her gentleness, her figure, her sexual optimism, her respect for men's cleverness, her domestication. She had lost her girlhood friends, her shyness, her literary aspirations, her obsession with clothes and her husband. It was a fair swop, she decided. Time had given her a greater measure of independence. She looked around the art gallery without seeing even one person that she really desired to see again. And yet they were her people: the ones she had known since her early twenties, the people who shared her tastes in cinema, travel, sport and books. Now she no longer wished to hear their opinions about the things she enjoyed and she only slightly wished to hear their opinions about the things she hated. The paintings here were awful, they didn't even show a childish exuberance; they were old, jaded and sad. She hated things that were too real. Ageing was real; as things grew older they became more real, and although age wasn't something she dreaded she didn't want to hurry in that direction.

Maria hoped that Loiseau wasn't going to be violent with the Englishman that he had taken away. Ten years ago she would have said something to Loiseau, but now she had learned discretion, and discretion had become more and more vital in Paris. So had violence, come to that. Maria concentrated on what the artist was saying to her. ' ... the relationships between the spirit of man and the material things with which he surrounds himself ... '

Maria had a slight feeling of claustrophobia; she also

had a headache. She should take an aspirin, and yet she didn't, even though she knew it would relieve the pain. As a child she had complained of pain and her mother had said that a woman's life is accompanied by constant pain. That's what it's like to be a woman, her mother had said, to know an ache or a pain all day, every day. Her mother had found some sort of stoic satisfaction in that statement, but the prospect had terrified Maria. It still terrified her and she was determined to disbelieve it. She tried to disregard all pains, as though by acknowledging them she might confess her feminine frailty. She wouldn't take an aspirin.

She thought of her ten-year-old son. He was living with her mother in Flanders. It was not good for a child to spend a lot of time with elderly people. It was just a temporary measure and yet all the time he was there she felt vaguely guilty about going out to dinner or the cinema, or even evenings like this.

'Take that painting near the door,' said the artist. ' "Holocaust quo vadis?" There you have the vulture that represents the ethereal and … '

Maria had had enough of him. He was a ridiculous fool; she decided to leave. The crowd had become more static now and that always increased her claustrophobia, as did people in the Métro standing motionless. She looked at his flabby face and his eyes, greedy and scavenging for admiration among this crowd who admired only themselves. 'I'm going now,' she said. 'I'm sure the show will be a big success.'

'Wait a moment,' he called, but she had timed her escape to coincide with a gap in the crush and she was through the emergency exit, across the *cour* and away. He didn't follow her. He probably already had his eye on some other woman who could become interested in art for a couple of weeks.

Maria loved her car, not sinfully, but proudly. She looked after it and drove it well. It wasn't far to the rue des Saussaies. She positioned the car by the side of the Ministry of the Interior. That was the exit they used at night. She hoped Loiseau wouldn't keep him there too long. This area near the Élysée Palace was alive with patrols and huge Berliot buses, full of armed cops, the motors running all night in spite of the price of petrol. They wouldn't do anything to her, of course, but their presence made her uncomfortable. She looked at her wristwatch. Fifteen minutes the Englishman had been there. Now, the sentry was looking back into the court-yard. This must be him. She flashed the headlights of the E-type. Exactly on time; just as Loiseau had told her.

7

The woman laughed. It was a pleasant musical laugh. She said, 'Not in an E-type. Surely no whore solicits from an E-type. Is it a girl's car?' It was the woman from the art gallery.

'Where I come from,' I said, 'they call them hair-dressers' cars.'

She laughed. I had a feeling that she had enjoyed my mistaking her for one of the motorized prostitutes that prowled this district. I got in alongside her and she drove past the Ministry of the Interior and out on to the Malesherbes. She said,

'I hope Loiseau didn't give you a bad time.'

'My resident's card was out of date.'

'Poof!' she scoffed. 'Do you think I'm a fool? You'd be at the Prefecture if that was the case, not the Ministry of the Interior.'

'So what do *you* think he wanted?'

She wrinkled her nose. 'Who can tell? Jean-Paul said you'd been asking questions about the clinic on the Avenue Foch.'

'Suppose I told you I wish I'd never heard of the Avenue Foch?'

She put her foot down and I watched the speedometer spin. There was a screech of tyres as she turned on to the Boulevard Haussmann. 'I'd believe you,' she said. 'I wish *I*'d never heard of it.'

I studied her. She was no longer a girl—perhaps about thirty—dark hair and dark eyes; carefully applied make-up; her clothes were like the car, not brand-new but of good quality. Something in her relaxed manner told me that she had been married and something in her overt friendliness told me she no longer was. She came into the Étoile without losing speed and entered the whirl of traffic effortlessly. She flashed the lights at a taxi that was on a collision course and he sheered away. In the Avenue Foch she turned into a driveway. The gates opened.

'Here we are,' she said. 'Let's take a look.'

The house was large and stood back in its own piece of ground. At dusk the French shutter themselves tightly against the night. This gaunt house was no exception.

Near to, the cracks in the plaster showed like wrinkles in a face carelessly made-up. The traffic was pounding down the Avenue Foch but that was over the garden wall and far away.

'So this is the house on the Avenue Foch,' I said.

'Yes,' said the girl.

The big gates closed behind us. A man with a flashlight came out of the shadows. He had a small mongrel dog on a chain.

'Go ahead,' said the man. He waved an arm without exerting himself. I guessed that the man was a one-time cop. They are the only people who can stand motionless without loitering. The dog was a German Shepherd in disguise.

We drove down a concrete ramp into a large underground garage. There were about twenty cars there of various expensive foreign makes: Ford GTs, Ferraris, a Bentley convertible. A man standing near the lift called, 'Leave the keys in.'

Maria slipped off her soft driving shoes and put on a pair of evening shoes. 'Stay close,' she said quietly.

I patted her gently. 'That's close enough,' she said.

When we got out of the lift on the ground floor, everything seemed red plush and cut glass—*un décor maison-fin-*

de-siècle — and all of it was tinkling: the laughter, the medals, the ice cubes, the coins, the chandeliers. The main lighting came from ornate gas lamps with pink glass shades; there were huge mirrors and Chinese vases on plinths. Girls in long evening dresses were seated decorously on the wide sweep of the staircase, and in an alcove a barman was pouring drinks as fast as he could work. It was a very fancy affair; it didn't have the Republican Guard in polished helmets lining the staircase with drawn sabres, but you had the feeling that they'd wanted to come.

Maria leaned across and took two glasses of champagne and some biscuits heaped with caviare. One of the men said, 'Haven't seen you for ages.' Maria nodded without much regret. The man said, 'You should have been in there tonight. One of them was nearly killed. He's hurt; badly hurt.'

Maria nodded. Behind me I heard a woman say, 'He must have been in agony. He wouldn't have screamed like that unless he had been in agony.'

'They always do that, it doesn't mean a thing.'

'I can tell a real scream from a fake one,' said the woman.

'How?'

'A real scream has no music, it slurs, it ... screeches. It's ugly.'

'The cuisine,' said a voice behind me, 'can be superb; the very finely sliced smoked pork served hot, cold citrus fruits divided in half, bowls of strange hot grains with cream upon it. And those large eggs that they have here in Europe, skilfully fried crisp on the outside and yet the yolk remains almost raw. Sometimes smoked fish of various kinds.' I turned to face them. The speaker was a middle-aged Chinese in evening dress. He had been speaking to a fellow countryman and as he caught my eye he said, 'I am

47

explaining to my colleague the fine Anglo-Saxon breakfast that I always enjoy so much.'

'This is Monsieur Kuang-t'ien,' said Maria, introducing us.

'And you, Maria, are exquisite this evening,' said M. Kuang-t'ien. He spoke a few lines of soft Mandarin.

'What's that?' asked Maria.

'It is a poem by Shao Hsŭn-mei, a poet and essayist who admired very much the poets of the West. Your dress reminded me of it.'

'Say it in French,' said Maria.

'It is indelicate, in parts.' He smiled apologetically and began to recite softly.

'Ah, lusty May is again burning,
A sin is born of a virgin's kiss;
Sweet tears tempt me, always tempt me
To feel between her breasts with my lips.

Here life is as eternal as death,
As the trembling happiness on a wedding night;
If she is not a rose, a rose all white,
Then she must be redder than the red of blood.'

Maria laughed. 'I thought you were going to say "she must be redder than the Chinese People's Republic".'

'Ah. Is not possible,' said M. Kuang-t'ien, and laughed gently.

Maria steered me away from the two Chinese. 'We'll see you later,' she called over her shoulder. 'He gives me the creeps,' she whispered.

'Why?'

' "Sweet tears", "if she isn't white she'll be red with blood", death "between breasts".' She shook away the thought of it. 'He has a sick sadistic streak in him that frightens me.'

A man came pushing through the crowd. 'Who's your friend?' he asked Maria.

'An Englishman,' said Maria. 'An old friend,' she added untruthfully.

'He looks all right,' said the man approvingly. 'But I wished to see you in those high patent shoes.' He made a clicking sound and laughed, but Maria didn't. All around us the guests were talking excitedly and drinking. 'Excellent,' said a voice I recognized. It was M. Datt. He smiled at Maria. Datt was dressed in a dark jacket, striped trousers and black tie. He looked remarkably calm, unlike so many of his guests, his brow was not flushed nor his collar wrinkled. 'Are you going in?' he asked Maria. He looked at his pocket watch. 'They will begin in two minutes.'

'I don't think so,' said Maria.

'Of course you are,' said Datt. 'You know you will enjoy it.'

'Not tonight,' said Maria.

'Nonsense,' said Datt gently. 'Three more bouts. One of them is a gigantic Negro. A splendid figure of a man with gigantic hands.'

Datt lifted one of his own hands to demonstrate, but his eyes watched Maria very closely. She became agitated under his gaze and I felt her grip my hand tightly as though in fear. A buzzer sounded and people finished their drinks and moved towards the rear door.

Datt put his hands on our shoulders and moved us the way the crowd went. As we reached the large double doors I saw into the salon. A wrestling ring was set up in the centre and around it were folding chairs formed up in rows. The salon itself was a magnificent room with golden caryatids, a decorated ceiling, enormous mirrors, fine tapestry and a rich red carpet. As the spectators settled the chandeliers began to dim. The atmosphere was expectant.

'Take a seat, Maria,' said Datt. 'It will be a fine fight; lots of blood.' Maria's palm was moist in mine.

'Don't be awful,' said Maria, but she let go of my hand and moved towards the seats.

'Sit with Jean-Paul,' said Datt. 'I want to speak with your friend.'

Maria's hand trembled. I looked around and saw Jean-Paul for the first time. He was seated alone. 'Go with Jean-Paul,' said Datt gently.

Jean-Paul saw us, he smiled. 'I'll sit with Jean-Paul,' said Maria to me.

'Agreed,' I said. By the time she was seated, the first two wrestlers were circling each other. One was an Algerian I would guess, the other had bright dyed yellow hair. The man with straw hair lunged forward. The Algerian slid to one side, caught him on the hip and butted him heavily with the top of his head. The crack of head meeting chin was followed by the sharp intake of breath by the audience. On the far side of the room there was a nervous titter of laughter. The mirrored walls showed the wrestlers repeated all around the room. The central light threw heavy shadows under their chins and buttocks, and their legs, painted dark with shadow, emerged into the light as they circled again looking for an opening. Hanging in each corner of the room there was a TV camera linked by land-line to monitor screens some distance away. The screens were showing the recorded image.

It was evident that the monitor screens were playing recordings, for the pictures were not very clear and the action on the screen took place a few seconds later than the actual fighting. Because of this time-lag between recording and playing back the audience were able to swing their eyes to the monitors each time there was an attack and see it take place again on the screen.

'Come upstairs,' said Datt.

'Very well.' There was a crash: they were on the mat and the fair man was in a leg lock. His face was contorted. Datt spoke without turning to look. 'This fighting is rehearsed. The fair-haired man will win after being nearly throttled in the final round.'

I followed him up the magnificent staircase to the first floor. There was a locked door. Clinic. Private. He unlocked the door and ushered me through. An old woman was standing in the corner. I wondered if I was interrupting one of Datt's interminable games of Monopoly.

'You were to come next week,' said Datt.

'Yes he was,' said the old woman. She smoothed her apron over her hips like a self-conscious maidservant.

'Next week would have been better,' said Datt.

'That's true. Next week—without the party—would have been better,' she agreed.

I said, 'Why is everyone speaking in the past tense?'

The door opened and two young men came in. They were wearing blue jeans and matching shirts. One of them was unshaven.

'What's going on now?' I asked.

'The footmen,' said Datt. 'Jules on the left. Albert on the right. They are here to see fair play. Right?' They nodded without smiling. Datt turned to me. 'Just lie down on the couch.'

'No.'

'What?'

'I said no I won't lie down on the couch.'

Datt tutted. He was a little put out. There wasn't any mockery or sadism in the tutting. 'There are four of us here,' he explained. 'We are not asking you to do anything unreasonable, are we? Please lie down on the couch.'

I backed towards the side table. Jules came at me and Albert was edging around to my left side. I came back until the edge of the table was biting my right hip so I knew exactly how my body was placed in relation to it. I watched their feet. You can tell a lot about a man from the way he places his feet. You can tell the training he has had, whether he will lunge or punch from a stationary position, whether he will pull you or try to provoke you into a forward movement. Jules was still coming on. His hands were flat and extended. About twenty hours of gymnasium karate. Albert had the old *course d'échalotte* look about him. He was used to handling heavyweight, over-confident drunks. Well, he'd find out what I was; yes, I thought: a heavyweight, over-confident drunk. Heavyweight Albert was coming on like a train. A boxer; look at his feet. A crafty boxer who would give you all the fouls; the butts, kidney jabs and back of the head stuff, but he fancied himself as a jab-and-move-around artist. I'd be surprised to see him aim a kick in the groin with any skill. I brought my hands suddenly into sparring position. Yes, his chin tucked in and he danced his weight around on the balls of his feet. 'Fancy your chances, Albert?' I jeered. His eyes narrowed. I wanted him angry. 'Come on soft boy,' I said. 'Bite on a piece of bare knuckle.'

I saw the cunning little Jules out of the corner of my eye-He was smiling. He was coming too, smooth and cool inch by inch, hands flat and trembling for the killer cut.

I made a slight movement to keep them going. If they once relaxed, stood up straight and began to think, they could eat me up.

Heavyweight Albert's hands were moving, foot forward for balance, right hand low and ready for a body punch while Jules chopped at my neck. That was the theory. Surprise for Albert: my metal heelpiece going into his instep. You were expecting a punch in the buffet or a kick in the groin, Albert, so you were surprised when a terrifying pain hit your instep. Difficult for the balancing too.

Albert leaned forward to console his poor hurt foot. Second surprise for Albert: under-swung flat hand on the nose; nasty. Jules is coming, cursing Albert for forcing his hand. Jules is forced to meet me head down. I felt the edge of the table against my hip. Jules thinks I'm going to lean into him. Surprise for Jules: I lean back just as he's getting ready to give me a hand edge on the corner of the neck. Second surprise for Jules: I do lean in after all and give him a fine glass paperweight on the earhole at a range of about eighteen inches. The paperweight seems none the worse for it. Now's the chance to make a big mistake. Don't pick up the paperweight. Don't pick up the paperweight. Don't pick up the paperweight. I didn't pick it up. Go for Datt, he's standing he's mobile and he's the one who is mentally the driving force in the room.

Down Datt. He's an old man but don't underrate him. He's large and weighty and he's been around. What's more he'll use anything available; the old maidservant is careful, discriminating, basically not aggressive. Go for Datt. Albert is rolling over and may come up to one side of my range of vision. Jules is motionless. Datt is moving around the desk; so it will have to be a missile. An ink-stand, too heavy. A pen-set will fly apart. A vase: unwieldy. An ashtray. I picked it up, Datt was still moving, very slowly now, watching me carefully, his mouth open and white hair disarrayed as though he had been in the scuffle. The ashtray is heavy and perfect. Careful, you don't want to kill him. 'Wait,' Datt says hoarsely. I waited. I waited about ten seconds, just long enough for the woman to come behind me with a candlestick. She was basically not aggressive, the maidservant. I was only unconscious thirty minutes, they told me.

8

I was saying 'You are not basically aggressive' as I regained consciousness.

'No,' said the woman as though it was a grave short-coming. 'It is true.' I couldn't see either of them from where I was full length on my back. She switched the tape recorder on. There was the sudden intimate sound of a girl sobbing. 'I want it recording,' she said, but the sound of the girl became hysterical and she began to scream as though someone was torturing her. 'Switch that damn thing off,' Datt called. It was strange to see him disturbed, he was usually so calm. She turned the volume control the wrong way and the sound of the screams went right through my head and made the floor vibrate.

'The other way,' screamed Datt. The sound abated, but the tape was still revolving and the sound could just be heard; the girl was sobbing again. The desperate sound was made even more helpless by its diminished volume, like someone abandoned or locked out.

'What is it?' asked the maidservant. She shuddered but seemed reluctant to switch off; finally she did so and the reels clicked to a standstill.

'What's it sound like?' said Datt. 'It's a girl sobbing and screaming.'

'My God,' said the maidservant.

'Calm down,' said Datt. 'It's for amateur theatricals. It's just for amateur theatricals,' he said to me.

'I didn't ask you,' I said.

'Well, I'm telling you.' The servant woman turned the reel over and rethreaded it. I felt fully conscious now and I sat up so that I could see across the room. The girl Maria was standing by the door, she had her shoes in her hand and a man's raincoat over her shoulders. She was staring blankly at the wall and looking miserable. There was a boy sitting near the gas fire. He was smoking a small cheroot, biting at the end which had become frayed like a rope end, so that each time he pulled it out of his mouth he twisted his face up to find the segments of leaf and discharge them on the tongue-tip. Datt and the old maidservant had dressed up in those old-fashioned-looking French medical gowns with high buttoned collars. Datt was very close to me and did a patent-medicine commercial while sorting through a trayful of instruments.

'Has he had the LSD?' asked Datt.

'Yes,' said the maid. 'It should start working soon.'

'You will answer any question we ask,' said Datt to me.

I knew he was right: a well-used barbiturate could nullify all my years of training and experience and make me as co-operatively garrulous as a tiny child. What the LSD would do was anyone's guess.

What a way to be defeated and laid bare. I shuddered, Datt patted my arm.

The old woman was assisting him. 'The Amytal,' said Datt, 'the ampoule, and the syringe.'

She broke the ampoule and filled the syringe. 'We must work fast,' said Datt. 'It will be useless in thirty minutes; it has a short life. Bring him forward, Jules, so that she can block the vein. Dab of alcohol, Jules, no need to be inhuman.'

I felt hot breath on the back of my neck as Jules laughed dutifully at Datt's little joke.

'Block the vein now,' said Datt. She used the arm muscle to compress the vein of the forearm and waited a moment while the veins rose. I watched the process with interest, the colours of the skin and the metal were shiny and unnaturally bright. Datt took the syringe and the old woman said, 'The small vein on the back of the hand. If it clots we've still got plenty of patent ones left.'

'A good thought,' said Datt. He did a triple jab under the skin and searched for the vein, dragging at the plunger until the blood spurted back a rich gusher of red into the glass hypodermic. 'Off,' said Datt. 'Off or he'll bruise. It's important to avoid that.'

She released the arm vein and Datt stared at his watch, putting the drug into the vein at a steady one c.c. per minute.

'He'll feel a great release in a moment, an orgastic response. Have the Megimide ready. I want him responding for at least fifteen minutes.'

M. Datt looked up at me. 'Who are you?' he asked in French. 'Where are you, what day is it?'

I laughed. His damned needle was going into someone else's arm, that was the only funny thing about it. I laughed again. I wanted to be absolutely sure about the arm. I watched the thing carefully. There was the needle in that patch of white skin but the arm didn't fit on to my shoulder. Fancy him jabbing someone else. I was laughing more now so that Jules steadied me. I must have been jostling whoever was getting the injection because Datt had trouble holding the needle in.

'Have the Megimide and the cylinder ready,' said M. Datt, who had hairs—white hairs—in his nostrils. 'Can't be too careful. Maria, quickly, come closer, we'll need you now, bring the boy closer; he'll be the witness if we need one.' M. Datt dropped something into the white enamel tray with a tremendous noise. I couldn't see Maria now, but I smelled the perfume—I'd bet it was *Ma Griffe*, heavy and exotic, oh boy! It's orange-coloured that smell. Orange-coloured with a sort of silky touch to it. 'That's good,' said M. Datt, and I heard Maria say orange-

56

coloured too. Everyone knows, I thought, everyone knows the colour of *Ma Griffe* perfume.

The huge glass orange fractured into a million prisms, each one a brilliant, like the Sainte Chapelle at high noon, and I slid through the coruscating light as a punt slides along a sleepy bywater, the white cloud low and the colours gleaming and rippling musically under me.

I looked at M. Datt's face and I was frightened. His nose had grown enormous, not just large but enormous, larger than any nose could possibly be. I was frightened by what I saw because I knew that M. Datt's face was the same as it had always been, and that it was my awareness that had distorted. Yet even knowing that the terrible disfigurement had happened inside my mind, not on M. Datt's face, did not change the image; M. Datt's nose had grown to a gigantic size.

'What day is it?' Maria was asking. I told her. 'It's just a gabble,' she said. 'Too fast to really understand.' I listened but I could hear no one gabbling. Her eyes were soft and unblinking. She asked me my age, my date of birth and a lot of personal questions. I told her as much, and more, than she asked. The scar on my knee and the day my uncle planted the pennies in the tall tree. I wanted her to know everything about me. 'When we die,' my grandmother told me, 'we shall all go to Heaven,' she surveyed her world, 'for surely this is Hell?' 'Old Mr Gardner had athlete's foot, whose was the other foot?' Recitation: 'Let me like a soldier fall ... '

'A desire,' said M. Datt's voice, 'to externalize, to confide.'

'Yes,' I agreed.

'I'll bring him up with the Megimide if he goes too far,' said M. Datt. 'He's fine like that. Fine response. Fine response.'

Maria repeated everything I said, as though Datt could

not hear it himself. She said each thing not once but twice. I said it, then she said it, then she said it again differently; sometimes very differently so that I corrected her, but she was indifferent to my corrections and spoke in that fine voice she had; a round reed-clear voice full of song and sorrow like an oboe at night.

Now and again there was the voice of Datt deep and distant, perhaps from the next room. They seemed to think and speak so slowly. I answered Maria leisurely but it was ages before the next question came. I tired of the long pauses eventually. I filled the gaps telling them anecdotes and interesting stuff I'd read. I felt I'd known Maria for years and I remember saying 'transference', and Maria said it too, and Datt seemed very pleased. I found it was quite easy to compose my answers in poetry — not all of it rhymed, mind you — but I phrased it carefully. I could squeeze those damned words like putty and hand them to Maria, but sometimes she dropped them on to the marble floor. They fell noiselessly, but the shadows of them reverberated around the distant walls and furniture. I laughed again, and wondered whose bare arm I was staring at. Mind you, that wrist was mine, I recognized the watch. Who'd torn that shirt? Maria kept saying something over and over, a question perhaps. Damned shirt cost me £3 10s. and now they'd torn it. The torn fabric was exquisite, detailed and jewel-like. Datt's voice said, 'He's going now: it's very short duration, that's the trouble with it.'

Maria said, 'Something about a shirt, I can't understand, it's so fast.'

'No matter,' said Datt. 'You've done a good job. Thank God you were here.'

I wondered why they were speaking in a foreign language. I had told them everything. I had betrayed my employers, my country, my department. They had opened me like a cheap watch, prodded the main spring and laughed at its simple construction. I had failed and failure closed over me like a darkroom blind coming down.

Dark. Maria's voice said, 'He's gone,' and I went, a white seagull gliding through black sky, while beneath me the even darker sea was welcoming and still. And deep, and deep and deep.

9

Maria looked down at the Englishman. He was contorted and twitching, a pathetic sight. She felt inclined to cuddle him close. So it was as easy as that to discover a man's most secret thoughts — a chemical reaction — extraordinary. He'd laid his soul bare to her under the influence of the Amytal and LSD, and now, in some odd way, she felt responsible — guilty almost — about his well-being. He shivered and she pulled the coat over him and tucked it around his neck. Looking around the damp walls of the dungeon she was in, she shivered too. She produced a compact and made basic changes to her make-up: the dramatic eyeshadow that suited last night would look terrible in the cold light of dawn. Like a cat, licking and washing in moments of anguish or distress. She removed all the make-up with a ball of cottonwool, erasing the green eyes and deep red lips. She looked at herself and pulled that pursed face that she did only when she looked in a mirror. She looked awful without make-up, like a Dutch peasant; her jaw was beginning to go. She followed the jawbone with her finger, seeking out that tiny niche halfway along the line of it. That's where the face goes, that niche becomes a gap and suddenly the chin and the jawbone separate and you have the face of an old woman.

She applied the moisture cream, the lightest of powder and the most natural of lipstick colours. The Englishman stirred and shivered; this time the shiver moved his whole body. He would become conscious soon. She hurried with her make-up, he mustn't see her like this. She felt a strange physical thing about the Englishman. Had she spent over thirty years not understanding what physical attraction was? She had always thought that beauty and physical attraction were the same thing, but now she was unsure. This man was heavy and not young—late thirties, she'd guess—and his body was thick and uncared for. Jean-Paul was the epitome of masculine beauty: young, slim, careful about his weight and his hips, artfully tanned —all over, she remembered—particular about his hairdresser, ostentatious with his gold wristwatch and fine rings, his linen, precise and starched and white, like his smile.

Look at the Englishman: ill-fitting clothes rumpled and torn, plump face, hair moth-eaten, skin pale; look at that leather wristwatch strap and his terrible old-fashioned shoes—so English. Lace-up shoes. She remembered the lace-up shoes she had as a child. She hated them, it was the first manifestation of her claustrophobia, her hatred of those shoes. Although she hadn't recognized it as such. Her mother tied the laces in knots, tight and restrictive. Maria had been extra careful with her son, he never wore laced shoes. Oh God, the Englishman was shaking like an epileptic now. She held his arms and smelled the ether and the sweat as she came close to him.

He would come awake quickly and completely. Men always did, they could snap awake and be speaking on the phone as though they had been up for hours. Man the hunter, she supposed, alert for danger; but they made no allowances. So many terrible rows with men began because she came awake slowly. The weight of his body excited her, she let it fall against her so that she took the weight of it. He's a big ugly man, she thought. She said 'ugly' again and that word attracted her, so did 'big' and so did 'man'. She said 'big ugly man' aloud.

*   *   *

I awoke but the nightmare continued. I was in the sort of dungeon that Walt Disney dreams up, and the woman was there saying 'Big ugly man' over and over. Thanks a lot, I thought, flattery will get you nowhere. I was shivering, and I came awake carefully; the woman was hugging me close, I must have been cold because I could feel the warmth of her. I'll settle for this, I thought, but if the girl starts to fade I'll close my eyes again, I need a dream.

It was a dungeon, that was the crazy thing. 'It really is a dungeon,' I said.

'Yes,' said Maria, 'it is.'

'What are *you* doing here then?' I said. I could accept the idea of me being in a dungeon.

'I'm taking you back,' she said. 'I tried to lift you out to the car but you were too heavy. How heavy are you?'

'Never mind how heavy I am,' I said. 'What's been going on?'

'Datt was questioning you,' she said. 'We can leave now.'

'I'll show you who's leaving,' I said, deciding to seek out Datt and finish off the ashtray exercise. I jumped off the hard bench to push open the heavy door of the dungeon. It was as though I was descending a non-existent staircase and by the time I reached the door I was on the wet ground, my legs twitching uselessly and unable to bear my weight.

'I didn't think you'd get even this far,' said Maria, coming across to me. I took her arm gratefully and helped myself upright by clawing at the door fixtures. Step by difficult step we inched through the cellar, past the rack, pincers and thumbscrews and the cold fireplace with the branding irons scattered around it. 'Who lives here?' I asked. 'Frankenstein?'

'Hush,' said Maria. 'Keep your strength for walking.'

'I had a terrible dream,' I said. It had been a dream of terrible betrayal and impending doom.

'I know,' said Maria. 'Don't think about it.'

The dawn sky was pale as though the leeches of my night had grown fat upon its blood. 'Dawns should be red,' I said to Maria.

'You don't look so good yourself,' she said, and helped me into the car.

She drove a couple of blocks from the house and parked under the trees amid the dead motor cars that litter the city. She switched the heater on and the warm air suffused my limbs.

'Do you live alone?' she asked.

'What's that, a proposal?'

'You aren't fit enough to be left alone.'

'Agreed,' I said. I couldn't shake off the coma of fear and Maria's voice came to me as I had heard it in the nightmare.

'I'll take you to my place, it's not far away,' she said.

'That's okay,' I said. 'I'm sure it's worth a detour.'

'It's worth a journey. Three-star food and drink,' she said. 'How about a *croque monsieur* and a baby?'*

'The *croque monsieur* would be welcome,' I agreed.

'But having the baby together might well be the best part,' she said.

She didn't smile, she kicked the accelerator and the power surged through the car like the blood through my reviving limbs. She watched the road, flashing the lights at each intersection and flipping the needle around the clock at the clear stretches. She loved the car, caressing the wheel and agog with admiration for it; and like a clever lover she coaxed it into effortless performance. She came down the Champs for speed and along the north side of the Seine before cutting up through Les Halles. The last

* baby: a small whisky.

of the smart set had abandoned their onion soup and now the lorries were being unloaded. The *fortes* were working like looters, stacking the crates of vegetables and boxes of fish. The lorry-drivers had left their cabs to patronize the brothels that crowd the streets around the Square des Innocents. Tiny yellow doorways were full of painted whores and arguing men in *bleu de travail*. Maria drove carefully through the narrow streets.

'You've seen this district before?' she asked.

'No,' I said, because I had a feeling that she wanted me to say that. I had a feeling that she got some strange titillation from bringing me this way to her home. 'Ten new francs,' she said, nodding towards two girls standing outside a dingy café. 'Perhaps seven if you argued.'

'The two?'

'Maybe twelve if you wanted the two. More for an exhibition.'

She turned to me. 'You are shocked.'

'I'm only shocked that you want me to be shocked,' I said.

She bit her lip and turned on to the Sebastopol and speeded out of the district. It was three minutes before she spoke again. 'You are good for me,' she said.

I wasn't sure she was right but I didn't argue.

That early in the morning the street in which Maria lived was little different from any other street in Paris; the shutters were slammed tight and not a glint of glass or ruffle of curtain was visible anywhere. The walls were colourless and expressionless as though every house in the street was mourning a family death. The ancient crumbling streets of Paris were distinguished socially only by the motor cars parked along the gutters. Here the R4s, corrugated *deux chevaux* and dented Dauphines were outnumbered by shiny new Jags, Buicks and Mercs.

Inside, the carpets were deep, the hangings lush, the

64

fittings shiny and the chairs soft. And there was that symbol of status and influence: a phone. I bathed in hot perfumed water and sipped aromatic broth, I was tucked into crisp sheets, my memories faded and I slept a long dreamless sleep.

When I awoke the radio was playing Françoise Hardy in the next room and Maria was sitting on the bed. She looked at me as I stirred. She had changed into a pink cotton dress and was wearing little or no make-up. Her hair was loose and combed to a simple parting in that messy way that takes a couple of hours of hairdressing expertise. Her face was kind but had the sort of wrinkles that come when you have smiled cynically about ten million times. Her mouth was small and slightly open like a doll, or like a woman expecting a kiss.

'What time is it?' I asked.

'It's past midnight,' she said. 'You've slept the clock round.'

'Get this bed on the road. What's wrong, have we run out of feathers?'

'We ran out of bedclothes; they are all around you.'

'Fill her up with bedclothes mister and if we forget to check the electric blanket you get a bolster free.'

'I'm busy making coffee. I've no time to play your games.'

She made coffee and brought it. She waited for me to ask questions and then she answered deftly, telling me as much as she wished without seeming evasive.

'I had a nightmare and awoke in a medieval dungeon.'

'You did,' said Maria.

'You'd better tell me all about it,' I said.

'Datt was terrified that you were spying on him. He said you have documents he wants. He said you had been making inquiries so he had to know.'

'What did he do to me?'

c   65

'He injected you with Amytal and LSD (it's the LSD that takes time to wear off). I questioned you. Then you went into a deep sleep and awoke in the cellars of the house. I brought you here.'

'What did I say?'

'Don't worry. None of those people speak English. I'm the only one that does. Your secrets are safe with me. Datt usually thinks of everything, but he was disconcerted when you babbled away in English. I translated.'

So that was why I'd heard her say everything twice. 'What did I say?'

'Relax. It didn't interest me but I satisfied Datt.'

I said, 'And don't think I don't appreciate it, but why should you do that for me?'

'Datt is a hateful man. I would never help him, and anyway, I took you to that house, I felt responsible for you.'

'And … ?'

'If I had told him what you really said he would have undoubtedly used amphetamine on you, to discover more and more. Amphetamine is dangerous stuff, horrible. I wouldn't have enjoyed watching that.'

'Thanks,' I said. I reached towards her, took her hand, and she lay down on the bed at my side. She did it without suspicion or arch looks, it was a friendly, rather than a sexual gesture. She lit a cigarette and gave me the packet and matches. 'Light it yourself,' she said. 'It will give you something to do with your hands.'

'What did I say?' I asked casually. 'What did I say that you didn't translate into French for Datt?'

'Nothing,' Maria said immediately. 'Not because you said nothing, but because I didn't hear it. Understand? I'm not interested in what you are or how you earn your living. If you are doing something that's illegal or dangerous, that's your worry. Just for the moment I feel a little responsible for you, but I've nearly worked off that
66

feeling. Tomorrow you can start telling your own lies and I'm sure you will do it remarkably well.'

'Is that a brush-off?'

She turned to me. 'No,' she said. She leaned over and kissed me.

'You smell delicious,' I said. 'What is it you're wearing?'

'Agony,' she said. 'It's an expensive perfume, but there are few humans not attracted to it.'

I tried to decide whether she was geeing me up, but I couldn't tell. She wasn't the sort of girl who'd help you by smiling, either.

She got off the bed and smoothed her dress over her hips.

'Do you like this dress?' she asked.

'It's great,' I said.

'What sort of clothes do you like to see women in?'

'Aprons,' I said. 'Fingers a-shine with those marks you get from handling hot dishes.'

'Yes, I can imagine,' she said. She stubbed out her cigarette.

'I'll help you if you want help but don't ask too much, and remember that I am involved with these people and I have only one passport and it's French.'

I wondered if that was a hint about what I'd revealed under the drugs, but I said nothing.

She looked at her wristwatch. 'It's very late,' she said. She looked at me quizzically. 'There's only one bed and I need my sleep.' I had been thinking of having a cigarette but I replaced them on the side table. I moved aside. 'Share the bed,' I invited, 'but I can't guarantee sleep.'

'Don't pull the Jean-Paul lover-boy stuff,' she said, 'it's not your style.' She grabbed at the cotton dress and pulled it over her head.

'What is my style?' I asked irritably.

'Check with me in the morning,' she said, and put the light out. She left only the radio on.

10

I stayed in Maria's flat but the next afternoon Maria went back to my rooms to feed Joey. She got back before the storm. She came in blowing on her hands and complaining of the cold.

'Did you change the water and put the cuttlefish bone in?' I asked.

'Yes,' she said.

'It's good for his beak,' I said.

'I know,' she said. She stood by the window looking out over the fast-darkening boulevard. 'It's primitive,' she said without turning away from the window. 'The sky gets dark and the wind begins to lift hats and boxes and finally dustbin lids, and you start to think this is the way the world will end.'

'I think politicians have other plans for ending the world,' I said.

'The rain is beginning. Huge spots, like rain for giants. Imagine being an ant hit by a ... '

The phone rang. ' ... raindrop like that.' Maria finished the sentence hurriedly and picked up the phone.

She picked it up as though it was a gun that might explode by accident. 'Yes,' she said suspiciously. 'He's here.' She listened, nodding, and saying 'yes'. 'The walk will do him good,' she said. 'We'll be there in about an hour.' She pulled an agonized face at me. 'Yes,' she said to the phone again. 'Well you must just whisper to him and then I won't hear your little secrets, will I?' There was a little gabble of electronic indignation, then Maria said, 'We'll get ready now or we'll be late,' and firmly replaced the receiver. 'Byrd,' she said. 'Your countryman Mr Martin Langley Byrd craves a word with you at the Café Blanc.' The noise of rain was like a vast crowd applauding frantically.

'Byrd,' I explained, 'is the man who was with me at the art gallery. The art people think a lot of him.'

'So he was telling me,' said Maria.

'Oh, he's all right,' I said. 'An ex-naval officer who becomes a bohemian is bound to be a little odd.'

'Jean-Paul likes him,' said Maria, as though it was the epitome of accolades. I climbed into my newly washed underwear and wrinkled suit. Maria discovered a tiny mauve razor and I shaved millimetre by millimetre and swamped the cuts with cologne. We left Maria's just as the rain shower ended. The concierge was picking up the potted plants that had been standing on the pavement.

'You are not taking a raincoat?' she asked Maria.

'No,' said Maria.

'Perhaps you'll only be out for a few minutes,' said the concierge. She pushed her glasses against the bridge of her nose and peered at me.

'Perhaps,' said Maria, and took my arm to walk away.

'It will rain again,' called the concierge.

'Yes,' said Maria.

'Heavily,' called the concierge. She picked up another pot and prodded the earth in it.

Summer rain is cleaner than winter rain. Winter rain strikes hard upon the granite, but summer rain is sibilant soft upon the leaves. This rainstorm pounced hastily like an inexperienced lover, and then as suddenly was gone. The leaves drooped wistfully and the air gleamed with green reflections. It's easy to forgive the summer rain; like first love, white lies or blarney, there's no malignity in it.

Byrd and Jean-Paul were already seated at the café. Jean-Paul was as immaculate as a shop-window dummy but Byrd was excited and dishevelled. His hair was awry and his eyebrows almost non-existent, as though he'd been too near a water-heater blow-back. They had chosen a seat near the side screens and Byrd was wagging a finger and talking excitedly. Jean-Paul waved to us and folded his ear with his fingers. Maria laughed. Byrd was wondering if Jean-Paul was making a joke against him, but deciding he wasn't, continued to speak.

'Simplicity annoys them,' Byrd said. 'It's just a rectangle, one of them complained, as though that was a criterion of art. Success annoys them. Even though I make almost no money out of my painting, that doesn't prevent the critics who feel my work is bad from treating it like an indecent assault, as though I have deliberately chosen to do bad work in order to be obnoxious. They have no kindness, no compassion, you see, that's why they call them critics — originally the word meant a captious fool; if they had compassion they would show it.'

'How?' asked Maria.

'By painting. That's what a painting is, a statement of love. Art is love, stricture is hate. It's obvious, surely. You see, a critic is a man who admires painters (he wants to be one) but cares little for paintings (which is why he isn't one). A painter, on the other hand, admires paintings, but doesn't like painters.' Byrd, having settled that problem, waved to a waiter. 'Four grands crèmes and some matches,' he ordered.

'I want black coffee,' said Maria.

'I prefer black too,' said Jean-Paul.

Byrd looked at me and made a little noise with his lips. 'You want black coffee?'

'White will suit me,' I said. He nodded an appreciation of a fellow countryman's loyalty. 'Two crèmes — grands crèmes — and two small blacks,' he ordered. The waiter arranged the beer mats, picked up some ancient checks and tore them in half. When he had gone Byrd leaned towards me. 'I'm glad,' he said — he looked around to see that the other two did not hear. They were talking to each other — 'I'm glad you drink white coffee. It's not good for the nerves, too much of this very strong stuff.' He lowered his voice still more. 'That's why they are all so argumentative,' he said in a whisper. When the coffees came Byrd arranged them on the table, apportioned the sugar, then took the check.

'Let me pay,' said Jean-Paul. 'It was my invitation.'

'Not on your life,' said Byrd. 'Leave this to me, Jean-Paul. I know how to handle this sort of thing, it's my part of the ship.'

Maria and I looked at each other without expression. Jean-Paul was watching closely to discover our relationship.

Byrd relished the snobbery of certain French phrases. Whenever he changed from speaking French into English I knew it was solely because he intended to introduce a long slab of French into his speech and give a knowing nod and slant his face significantly, as if we two were the only people in the world who understood the French language.

'Your inquiries about this house,' said Byrd. He raised his forefinger. 'Jean-Paul has remarkable news.'

'What's that?' I asked.

'Seems, my dear fellow, that there's something of a mystery about your friend Datt and that house.'

'He's not a friend of mine,' I said.

'Quite quite,' said Byrd testily. 'The damned place is a brothel, what's more … '

'It's not a brothel,' said Jean-Paul as though he had explained this before. 'It's a *maison de passe*. It's a house that people go to when they already have a girl with them.'

'Orgies,' said Byrd. 'They have orgies there. Frightful

71

goings on Jean-Paul tells me, drugs called LSD, pornographic films, sexual displays ... '

Jean-Paul took over the narrative. 'There are facilities for every manner of perversion. They have hidden cameras there and even a great mock torture-chamber where they put on shows ... '

'For masochists,' said Byrd. 'Chaps who are abnormal, you see.'

'Of course he sees,' said Jean-Paul. 'Anyone who lives in Paris knows how widespread are such parties and exhibitions.'

'*I* didn't know,' said Byrd. Jean-Paul said nothing. Maria offered her cigarettes around and said to Jean-Paul, 'Where did Pierre's horse come in yesterday?'

'A friend of theirs with a horse,' Byrd said to me.

'Yes,' I said.

'Nowhere,' said Jean-Paul.

'Then I lost my hundred nouveaux,' said Maria.

'Foolish,' said Byrd to me. He nodded.

'My fault,' said Jean-Paul.

'That's right,' said Maria. 'I didn't give it a second look until you said it was a certainty.'

Byrd gave another of his conspiratorial glances over the shoulder.

'You,' he pointed to me as though he had just met me on a footpath in the jungle, 'work for the German magazine *Stern*.'

'I work for several German magazines,' I admitted. 'But not so loud, I don't declare all of it for tax.'

'You can rely upon me,' said Byrd. 'Mum's the word.'

'Mum's the word,' I said. I relished Byrd's archaic vocabulary.

'You see,' said Byrd, 'when Jean-Paul told me this fascinating stuff about the house on Avenue Foch I said that you would probably be able to advance him a little of the ready if you got a story out of it.'

'I might,' I agreed.

'My word,' said Byrd, 'what with your salary from the travel agency and writing pieces for magazines you must be minting it. Absolutely minting it, eh?'

'I do all right,' I admitted.

'All right. I should think you do. I don't know where you stack it all if you are not declaring it for tax. What do you do, hide it under your bed?'

'To tell you the truth,' I said, 'I've sewn it into the seat of my armchair.'

Byrd laughed. 'Old Tastevin will be after you, tearing his furniture.'

'It was his idea,' I joked, and Byrd laughed again, for Tastevin had a reputation for being a skinflint.

'Get you in there with a camera,' mused Byrd. 'Be a wonderful story. What's more it would be a public service. Paris is rotten to the core you see. It's time it was given a shaking up.'

'It's an idea,' I agreed.

'Would a thousand quid be too much?' he asked.

'Much too much,' I said.

Byrd nodded. 'I thought it might be. A hundred more like it eh?'

'If it's a good story with pictures I could get five hundred pounds out of it. I'd pay fifty for an introduction and guided tour with co-operation, but the last time I was there I was persona non grata.'

'Precisely, old chap,' said Byrd. 'You were manhandled, I gather, by that fellow Datt. All a mistake, wasn't it?'

'It was from my point of view,' I said. 'I don't know how Monsieur Datt feels about it.'

'He probably feels *désolé*,' said Byrd. I smiled at the idea.

'But really,' said Byrd, 'Jean-Paul knows all about it. He

73

could arrange for you to do your story, but meanwhile mum's the word, eh? Say nothing to anyone about any aspect. Are we of one mind?'

'Are you kidding me?' I said. 'Why would Datt agree to expose his own activities?'

'You don't understand the French, my boy.'

'So everyone keeps telling me.'

'But really. This house is owned and controlled by the Ministry of the Interior. They use it as a check and control on foreigners—especially diplomats—blackmail you might almost say. Bad business, shocking people, eh? Well they are. Some other French johnnies in government service—Loiseau is one—would like to see it closed down. Now do you see, my dear chap, now do you see?'

'Yes,' I said. 'But what's in it for you?'

'Don't be offensive, old boy,' said Byrd. 'You asked me about the house. Jean-Paul is in urgent need of the ready; ergo, I arrange for you to make a mutually beneficial pact.' He nodded. 'Suppose we say fifty on account, and another thirty if it gets in to print?'

A huge tourist bus crawled along the boulevard, the neon light flashing and dribbling down its glasswork. Inside, the tourists sat stiff and anxious, crouching close to their loudspeakers and staring at the wicked city.

'Okay,' I said. I was amazed that he was such an efficient bargain-maker.

'In any magazine anywhere,' Byrd continued. 'With ten per cent of any subsequent syndication.'

I smiled. Byrd said, 'Ah, you didn't expect me to be adept at bargaining eh?'

'No,' I said.

'You've a lot to learn about me. Waiter,' he called. 'Four kirs.' He turned to Jean-Paul and Maria. 'We have concluded an agreement. A small celebration is now indicated.'

74

The white wine and cassis came. 'You will pay,' Byrd said to me, 'and take it out of our down payment.'

'Will we have a contract?' asked Jean-Paul.

'Certainly not,' said Byrd. 'An Englishman's word is his bond. Surely you know that, Jean-Paul. The whole essence of a contract is that it's mutually beneficial. If it isn't, no paper in the world will save you. Besides,' he whispered to me in English, 'give him a piece of paper like that and he'll be showing everyone; he's like that. And that's the last thing you want, eh?'

'That's right,' I said. That's right, I thought. My employment on a German magazine was a piece of fiction that the office in London had invented for the rare times when they had to instruct me by mail. No one could have known about it unless they had been reading my mail. If Loiseau had said it, I wouldn't have been surprised, but Byrd … !

Byrd began to explain the theory of pigment to Jean-Paul in the shrill voice that he adopted whenever he talked art. I bought them another kir before Maria and I left to walk back to her place.

We picked our way through the dense traffic on the boulevard.

'I don't know how you can be so patient with them,' Maria said. 'That pompous Englishman Byrd and Jean-Paul holding his handkerchief to protect his suit from wine stains.'

'I don't know them well enough to dislike them,' I explained.

'Then don't believe a word they say,' said Maria.

'Men were deceivers ever.'

'You are a fool.' said Maria. 'I'm not talking about amours, I'm talking about the house on Avenue Foch; Byrd and Jean-Paul are two of Datt's closest friends. Thick as thieves.'

'Are they?' I said. From the far side of the boulevard I looked back. The wiry little Byrd—as volatile as when we'd joined him—was still explaining the theory of pigment to Jean-Paul.

'*Comédiens*,' Maria pronounced. The word for 'actor' also means a phoney or impostor. I stood there a few minutes, looking. The big Café Blanc was the only brightly lit place on the whole tree-lined boulevard. The white coats of the waiters gleamed as they danced among the tables laden with coffee pots, *citron pressé* and soda siphons. The customers were also active, they waved their hands, nodded heads, called to waiters and to each other. They waved ten-franc notes and jangled coins. At least four of them kissed. It was as though the wide dark boulevard was a hushed auditorium, respecting and attentive, watching the drama unfold on the stage-like *terrasse* of the Café Blanc. Byrd leaned close to Jean-Paul. Jean-Paul laughed.

11

We walked and talked and forgot the time. 'Your place,'
I said finally to Maria. 'You have central heating, the sink
is firmly fixed to the wall, you don't share the w.c. with
eight other people and there are gramophone records I
haven't even read the labels on yet. Let's go to your
place.'

'Very well,' she said, 'since you are so flattering about
its advantages.' I kissed her ear gently. She said, 'But
suppose the landlord throws you out?'

'Are you having an affair with your landlord?'

She smiled and gave me a forceful blow that many
French women conveniently believe is a sign of affection.

'I'm not washing any more shirts,' she said. 'We'll take
a cab to your place to pick up some linen.'

We bargained with three taxi-drivers, exchanging their
directional preferences with ours; finally one of them
weakened and agreed to take us to the Petit Légionnaire.

I let myself into my room with Maria just behind me.
Joey chirped politely when I switched on the light.

'My God,' said Maria, 'someone's turned you over.'

I picked up a heap of shirts that had landed in the
fireplace.

'Yes,' I said. Everything from the drawers and cupboards had been tipped on to the floor. Letters and cheque
stubs were scattered across the sofa and quite a few things
were broken. I let the armful of shirts fall to the floor again,
I didn't know where to begin on it. Maria was more
methodical, she began to sort through the clothes, folding
them and putting trousers and jackets on the hangers. I

picked up the phone and dialled the number Loiseau had given me.

'*Un sourire est différent d'un rire,*' I said. France is one place where the romance of espionage will never be lost, I thought. Loiseau said 'Hello.'

'Have you turned my place over, Loiseau?' I said.

'Are you finding the natives hostile?' Loiseau asked.

'Just answer the question,' I asked.

'Why don't you answer mine?' said Loiseau.

'It's my jeton,' I said. 'If you want answers you buy your own call.'

'If my boys had done it you wouldn't have noticed.'

'Don't get blasé, Loiseau. The last time your boys did it—five weeks back—I did notice. Tell 'em if they must smoke, to open the windows; that cheap pipe tobacco makes the canary's eyes water.'

'But they are very tidy,' said Loiseau. 'They wouldn't make a mess. If it's a mess you are complaining of.'

'I'm not complaining about anything,' I said. 'I'm just trying to get a straight answer to a simple question.'

'It's too much to ask of a policeman,' said Loiseau. 'But if there is anything damaged I'd send the bill to Datt.'

'If anything gets damaged it's likely to be Datt,' I said.

'You shouldn't have said that to me,' said Loiseau. 'It was indiscreet, but *bonne chance* anyway.'

'Thanks,' I said and hung up.

'So it wasn't Loiseau?' said Maria, who had been listening.

'What makes you think that?' I asked.

She shrugged, 'The mess here. The police would have been careful. Besides, if Loiseau admitted that the police have searched your home other times why should he deny that they did it this time?'

'Your guess is as good as mine,' I said. 'Perhaps Loiseau did it to set me at Datt's throat.'

'So you were deliberately indiscreet to let him think he'd succeeded?'

'Perhaps.' I looked into the torn seat of the armchair. The horse-hair stuffing had been ripped out and the case of documents that the courier had given me had disappeared. 'Gone,' said Maria.

'Yes,' I said. 'Perhaps you did translate my confession correctly after all.'

'It was an obvious place to look. In any case I was not the only person to know your "secret": this evening you told Byrd that you kept your money there.'

'That's true, but was there time for anyone to act on that?'

'It was two hours ago,' said Maria. 'He could have phoned. There was plenty of time.'

We began to sort out the mess. Fifteen minutes passed, then the phone rang. It was Jean-Paul.

'I'm glad to catch you at home,' he said. 'Are you alone?'

I held a finger up to my lips to caution Maria. 'Yes,' I said. 'I'm alone. What is it?'

'There's something I wanted to tell you without Byrd hearing.'

'Go ahead.'

'Firstly. I have good connections in the underworld and the police. I am certain that you can expect a burglary within a day or so. Anything you treasure should be put into a bank vault for the time being.'

'You're too late,' I said. 'They were here.'

'What a fool I am. I should have told you earlier this evening. It might have been in time.'

'No matter,' I said. 'There was nothing here of value except the typewriter.' I decided to solidify the freelance-writer image a little. 'That's the only essential thing. What else did you want to tell me?'

'Well that policeman, Loiseau, is a friend of Byrd.'

'I know,' I said. 'Byrd was in the war with Loiseau's brother.'

'Right,' said Jean-Paul. 'Now Inspector Loiseau was asking Byrd about you earlier today. Byrd told Inspector Loiseau that … '

'Well, come on.'

'He told him you are a spy. A spy for the West Germans.'

'Well that's good family entertainment. Can I get invisible ink and cameras at a trade discount?'

'You don't know how serious such a remark can be in France today. Loiseau is forced to take notice of such a remark no matter how ridiculous it may seem. And it's impossible for you to *prove* that it's not true.'

'Well thanks for telling me,' I said. 'What do you suggest I do about it?'

'There is nothing you can do for the moment,' said Jean-Paul. 'But I shall try to find out anything else Byrd says of you, and remember that I have very influential friends among the police. Don't trust Maria whatever you do.'

Maria's ear went even closer to the receiver. 'Why's that?' I asked. Jean-Paul chuckled maliciously. 'She's Loiseau's ex-wife, that's why. She too is on the payroll of the Sûreté.'

'Thanks,' I said. 'See you in court.'

Jean-Paul laughed at that remark — or perhaps he was still laughing at the one before.

12

Maria applied her make-up with unhurried precision. She was by no means a cosmetics addict but this morning she was having lunch with Chief Inspector Loiseau. When you had lunch with an ex-husband you made quite sure that he realized what he had lost. The pale-gold English wool suit that she had bought in London. He'd always thought her a muddle-headed fool so she'd be as slick and businesslike as possible. And the new plain-front shoes; no jewellery. She finished the eyeliner and the mascara and began to apply the eye-shadow. Not too much; she had been wearing much too much the other evening at the art gallery. You have a perfect genius, she told herself severely, for getting yourself involved in situations where you are a minor factor instead of a major factor. She smudged the eye-shadow, cursed softly, removed it and began again. Will the Englishman appreciate the risk you are taking? Why not tell M. Datt the truth of what the Englishman said? The Englishman is interested only in his work, as Loiseau was interested only in *his* work. Loiseau's love-making was efficient, just as his working day was. How can a woman compete with a man's work? Work is abstract and intangible, hypnotic and lustful; a woman is no match for it. She remembered the nights she had tried to fight Loiseau's work, to win him away from the police and its interminable paperwork and its relentless demands upon their time together. She remembered the last bitter argument about it. Loiseau had kissed her passionately in a way he had never done before and they had made love and she had clung to him, crying silently in the sudden release of tension, for at that moment she knew that they would separate and divorce, and she had been right.

Loiseau still owned a part of her, that's why she had to keep seeing him. At first they had been arranging details of the legal separation, custody of the boy, then agreements about the house. Then Loiseau had asked her to do small tasks for the police department. She knew that he could not face the idea of losing her completely. They had become dispassionate and sincere, for she no longer feared losing him; they were like brother and sister now, and yet ... she sighed. Perhaps it all could have been different; Loiseau still had an insolent confidence that made her pleased, almost proud, to be with him. He was a man, and that said everything there was to say about him. Men were unreasonable. Her work for the Sûreté had become quite important. She was pleased with the chance to show Loiseau how efficient and businesslike she could be, but Loiseau would never acknowledge it. Men were unreasonable. All men. She remembered a certain sexual mannerism of his, and smiled. All men set tasks and situations in which anything a woman thinks, says, or does will be wrong. Men demand that women should be inventive, shameless whores, and then reject them for not being motherly enough. They want them to attract their men friends and then they get jealous about it.

She powdered her lipstick to darken it and then pursed her lips and gave her face one final intent glare. Her eyes were good, the pupils were soft and the whites gleaming. She went to meet her ex-husband.

13

Loiseau had been smoking too much and not getting enough sleep. He kept putting a finger around his metal wristwatch band; Maria remembered how she had dreaded those nervous mannerisms that always preceded a row. He gave her coffee and remembered the amount of sugar she liked. He remarked on her suit and her hair and liked the plain-fronted shoes. She knew that sooner or later he would mention the Englishman.

'Those same people have always fascinated you,' he said. 'You are a gold-digger for brains, Maria. You are drawn irresistibly to men who think only of their work.'

'Men like you,' said Maria. Loiseau nodded.

He said, 'He'll just bring you trouble, that Englishman.'

'I'm not interested in him,' said Maria.

'Don't lie to me,' said Loiseau cheerfully. 'Reports from seven hundred policemen go across this desk each week. I also get reports from informers and your concierge is one of them.'

'The bitch.'

'It's the system,' said Loiseau. 'We have to fight the criminal with his own weapons.'

'Datt gave him an injection of something to question him.'

'I know,' said Loiseau.

'It was awful,' said Maria.

'Yes, I've seen it done.'

'It's like a torture. A filthy business.'

'Don't lecture me,' said Loiseau. 'I don't like Amytal injections and I don't like Monsieur Datt or that clinic, but there's nothing I can do about it.' He sighed. 'You know that, Maria.' But Maria didn't answer. 'That house is safe from even my wide powers.' He smiled as if the idea of him endangering anything was absurd. 'You deliberately translated the Englishman's confession incorrectly, Maria.' Loiseau accused her.

Maria said nothing. Loiseau said, 'You told Monsieur Datt that the Englishman is working under my orders. Be careful what you say or do with these people. They are dangerous—all of them are dangerous; your flashy boy-friend is the most dangerous of all.'

'Jean-Paul you mean?'

'The playboy of the Buttes Chaumont,' said Loiseau sarcastically.

'Don't keep calling him my boy-friend,' said Maria.

'Come come, I know all about you,' said Loiseau, using a phrase and a manner that he employed in interrogations. 'You can't resist these flashy little boys and the older you get the more vulnerable you become to them.' Maria was determined not to show anger. She knew that Loiseau was watching her closely and she felt her cheeks flushing in embarrassment and anger.

'He wants to work for me,' said Loiseau.

'He likes to feel important,' explained Maria, 'as a child does.'

'You amaze me,' said Loiseau, taking care to be un-amazed. He stared at her in a way that a Frenchman stares at a pretty girl on the street. She knew that he fancied her sexually and it comforted her, not to frustrate him, but because to be able to interest him was an important part of their new relationship. She felt that in some ways this new feeling she had for him was more important than their marriage had been, for now they were friends, and friendship is less infirm and less fragile than love.

'You mustn't harm Jean-Paul because of me,' said Maria.

'I'm not interested in Drugstore cowboys,' said Loiseau.

'At least not until they are caught doing something illegal.'

Maria took out her cigarettes and lit one as slowly as she knew how. She felt all the old angers welling up inside her. This was the Loiseau she had divorced; this stern, unyielding man who thought that Jean-Paul was an effeminate gigolo merely because he took himself less seriously than Loiseau ever could. Loiseau had crushed her, had reduced her to a piece of furniture, to a dossier – the dossier on Maria; and now the dossier was passed over to someone else and Loiseau thought the man concerned would not handle it as competently as he himself had done. Long ago Loiseau had produced a cold feeling in her and now she felt it again. This same icy scorn was poured upon anyone who smiled or relaxed; self-indulgent, complacent, idle – these were Loiseau's words for anyone without his self-flagellant attitude to work. Even the natural functions of her body seemed something against the law when she was near Loiseau. She remembered the lengths she went to to conceal the time of her periods in case he should call her to account for them, as though they were the mark of some ancient sin.

She looked up at him. He was still talking about Jean-Paul. How much had she missed – a word, a sentence, a lifetime? She didn't care. Suddenly the room seemed cramped and the old claustrophobic feeling that made her unable to lock the bathroom door – in spite of Loiseau's rages about it – made this room unbearably small. She wanted to leave.

'I'll open the door,' she said. 'I don't want the smoke to bother you.'

'Sit down,' he said. 'Sit down and relax.'

She felt she must open the door.

'Your boy-friend Jean-Paul is a nasty little casserole,'* said Loiseau, 'and you might just as well face up to it. You

* Informer.

85

accuse me of prying into other people's lives: well perhaps that's true, but do you know what I see in those lives? I see things that shock and appal me. That Jean-Paul. What is he but a toe-rag for Datt, running around like a filthy little pimp. He is the sort of man that makes me ashamed of being a Frenchman. He sits all day in the Drugstore and the other places that attract the foreigners. He holds a foreign newspaper pretending that he is reading it — although he speaks hardly a word of any foreign language — hoping to get into conversation with some pretty little girl secretary or better still a foreign girl who can speak French. Isn't that a pathetic thing to see in the heart of the most civilized city in the world? This lout sitting there chewing Hollywood chewing-gum and looking at the pictures in *Playboy*. Speak to him about religion and he will tell you how he despises the Catholic Church. Yet every Sunday when he's sitting there with his hamburger looking so *transatlantique*, he's just come from Mass. He prefers foreign girls because he's ashamed of the fact that his father is a metal-worker in a junk yard and foreign girls are less likely to notice his coarse manners and his phoney voice.'

Maria had spent years hoping to make Loiseau jealous and now, years after their divorce had been finalized, she had succeeded. For some reason the success brought her no pleasure. It was not in keeping with Loiseau's calm, cold, logical manner. Jealousy was weakness, and Loiseau had very few weaknesses.

Maria knew that she must open the door or faint. Although she knew this slight dizziness was claustrophobia she put out the half-smoked cigarette in the hope that it would make her feel better. She stubbed it out viciously. It made her feel better for about two minutes. Loiseau's voice droned on. How she hated this office. The pictures of Loiseau's life, photos of him in the army; slimmer and handsome, smiling at the photographer as if to say 'This is the best time of our lives, no wives, no responsibility.' The office actually smelled of Loiseau's work; she remembered that brown card that wrapped the dossiers and the smell of the old files that had come up from the cellars after goodness knows how many years. They smelled of stale vinegar. It must have been something in the paper, or perhaps the finger-print ink.

'He's a nasty piece of work, Maria,' said Loiseau. 'I'd even go so far as to say evil. He took three young German girls out to that damned cottage he has near Barbizon. He was with a couple of his so-called artist friends. They raped those girls, Maria, but I couldn't get them to give evidence. He's an evil fellow; we have too many like him in Paris.'

Maria shrugged, 'The girls should not have gone there, they should have known what to expect. Girl tourists— they only come here to be raped; they think it's romantic to be raped in Paris.'

'Two of these girls were sixteen years old, Maria, they were children; the other only eighteen. They'd asked your boy-friend the way to their hotel and he offered them a lift there. Is this what has happened to our great and beautiful city, that a stranger can't ask the way without risking assault?'

Outside the weather was cold. It was summer and yet the wind had an icy edge. Winter arrives earlier each year, thought Maria. Thirty-two years old, it's August again but already the leaves die, fall and are discarded by the wind. Once August was hot midsummer, now August was the beginning of autumn. Soon all the seasons would merge, spring would not arrive and she would know the menopausal womb-winter that is half-life.

'Yes,' said Maria. 'That's what has happened.' She shivered.

14

It was two days later when I saw M. Datt again. The courier was due to arrive any moment. He would probably be grumbling and asking for my report about the house on the Avenue Foch. It was a hard grey morning, a slight haze promising a scorching hot afternoon. In the Petit Légionnaire there was a pause in the business of the day, the last *petit déjeuner* had been served but it was still too early for lunch. Half a dozen customers were reading their newspapers or staring across the street watching the drivers argue about parking space. M. Datt and both the Tastevins were at their usual table, which was dotted with coffee pots, cups and tiny glasses of Calvados. Two taxi-drivers played 'ping-foot', swivelling the tiny wooden footballers to smack the ball across the green felt cabinet. M. Datt called to me as I came down for breakfast.

'This is terribly late for a young man to wake,' he called jovially. 'Come and sit with us.' I sat down, wondering why M. Datt had suddenly become so friendly. Behind me the 'ping-foot' players made a sudden volley. There was a clatter as the ball dropped through the goal-mouth and a mock cheer of triumph.

'I owe you an apology,' said M. Datt. 'I wanted to wait a few days before delivering it so that you would find it in yourself to forgive me.'

'That humble hat doesn't fit,' I said. 'Go a size larger.'

M. Datt opened his mouth and rocked gently. 'You have a fine sense of humour,' he proclaimed once he had got himself under control.

'Thanks,' I said. 'You are quite a joker yourself.'

M. Datt's mouth puckered into a smile like a carelessly ironed shirt-collar. 'Oh I see what you mean,' he said suddenly and laughed. 'Ha-ha-ha,' he laughed. Madame Tastevin had spread the Monopoly board by now and dealt us the property cards to speed up the game. The courier was due to arrive, but getting closer to M. Datt was the way the book would do it.

'Hotels on Lecourbe and Belleville,' said Madame Tastevin.

'That's what you always do,' said M. Datt. 'Why don't you buy railway stations instead?'

We threw the dice and the little wooden discs went trotting around the board, paying their rents and going to prison and taking their chances just like humans. 'A voyage of destruction,' Madame Tastevin said it was.

'That's what all life is,' said M. Datt. 'We start to die on the day we are born.'

My chance card said '*Faites des réparations dans toutes vos maisons*' and I had to pay 2,500 francs on each of my houses. It almost knocked me out of the game but I scraped by. As I finished settling up I saw the courier cross the *terrasse*. It was the same man who had come last time. He took it very slow and stayed close to the wall. A coffee crème and a slow appraisal of the customers before contacting me. Professional. Sift the tails off and duck from trouble. He saw me but gave no sign of doing so.

'More coffee for all of us,' said Madame Tastevin. She watched the two waiters laying the tables for lunch, and now she called out to them, 'That glass is smeary', 'Use the pink napkins, save the white ones for evening.' 'Be sure there is enough terrine today. I'll be angry if we run short.' The waiters were keen that Madame shouldn't get angry, they moved anxiously, patting the cloths and making microscopic adjustments to the placing of the cutlery.

The taxi-drivers decided upon another game and there was a rattle of wooden balls as the coin went into the slot.

The courier had brought out a copy of *L'Express* and was reading it and sipping abstractedly at his coffee. Perhaps he'll go away, I thought, perhaps I won't have to listen to his endless official instructions. Madame Tastevin was in dire straits, she mortgaged three of her properties. On the cover of *L'Express* there was a picture of the American Ambassador to France shaking hands with a film star at a festival.

M. Datt said, 'Can I smell a terrine cooking? What a good smell.'

Madame nodded and smiled. 'When I was a girl all Paris was alive with smells; oil paint and horse sweat, dung and leaky gas lamps and everywhere the smell of superb French cooking. Ah!' She threw the dice and moved. 'Now,' she said, 'it smells of diesel, synthetic garlic, hamburgers and money.'

M. Datt said, 'Your dice.'

'Okay.' I told him. 'But I must go upstairs in a moment. I have so much work to do.' I said it loud enough to encourage the courier to order a second coffee.

Landing on the Boul. des Capucines destroyed Madame Tastevin.

'I'm a scientist,' said M. Datt, picking up the pieces of Madame Tastevin's bankruptcy. 'The scientific method is inevitable and true.'

'True to what?' I asked. 'True to scientists, true to history, true to fate, true to what?'

'True to itself,' said Datt.

'The most evasive truth of all,' I said.

M. Datt turned to me, studied my face and wet his lips before beginning to talk. 'We have begun in a bad ... a silly way.' Jean-Paul came into the café—he had been having lunch there every day lately. He waved airily to us and bought cigarettes at the counter.

'But there are certain things that I don't understand,' Datt continued. 'What are you doing carrying a case-load of atomic secrets?'

'And what are you doing stealing it?'

Jean-Paul came across to the table, looked at both of us and sat down.

'Retrieving,' said Datt. 'I retrieved it for you.'

'Then let's ask Jean-Paul to remove his gloves,' I said.

Jean-Paul watched M. Datt anxiously. 'He knows,' said M. Datt. 'Admit it, Jean-Paul.'

'On account,' I explained to Jean-Paul, 'of how we began in a bad and silly way.'

'I said that,' said M. Datt to Jean-Paul. 'I said we had started in a bad and silly way and now we want to handle things differently.'

I leaned across and peeled back the wrist of Jean-Paul's cotton gloves. The flesh was stained violet with 'nin'.*

'Such an embarrassment for the boy,' said M. Datt smiling. Jean-Paul glowered at him.

'Do you want to buy the documents?' I asked.

M. Datt shrugged. 'Perhaps. I will give you ten thousand new francs, but if you want more than that I would not be interested.'

'I'll need double that,' I said.

'And if I decline?'

'You won't get every second sheet, which I removed and deposited elsewhere.'

'You are no fool,' said M. Datt. 'To tell you the truth the documents were so easy to get from you that I

---

* Ninhydrine: a colour reagent, reddish-black powder. Hands become violet because of amino acid in the skin. It takes three days before it comes off. Washing makes it worse.

suspected their authenticity. I'm glad to find you are no fool.'

'There are more documents,' I said. 'A higher percentage will be Xerox copies but you probably won't mind that. The first batch had a high proportion of originals to persuade you of their authenticity, but it's too risky to do that regularly.'

'Whom do you work for?'

'Never mind who I work for. Do you want them or not?'

M. Datt nodded, smiled grimly and said, 'Agreed, my friend. Agreed.' He waved an arm and called for coffee. 'It's just curiosity. Not that your documents are anything like my scientific interests. I shall use them merely to stimulate my mind. Then they will be destroyed. You can have them back ... ' The courier finished his coffee and then went upstairs, trying to look as though he was going no farther than the toilets on the first floor.

I blew my nose noisily and then lit a cigarette. 'I don't care what you do with them, monsieur. My fingerprints are not on the documents and there is no way to connect them with me; do as you wish with them. I don't know if these documents connect with your work. I don't even know what your work is.'

'My present work is scientific,' explained Datt. 'I run my clinic to investigate the patterns of human behaviour. I could make much more money elsewhere, my qualifications are good. I am an analyst. I am still a good doctor. I could lecture on several different subjects: upon oriental art, Buddhism or even Marxist theory. I am considered an authority on Existentialism and especially upon Existentialist psychology; but the work I am doing now is the work by which I will be known. The idea of being remembered after death becomes important as one gets old.' He threw the dice and moved past Départ. 'Give me my twenty thousand francs,' he said.

92

'What do you do at this clinic?' I peeled off the toy money and passed it to him. He counted it and stacked it up.

'People are blinded by the sexual nature of my work. They fail to see it in its true light. They think only of the sex activity.' He sighed. 'It's natural, I suppose. My work is important merely because people cannot consider the subject objectively. I can; so I am one of the few men who can control such a project.'

'You analyse the sexual activity?'

'Yes,' said Datt. 'No one does anything they do not wish to do. We do employ girls but most of the people who go to the house go there as couples, and they leave in couples. I'll buy two more houses.'

'The same couples?'

'Not always,' said Datt. 'But that is not necessarily a thing to be deplored. People are mentally in bondage, and their sexual activity is the cipher which can help to explain their problems. You're not collecting your rent.' He pushed it over to me.

'You are sure that you are not rationalizing the owner-ship of a whorehouse?'

'Come along there now and see,' said Datt. 'It is only a matter of time before you land upon my hotels in the Avenue de la République.' He shuffled his property cards together. 'And then you are no more.'

'You mean the clinic is operating at noon?'

'The human animal,' said Datt, 'is unique in that its sexual cycle continues unabated from puberty to death.' He folded up the Monopoly board.

It was getting hotter now, the sort of day that gives rheumatism a jolt and expands the Eiffel Tower six inches. 'Wait a moment,' I said to Datt. 'I'll go up and shave. Five minutes?'

'Very well,' said Datt. 'But there's no real need to shave, you won't be asked to participate.' He smiled.

I hurried upstairs, the courier was waiting inside my room. 'They bought it?'

'Yes,' I said. I repeated my conversation with M. Datt.

'You've done well,' he said.

'Are you running me?' I lathered my face carefully and began shaving.

'No. Is that where they took it from, where the stuffing is leaking out?'

'Yes. Then who is?'

'You know I can't answer that. You shouldn't even ask me. Clever of them to think of looking there.'

'I told them where it was. I've never asked before,' I said, 'but whoever is running me seems to know what these people do even before I know. It's someone close, someone I know. Don't keep poking at it. It's only roughly stitched back.'

'That at least is wrong,' said the courier. 'It's no one you know or have ever met. How did you know who took the case?'

'You're lying. I told you not to keep poking at it. Nin; it colours your flesh. Jean-Paul's hands were bright with it.'

'What colour?'

'You'll be finding out,' I said. 'There's plenty of nin still in there.'

'Very funny.'

'Well who told you to poke your stubby peasant fingers into my stuffing?' I said. 'Stop messing about and listen carefully. Datt is taking me to the clinic, follow me there.'

'Very well,' said the courier without enthusiasm. He wiped his hands on a large handkerchief.

'Make sure I'm out again within the hour.'

'What am I supposed to do if you are not out within the hour?' he asked.

'I'm damned if I know,' I said. They never ask questions

94

like that in films. 'Surely you have some sort of emergency procedure arranged?'

'No,' said the courier. He spoke very quietly, 'I'm afraid I haven't. I just do the reports and pop them into the London dip mail secret tray. Sometimes it takes three days.'

'Well this could be an emergency,' I said. 'Something should have been arranged beforehand.' I rinsed off the last of the soap and parted my hair and straightened my tie.

'I'll follow you anyway,' said the courier encouragingly. 'It's a fine morning for a walk.'

'Good,' I said. I had a feeling that if it had been raining he would have stayed in the café. I dabbed some lotion on my face and then went downstairs to M. Datt. Upon the great bundle of play-money he had left the waiter's tip: one franc.

Summer was here again; the pavement was hot, the streets were dusty and the traffic cops were in white jackets and dark glasses. Already the tourists were everywhere, in two styles: beards, paper parcels and bleached jeans, or straw hats, cameras and cotton jackets. They were sitting on the benches complaining loudly, 'So he explained that it was one hundred new francs or it would be ten thousand old francs, and I said, "Gracious me I sure can understand why you people had that revolution." '

Another tourist said, 'But you don't speak the language.'

A man replied, 'I don't have to speak the language to know what that waiter meant.'

As we walked I turned to watch them and caught a sight of the courier strolling along about thirty yards behind us.

'It will take me another five years to complete my work,' said Datt. 'The human mind and the human body; remarkable mechanisms but often ill-matched.'

'Very interesting,' I said. Datt was easily encouraged.

'At present my researches are concerned with simulating the registering of pain, or rather the excitement caused by someone pretending to have sudden physical pain. You perhaps remember that scream I had on the tape recorder. Such a sound can cause a remarkable mental change in a man if used in the right circumstances.'

'The right circumstances being that film-set-style torture chamber where I was dumped after treatment.'

'Exactly,' said Datt. 'You have hit it. Even if they can see that it's a recording and even if we tell them that the girl was an actress, even then the excitement they get from it is not noticeably lessened. Curious, isn't it?'

'Very,' I said.

The house on the Avenue Foch quivered in the heat of the morning. The trees before it moved sensuously as though anxious to savour the hot sun. The door was opened by a butler; we stepped inside the entrance hall. The marble was cold and the curve of the staircase twinkled where sunbeams prodded the rich colours of the carpeting. High above us the chandeliers clinked with the draught from the open door.

The only sound was a girl's scream. I recognized it as the tape-recording that Datt had mentioned. The screams were momentarily louder as a door opened and closed again somewhere on the first floor beyond the top of the staircase.

'Who is up there?' said Datt as he handed his umbrella and hat to the butler.

'Monsieur Kuang-t'ien,' said the butler.

'A charming fellow,' said Datt. 'Major-domo of the Chinese Embassy here in Paris.'

Somewhere in the house a piano played Liszt, or perhaps it was a recording.

I looked towards the first floor. The screams continued,

muffled by the door that had now closed again. Suddenly, moving noiselessly like a figure in a fantasy, a young girl ran along the first-floor balcony and came down the stairs, stumbling and clinging to the banister rail. She half-fell and half-ran, her mouth open in the sort of soundless scream that only nightmares produce. The girl was naked but her body was speckled with patches of bright wet blood. She must have been stabbed twenty, perhaps thirty times, and the blood had produced an intricate pattern of rivulets like a tight bodice of fine red lace. I remembered M. Kuang-t'ien's poem: 'If she is not a rose all white, then she must be redder than the red of blood.'

No one moved until Datt made a half-hearted attempt to grab her, but he was so slow that she avoided him effortlessly and ran through the door. I recognized her face now; it was the model that Byrd had painted, Annie.

'Get after her.' Datt called his staff into action with the calm precision of a liner captain pulling into a pier. 'Go upstairs, grab Kuang-t'ien, disarm him, clean the knife and hide it. Put him under guard, then phone the Press Officer at the Chinese Embassy. Don't tell him anything, but he must stay in his office until I call him to arrange a meeting. Albert, get on my personal phone and call the Ministry of the Interior. Tell them we'll need some C.R.S. policemen here. I don't want the Police Municipale poking around too long. Jules, get my case and the drug box and have the transfusion apparatus ready; I'll take a look at the girl.' Datt turned, but stopped and said softly, 'And Byrd, get Byrd here immediately; send a car for him.'

He hurried after the footmen and butler who were running across the lawn after the bleeding girl. She glanced over her shoulder and gained fresh energy from the closeness of the pursuit. She grabbed at the gatepost and swung out on to the hot dusty pavement of the Avenue

Foch, her heart pumping the blood patches into shiny bulbous swellings that burst and dribbled into vertical stripes.

'Look!' I heard the voices of passers-by calling.

Someone else called 'Hello darling', and there was a laugh and a lot of wolf-whistles. They must have been the last thing the girl heard as she collapsed and died on the hot dusty, Parisian pavement under the trees in the Avenue Foch. A bewhiskered old crone carrying two *baguettes* came shuffling in her threadbare carpet-slippers. She pushed through the onlookers and leaned down close to the girl's head. 'Don't worry chérie, I'm a nurse,' she croaked. 'All your injuries are small and superficial.' She pushed the loaves of bread tighter under her armpit and tugged at her corset bottom. 'Just superficial,' she said again, 'so don't make so much fuss.' She turned very slowly and went shuffling off down the street muttering to herself.

There were ten or twelve people around her by the time I reached the body. The butler arrived and threw a car blanket over her. One of the bystanders said '*Tant pis*', and another said that the *jolie pépée* was well barricaded. His friend laughed.

A policeman is never far away in Paris and they came quickly, the blue-and-white corrugated van disgorging cops like a gambler fanning a deck of cards. Even before the van came to a halt the police were sorting through the bystanders, asking for papers, detaining some, prodding others away. The footmen had wrapped the girl's body in the blanket and began to heave the sagging bundle towards the gates of the house.

'Put it in the van,' said Datt. One of the policemen said, 'Take the body to the house.' The two men carrying the dead girl stood undecided.

'In the van,' said Datt.

'I get my orders from the Commissaire de Police,' said the cop. 'We are on the radio now.' He nodded towards the van.

Datt was furious. He struck the policeman a blow on the arm. His voice was sibilant and salivatory. 'Can't you see that you are attracting attention, you fool? This is a political matter. The Ministry of the Interior are concerned. Put the body in the van. The radio will confirm my ruling.' The policeman was impressed by Datt's anger. Datt pointed at me. 'This is one of the officers working with Chief Inspector Loiseau of the Sûreté. Is that good enough for you?'

'Very well,' said the policeman. He nodded to the two men, who pushed the body on to the floor of the police van. They closed the door.

'Journalists may arrive,' said Datt to the policeman. 'Leave two of your men on guard here and make sure they know about article ten.'

'Yes,' said the policeman docilely.

'Which way are you going?' I asked the driver.

'The meat goes to the Medico-Legal,' he said.

'Ride me to the Avenue de Marigny,' I said. 'I'm going back to my office.'

By now the policeman in charge of the vehicle was brow-beaten by Datt's fierce orders. He agreed to my riding in the van without a word of argument. At the corner of the Avenue de Marigny I stopped the van and got out. I needed a large brandy.

15

I expected the courier from the Embassy to contact me again that same day but he didn't return until the next morning. He put his document case on top of the wardrobe and sank into my best armchair.

He answered an unasked question. 'It's a whorehouse,' he pronounced. 'He calls it a clinic but it's more like a whorehouse.'

'Thanks for your help,' I said.

'Don't get snotty—you wouldn't want me telling you what to say in your reports.'

'That's true,' I admitted.

'Certainly it's true. It's a whorehouse that a lot of the Embassy people use. Not just our people—the Americans, etc., use it.'

I said, 'Straighten me up. Is this just a case of one of our Embassy people getting some dirty pictures back from Datt? Or something like that?'

The courier stared at me. 'I'm not allowed to talk about anything like that,' he said.

'Don't give me that stuff,' I said. 'They killed that girl yesterday.'

'In passion,' explained the courier. 'It was part of a kinky sex act.'

'I don't care if it was done as a publicity stunt,' I said. 'She's dead and I want as much information as I can get to avoid trouble. It's not just for my own skin; it's in the interests of the department that I avoid trouble.'

The courier said nothing, but I could see he was weakening.

I said, 'If I'm heading into that house again just to recover some pictures of a secretary on the job, I'll come back and haunt you.'

'Give me some coffee,' said the courier, and I knew he had decided to tell me whatever he knew. I boiled the kettle and brewed up a pint of strong black coffee.

'Kuang-t'ien,' said the courier, 'the man who knifed the girl: do you know who he is?'

'Major-domo at the Chinese Embassy, Datt said.'

'That's his cover. His name is Kuang-t'ien, but he's one of the top five men in the Chinese nuclear programme.'

'He speaks damn good French.'

'Of course he does. He was trained at the Laboratoire Curie, here in Paris. So was his boss, Chien San-chiang, who is head of the Atomic Energy Institute in Peking.'

'You seem to know a lot about it,' I said.

'I was evaluating it this time last year.'

'Tell me more about this man who mixes his sex with switchblades.'

He pulled his coffee towards him and stirred it thoughtfully. Finally he began.

'Four years ago the U2 flights picked up the fourteen-acre gaseous diffusion plant taking hydro-electric power from the Yellow River not far from Lanchow. The experts had predicted that the Chinese would make their bombs as the Russians and French did, and as we did too: by producing plutonium in atomic reactors. But the Chinese didn't; our people have been close. I've seen the photos. Very close. That plant proves that they are betting all or nothing on hydrogen. They are going full steam ahead on their hydrogen research programme. By concentrating on the light elements generally and by pushing the megaton instead of the kiloton bomb they could be the leading nuclear power in eight or ten years if their hydrogen research pays off. This man Kuang-t'ien is their best authority on hydrogen. See what I mean?'

I poured more coffee and thought about it. The courier got his case down and rummaged through it. 'When you left the clinic yesterday did you go in the police van?'

'Yes.'

'Um. I thought you might have. Good stunt that. Well, I hung around for a little while, then when I realized that you'd gone I came back here. I hoped you'd come back, too.'

'I had a drink,' I said. 'I put my mind in neutral for an hour.'

'That's unfortunate,' said the courier. 'Because while you were away you had a visitor. He asked for you at the counter, then hung around for nearly an hour, but when you didn't come back he took a cab to the Hotel Lotti.'

'What was he like?'

The courier smiled his mirthless smile and produced some ten-by-eight glossy pictures of a man drinking coffee in the afternoon sunlight. It wan't a good-quality photograph. The man was about fifty, dressed in a light-weight suit with a narrow-brimmed felt hat. His tie had a small monogram that was unreadable and his cufflinks were large and ornate. He had large black sunglasses which in one photo he had removed to polish. When he drank coffee he raised his little finger high and pursed his lips.

'Ten out of ten,' I said. 'Good stuff: waiting till he took the glasses off. But you could use a better D and P man.'

'They are just rough prints,' said the courier. 'The negs are half-frame but they are quite good.'

'You are a regular secret agent,' I said admiringly. 'What did you do—shoot him in the ankle with the toe-cap gun, send out a signal to H.Q. on your tooth and play the whole thing back on your wristwatch?'

He rummaged through his papers again, then slapped a copy of *L'Express* upon the table top. Inside there was a photo of the U.S. Ambassador greeting a group of American businessmen at Orly airport. The courier looked up at me briefly.

'Fifty per cent of this group of Americans work—or did work—for the Atomic Energy Commission. Most of the remainder are experts on atomic energy or some allied subject. Bertram: nuclear physics at M.I.T. Bestbridge: radiation sickness of 1961. Waldo: fall-out experiments and work at the Hiroshima hospital. Hudson: hydrogen research—now he works for the U.S. Army.' He marked Hudson's face with his nail. It was the man he'd photographed.

'Okay,' I said. 'What are you trying to prove?'

'Nothing. I'm just putting you in the picture. That's what you wanted, isn't it?'

'Yes,' I said. 'Thanks.'

'I'm just juxtaposing a hydrogen expert from Peking with a hydrogen expert from the Pentagon. I'm wondering why they are both in the same city at the same time and especially why they both cross your path. It's the sort of thing that makes me nervous.' He gulped down the rest of his coffee.

'You shouldn't drink too much of that strong black coffee,' I said. 'It'll be keeping you awake at night.'

The courier picked up his photos and copy of *L'Express*. 'I've got a system for getting to sleep,' he said. 'I count reports I've filed.'

'Watch resident agents jumping to conclusions,' I said.

'It's not soporific.' He got to his feet. 'I've left the most important thing until last,' he said.

'Have you?' I said, and wondered what was more important than the Chinese People's Republic preparing for nuclear warfare.

'The girl was ours.'

'What girl was whose?'

'The murdered girl was working for us, for the department.'

'A floater?'

'No. Permanent; warranty contract, the lot.'

'Poor kid,' I said. 'Was she pumping Kuang-t'ien?'

'It's nothing that's gone through the Embassy. They know nothing about her there.'

'But you knew?'

'Yes.'

'You are playing both ends.'

'Just like you.'

'Not at all. I'm just London. The jobs I do for the Embassy are just favours. I can decline if I want to. What do London want me to do about the girl?'

He said, 'She has an apartment on the left bank. Just check through her personal papers, her possessions. You know the sort of thing. It's a long shot but you might find something. These are her keys—the department held duplicates for emergencies—small one for mail box, large ones front door and apartment door.'

'You're crazy. The police were probably turning it over within thirty minutes of her death.'

'Of course they were. I've had the place under observation. That's why I waited a bit before telling you. London is pretty certain that no one—not Loiseau nor Datt nor anyone—knew that the girl worked for us. It's probable that they just made a routine search.'

'If the girl was a permanent she wouldn't leave anything lying around,' I said.

'Of course she wouldn't. But there may be one or two little things that could embarrass us all ... ' He looked around the grimy wallpaper of my room and pushed my ancient bedstead. It creaked.

'Even the most careful employee is tempted to have something close at hand.'

'That would be against orders.'

'Safety comes above orders,' he said. I shrugged my grudging agreement. 'That's right,' he said. 'Now you see why they want you to go. Go and probe around there as though it's your room and you've just been killed. You might find something where anyone else would fail. There's an insurance of about thirty thousand new francs if you find someone who you think should get it.' He wrote the address on a slip of paper and put it on the table. 'I'll be in touch,' he said. 'Thanks for the coffee, it was very good.'

'If I start serving instant coffee,' I said, 'perhaps I'll get a little less work.'

16

The dead girl's name was Annie Couzins. She was twenty-four and had lived in a new piece of speculative real estate not far from the Boul. Mich. The walls were close and the ceilings were low. What the accommodation agents described as a studio apartment was a cramped bed-sitting room. There were large cupboards containing a bath, a toilet and a clothes rack respectively. Most of the construction money had been devoted to an entrance hall lavished with plate glass, marble and bronze-coloured mirrors that made you look tanned and rested and slightly out of focus.

Had it been an old house or even a pretty one, then perhaps some memory of the dead girl would have remained there, but the room was empty, contemporary and pitiless. I examined the locks and hinges, probed the mattress and shoulder pads, rolled back the cheap carpet and put a knife blade between the floorboards. Nothing. Perfume, lingerie, bills, a postcard greeting from Nice, ' … some of the swimsuits are divine …', a book of dreams, six copies of *Elle*, laddered stockings, six medium-price dresses, eight and a half pairs of shoes, a good English wool overcoat, an expensive transistor radio tuned to France Musique, tin of Nescafé, tin of powdered milk, saccharine, a damaged handbag containing spilled powder and a broken mirror, a new saucepan. Nothing to show what she was, had been, feared, dreamed of or wanted.

The bell rang. There was a girl standing there. She may have been twenty-five but it was difficult to say. Big cities leave a mark. The eyes of city-dwellers scrutinize rather than see; they assess the value and the going-rate and try to separate the winners from the losers. That's what this girl tried to do.

'Are you from the police?' she asked.

'No. Are you?'

'I'm Monique. I live next door in apartment number eleven.'

'I'm Annie's cousin, Pierre.'

'You've got a funny accent. Are you a Belgian?' She gave a little giggle as though being a Belgian was the funniest thing that could happen to anyone.

'Half Belgian,' I lied amiably.

'I can usually tell. I'm very good with accents.'

'You certainly are,' I said admiringly. 'Not many people detect that I'm half Belgian.'

'Which half is Belgian?'

'The front half.'

She giggled again. 'Was your mother or your father Belgian I mean.'

'Mother. Father was a Parisian with a bicycle.'

She tried to peer into the flat over my shoulder. 'I would invite you in for a cup of coffee,' I said, 'but I mustn't disturb anything.'

'You're hinting. You want me to invite you for coffee.'

'Damned right I do.' I eased the door closed. 'I'll be there in five minutes.'

I turned back to cover up my searching. I gave a last look to the ugly cramped little room. It was the way I'd go one day. There would be someone from the department making sure that I hadn't left 'one or two little things that could embarrass us all'. Goodbye, Annie, I thought. I didn't know you but I know you now as well as anyone knows me. You won't retire to a little *tabac* in Nice and get a monthly cheque from some phoney insurance company. No, you can be resident agent in hell, Annie, and your bosses will be sending directives from Heaven telling you to clarify your reports and reduce your expenses.

I went to apartment number eleven. Her room was like Annie's: cheap gilt and film-star photos. A bath towel on the floor, ashtrays overflowing with red-marked butts, a plateful of garlic sausage that had curled up and died.

Monique had made the coffee by the time I got there. She'd poured boiling water on to milk powder and instant coffee and stirred it with a plastic spoon. She was a tough girl under the giggling exterior and she surveyed me carefully from behind fluttering eyelashes.

'I thought you were a burglar,' she said, 'then I thought you were the police.'

'And now?'

'You're Annie's cousin Pierre. You're anyone you want to be, from Charlemagne to Tin-Tin, it's no business of mine, and you can't hurt Annie.'

I took out my notecase and extracted a one-hundred new-franc note. I put it on the low coffee table. She stared at me thinking it was some kind of sexual proposition.

'Did you ever work with Annie at the clinic?' I asked.
'No.'

I placed another note down and repeated the question.
'No,' she said.

I put down a third note and watched her carefully. When she again said no I leaned forward and took her hand roughly. 'Don't no me,' I said. 'You think I came here without finding out first?'

She stared at me angrily. I kept hold of her hand. 'Sometimes,' she said grudingly.

'How many?'

'Ten, perhaps twelve.'

'That's better,' I said. I turned her hand over, pressed my finger against the back of it to make her fingers open and slapped the three notes into her open palm. I let go of her and she leaned back out of reach, rubbing the back of her hand where I had held it. They were slim, bony hands with rosy knuckles that had known buckets of cold water and Marseilles soap. She didn't like her hands. She put them inside things and behind them and hid them under her folded arms.

'You bruised me,' she complained.

'Rub money on it.'

'Ten, perhaps twelve, times,' she admitted.

'Tell me about the place. What went on there?'

'You are from the police.'

'I'll do a deal with you, Monique. Slip *me* three hundred and I'll tell you all about what *I* do.'

She smiled grimly. 'Annie wanted an extra girl sometimes, just as a hostess ... the money was useful.'

'Did Annie have plenty of money?'

'Plenty? I never knew anyone who had plenty. And even if they did it wouldn't go very far in this town. She didn't go to the bank in an armoured car if that's what you mean.' I didn't say anything.

Monique continued, 'She did all right but she was silly with it. She gave it to anyone who spun her a yarn. Her parents will miss her, so will Father Marconi; she was always giving to his collections for kids and missions and cripples. I told her over and over, she was silly with it. You're not Annie's cousin, but you throw too much money around to be the police.'

'The men you met there. You were told to ask them things and to remember what they said.'

'I didn't go to bed with them ... '

'I don't care if you took *thé anglais* with them and dunked the *gâteau sec*, what were your instructions?' She hesitated, and I placed five more one hundred franc notes on the table but kept my fingers on them.

'Of course I made love to the men, just as Annie did,

but they were all refined men. Men of taste and culture.'

'Sure they were,' I said. 'Men of real taste and culture.'

'It was done with tape recorders. There were two switches on the bedside lamps. I was told to get them talking about their work. So boring, men talking about their work, but are they ready to do it? My God they are.'

'Did you ever handle the tapes?'

'No, the recording machines were in some other part of the clinic.' She eyed the money.

'There's more to it than that. Annie did more than that.'

'Annie was a fool. Look where it got her. That's where it will get me if I talk too much.'

'I'm not interested in you,' I said. 'I'm only interested in Annie. What else did Annie do?'

'She substituted the tapes. She changed them. Sometimes she made her own recordings.'

'She took a machine into the house?'

'Yes. It was one of those little ones, about four hundred new francs they cost. She had it in her handbag. I found it there once when I was looking for her lipstick to borrow.'

'What did Annie say about it?'

'Nothing. I never told her. And I never opened her handbag again either. It was her business, nothing to do with me.'

'The miniature recorder isn't in her flat now.'

'I didn't pinch it.'

'Then who do you think did?'

'I told her not once. I told her a thousand times.'

'What did you tell her?'

She pursed up her mouth in a gesture of contempt. 'What do you think I told her, M. Annie's cousin Pierre? I told her that to record conversations in such a house was a dangerous thing to do. In a house owned by people like those people.'

'People like what people?'

'In Paris one does not talk of such things, but it's said that the Ministry of the Interior or the S.D.E.C.E.* own the house to discover the indiscretions of foolish aliens.' She gave a tough little sob, but recovered herself quickly.

'You were fond of Annie?'

'I never got on well with women until I got to know her. I was broke when I met her, at least I was down to only ten francs. I had run away from home. I was in the laundry asking them to split the order because I didn't have enough to pay. The place where I lived had no running water. Annie lent me the money for the whole laundry bill—twenty francs—so that I had clean clothes while looking for a job. She gave me the first warm coat I ever had. She showed me how to put on my eyes. She listened to my stories and let me cry. She told me not to live the life that she had led, going from one man to another. She would have shared her last cigarette with a stranger. Yet she never asked me questions. Annie was an angel.'

'It certainly sounds like it.'

'Oh I know what you're thinking. You're thinking that Annie and I were a couple of Lesbians.'

'Some of my best lovers are Lesbians,' I said.

Monique smiled. I thought she was going to cry all over me but she sniffed and smiled. 'I don't know if we were or not,' she said.

'Does it matter?'

'No, it doesn't matter. Anything would be better than to have stayed in the place I was born. My parents are still there; it's like living through a siege, besieged by the cost of necessities. They are careful how they use detergent, coffee is measured out. Rice, pasta and potatoes eke out tiny bits of meat. Bread is consumed, meat is revered and Kleenex tissues never afforded. Unnecessary lights are

* Service de Documentation Extérieure et Contre-Espionage.

switched off immediately, they put on a sweater instead of the heating. In the same building families crowd into single rooms, rats chew enormous holes in the woodwork—there's no food for them to chew on—and the w.c. is shared by three families and it usually doesn't flush. The people who live at the top of the house have to walk down two flights to use a cold water tap. And yet in this same city I get taken out to dinner in three-star restaurants where the bill for two dinners would keep my parents for a year. At the Ritz a man friend of mine paid nine francs a day to them for looking after his dog. That's just about half the pension my father gets for being blown up in the war. So when you people come snooping around here, flashing your money and protecting the République Française's rocket programme, atomic plants, supersonic bombers and nuclear submarines or whatever it is you're protecting, don't expect too much from my patriotism.'

She bit her lip and glared at me, daring me to contradict her, but I didn't contradict. 'It's a lousy rotten town,' I agreed.

'And dangerous,' she said.

'Yes,' I said. 'Paris is all of those things.'

She laughed. 'Paris is like me, cousin Pierre; it's no longer young, and too dependent upon visitors who bring money. Paris is a woman with a little too much alcohol in her veins. She talks a little too loud and thinks she is young and gay. But she has smiled too often at strange men and the words "I love you" trip too easily from her tongue. The ensemble is chic and the paint is generously applied, but look closely and you'll see the cracks showing through.'

She got to her feet, groped along the bedside table for a match and lit her cigarette with a hand that trembled very slightly. She turned back to me. 'I saw the girls I knew taking advantage of offers that came from rich men they could never possibly love. I despised the girls and wondered how they could bring themselves to go to bed with such unattractive men. Well, now I know.' The smoke was getting in her eyes. 'It was fear. Fear of being a woman instead of a girl, a woman whose looks are slipping away rapidly, leaving her alone and unwanted in this vicious town.' She was crying now and I stepped closer to her and touched her arm. For a moment she seemed about to let her head fall upon my shoulder, but I felt her body tense and unyielding. I took a business card from my top pocket and put it on the bedside table next to a box of chocolates. She pulled away from me irritably. 'Just phone if you want to talk more,' I said.

'You're English,' she said suddenly. It must have been something in my accent or syntax. I nodded.

'It will be strictly business,' she said. 'Cash payments.'

'You don't have to be so tough on yourself,' I said. She said nothing.

'And thanks,' I said.

'Get stuffed,' said Monique.

17

First there came a small police van, its klaxon going. Co-operating with it was a blue-uniformed man on a motor-cycle. He kept his whistle in his mouth and blew repeatedly. Sometimes he was ahead of the van, sometimes behind it. He waved his right hand at the traffic as if by just the draught from it he could force the parked cars up on the pavement. The noise was deafening. The traffic ducked out of the way, some cars went willingly, some grudgingly, but after a couple of beeps on the whistle they crawled up on the stones, the pavement and over traffic islands like tortoises. Behind the van came the flying column: three long blue buses jammed with Garde Mobile men who stared at the cringing traffic with a bored look on their faces. At the rear of the column came a radio car. Loiseau watched them disappear down the Faubourg St Honoré. Soon the traffic began to move again. He turned away from the window and back to Maria. 'Dangerous,' pronounced Loiseau. 'He's playing a dangerous game. The girl is killed in his house, and Datt is pulling every political string he can find to prevent an investigation taking place. He'll regret it.' He got to his feet and walked across the room.

'Sit down, darling,' said Maria. 'You are just wasting calories in getting annoyed.'

'I'm not Datt's boy,' said Loiseau.

'And no one will imagine that you are,' said Maria. She wondered why Loiseau saw everything as a threat to his prestige.

'The girl is entitled to an investigation,' explained

Loiseau. 'That's why I became a policeman. I believe in equality before the law. And now they are trying to tie my hands. It makes me furious.'

'Don't shout,' said Maria. 'What sort of effect do you imagine that has upon the people that work for you, hearing you shouting?'

'You are right,' said Loiseau. Maria loved him. It was when he capitulated so readily like that that she loved him so intensely. She wanted to care for him and advise him and make him the most successful policeman in the whole world. Maria said, 'You are the finest policeman in the whole world.'

He smiled. 'You mean with your help I could be.' Maria shook her head. 'Don't argue,' said Loiseau. 'I know the workings of your mind by now.'

Maria smiled too. He did know. That was the awful thing about their marriage. They knew each other too well. To know all is to forgive nothing.

'She was one of my girls,' said Loiseau. Maria was surprised. Of course Loiseau had girls, he was no monk, but it surprised her to hear him talk like that to her. 'One of them?' She deliberately made her voice mocking.

'Don't be so bloody arch, Maria. I can't stand you raising one eyebrow and adopting that patronizing tone. One of my girls.' He said it slowly to make it easy for her to understand. He was so pompous that Maria almost giggled. 'One of my girls, working for me as an informant.'

'Don't all the tarts do that?'

'She wasn't a tart, she was a highly intelligent girl giving us first-class information.'

'Admit it, darling,' Maria cooed, 'you were a tiny bit infatuated with her.' She raised an eyebrow quizzically.

'You stupid cow,' said Loiseau. 'What's the good of treating you like an intelligent human.' Maria was shocked by the rusty-edged hatred that cut her. She had

115

made a kind, almost loving remark. Of course the girl had fascinated Loiseau and had in turn been fascinated by him. The fact that it was true was proved by Loiseau's anger. But did his anger have to be so bitter? Did he have to wound her to know if blood flowed through her veins?

Maria got to her feet. 'I'll go,' she said. She remembered Loiseau once saying that Mozart was the only person who understood him. She had long since decided that that at least was true.

'You said you wanted to ask me something.'

'It doesn't matter.'

'Of course it matters. Sit down and tell me.'

She shook her head. 'Another time.'

'Do you have to treat me like a monster, just because I won't play your womanly games?'

'No,' she said.

There was no need for Maria to feel sorry for Loiseau. He didn't feel sorry for himself and seldom for anyone else. He had pulled the mechanism of their marriage apart and now looked at it as if it were a broken toy, wondering why it didn't work. Poor Loiseau. My poor, poor, darling Loiseau. I at least can build again, but you don't know what you did that killed us.

'You're crying, Maria. Forgive me. I'm so sorry.'

'I'm not crying and you're not sorry.' She smiled at him. 'Perhaps that's always been our problem.'

Loiseau shook his head but it wasn't a convincing denial.

Maria walked back towards the Faubourg St Honoré. Jean-Paul was at the wheel of her car.

'He made you cry,' said Jean-Paul. 'The rotten swine.'

'I made myself cry,' said Maria.

Jean-Paul put his arm around her and held her tight. It was all over between her and Jean-Paul, but feeling his arm around her was like a shot of cognac. She stopped feeling sorry for herself and studied her make-up.

'You look magnificent,' said Jean-Paul. 'I would like to take you away and make love to you.'

There was a time when that would have affected her, but she had long since decided that Jean-Paul seldom *wanted* to make love to anyone, although he did it often enough, heaven knows. But it was a good thing to hear when you have just argued with an ex-husband. She smiled at Jean-Paul and he took her hand in his large tanned one and turned it around like a bronze sculpture on a turntable. Then he released it and grabbed at the controls of the car. He wasn't as good a driver as Maria was, but she preferred to be his passenger rather than drive herself. She lolled back and pretended that Jean-Paul was the capable tanned he-man that he looked. She watched the pedestrians, and intercepted the envious glances. They were a perfect picture of modern Paris: the flashy automobile, Jean-Paul's relaxed good looks and expensive clothes, her own well-cared-for appearance—for she was as sexy now as she had ever been. She leaned her head close upon Jean-Paul's shoulder. She could smell his after-shave perfume and the rich animal smell of the leather seats. Jean-Paul changed gear as they roared across the Place de la Concorde. She felt his arm muscles ripple against her cheek.

'Did you ask him?' asked Jean-Paul.

'No,' she said. 'I couldn't. He wasn't in the right mood.'

'He's never in the right mood, Maria. And he's never going to be. Loiseau knows what you want to ask him and he precipitates situations so that you never will ask him.'

'Loiseau isn't like that,' said Maria. She had never thought of that. Loiseau was clever and subtle; perhaps it was true.

'Look,' said Jean-Paul, 'during the last year that house on the Avenue Foch has held exhibitions, orgies, with

117

perversions, blue movies and everything, but has never had any trouble from the police. Even when a girl dies there, there is still little or no trouble. Why? Because it has the protection of the French Government. Why does it have protection? Because the activities at the house are filmed and photographed for official dossiers.'

'I'm not sure you're right. Datt implies that, but I'm not sure.'

'Well I am sure,' said Jean-Paul. 'I'll bet you that those films and photos are in the possession of the Ministry of the Interior. Loiseau probably sees every one of them. They probably have a private showing once a week. Loiseau probably saw that film of you and me within twenty-four hours of its being taken.'

'Do you think so?' said Maria. A flush of fear rose inside her, radiating panic like a two-kilowatt electric fire. Jean-Paul's large cool hand gripped her shoulder. She wished he would grip her harder. She wanted him to hurt her so that her sins would be expiated and erased by the pain. She thought of Loiseau seeing the film in the company of other policemen. Please God it hadn't happened. Please please God. She thought she had agonized over every aspect of her foolishness, but this was a new and most terrible one.

'But why would they keep the films?' Maria asked, although she knew the answer.

'Datt selects the people who use that house. Datt is a psychiatrist, a genius ... '

' ... an evil genius.'

'Perhaps an evil genius,' said Jean-Paul objectively. 'Perhaps an evil genius, but by gathering a select circle of people—people of great influence, of prestige and diplomatic power—Datt can compile remarkable assessments and predictions about their behaviour in everything they do. Many major shifts of French Government policy have

118

been decided by Datt's insights and analysis of sexual behaviour.'

'It's vile,' said Maria.

'It's the world in our time.'

'It's France in our time,' Maria corrected. 'Foul man.'

'He's not foul,' said Jean-Paul. 'He is not responsible for what those people do. He doesn't even encourage them. As far as Datt is concerned his guests could behave with impeccable decorum; he would be just as happy to record and analyse their attitudes.'

'*Voyeur.*'

'He's not even a *voyeur*. That's the odd thing. That's what makes him of such great importance to the Ministry. And that's why your ex-husband could do nothing to retrieve that film even if he wished to.'

'And what about you?' asked Maria casually.

'Be reasonable,' said Jean-Paul. 'It's true I do little jobs for Datt but I am not his *confidant*. I've no idea of what happens to the film ... '

'They burn them sometimes,' Maria remembered. 'And often they are taken away by the people concerned.'

'You have never heard of duplicate prints?'

Maria's hopes sank. 'Why didn't you ask for that piece of film of us?'

'Because you said let them keep it. Let them show it every Friday night, you said.'

'I was drunk,' said Maria. 'It was a joke.'

'It's a joke for which we are both paying dearly.'

Maria snorted. 'You love the idea of people seeing the film. It's just the image you love to project. The great lover ... ' She bit her tongue. She had almost added that the film was his sole documentary proof of heterosexuality, but she closed her eyes. 'Loiseau could get the film back,' she said. She was sure, sure, sure that Loiseau hadn't seen that piece of film, but the memory of the fear remained.

'Loiseau *could* get it,' she said desperately, wanting Jean-Paul to agree on this one, very small point.

'But he won't,' said Jean-Paul. 'He won't because I'm involved and your ex-husband hates me with a deep and illogical loathing. The trouble is that I can understand why he does. I'm no good for you, Maria. You would probably have managed the whole thing excellently except that Loiseau is jealous of your relationship with me. Perhaps we should cease to see each other for a few months.'

'I'm sure we should.'

'But I couldn't bear it, Maria.'

'Why the hell not? We don't love each other. I am only a suitable companion and you have so many other women you'd never even notice my absence.' She despised herself even before she'd completed the sentence. Jean-Paul detected her motive immediately, of course, and responded.

'My darling little Maria.' He touched her leg lightly and sexlessly. 'You are different from the others. The others are just stupid little tarts that amuse me as decorations. They are not women. You are the only real woman I know. You are the woman I love, Maria.'

'Monsieur Datt himself,' said Maria, '*he* could get the film.' Jean-Paul pulled into the side of the road and double parked.

'We've played this game long enough, Maria,' he said.

'What game?' asked Maria. Behind them a taxi-driver swore bitterly as he realized they were not going to move.

'The how-much-you-hate-Datt game,' said Jean-Paul.

'I do hate him.'

'He's your father, Maria.'

'He's not my father, that's just a stupid story that he told you for some purpose of his own.'

'Then where is your father?'

'He was killed in 1940 in Bouillon, Belgium, during the fighting with the Germans. He was killed in an air raid.'

'He would have been about the same age as Datt.'

'So would a million men,' said Maria. 'It's such a stupid lie that it's not worth arguing about. Datt hoped I'd swallow that story but now even he no longer speaks of it. It's a stupid lie.'

Jean-Paul smiled uncertainly. 'Why?'

'Oh Jean-Paul. Why. You know how his evil little mind works. I was married to an important man in the Sûreté. Can't you see how convenient it would be to have me thinking he was my father? A sort of insurance, that's why.'

Jean-Paul was tired of this argument. 'Then he's not your father. But I still think you should co-operate.'

'Co-operate how?'

'Tell him a few snippets of information.'

'Could he get the film if it was really worth while?'

'I can ask him.' He smiled. 'Now you are being sensible, my love,' he said. Maria nodded as the car moved forward into the traffic. Jean-Paul planted a brief kiss on her forehead. A taxi-driver saw him do it and tooted a small illegal toot on the horn. Jean-Paul kissed Maria's forehead again a little more ardently. The great Arc de Triomphe loomed over them as they roared around the Étoile like soapsuds round the kitchen sink. A hundred tyres screamed an argument about centrifugal force, then they were into the Grande Armée. The traffic had stopped at the traffic lights. A man danced nimbly between the cars, collecting money and whipping newspapers from window to window like a fan dancer. As the traffic lights changed the cars slid forward. Maria opened her paper; the ink was still wet and it smudged under her thumb. 'American tourist disappears,' the headline said. There was a photograph of Hudson, the American hydrogen-research man. The newspaper said he was a frozen foods executive named Parks, which was the story the U.S. Embassy had given out. Neither the face nor either name meant anything to Maria.

'Anything in the paper?' asked Jean-Paul. He was fighting a duel with a Mini-Cooper. 'No,' said Maria. She rubbed the newsprint on her thumb. 'There never is at this time of year. The English call it the silly season.'

18

Les Chiens is everything that delights the yeh yeh set. It's dark, hot, and squirming like a tin of live bait. The music is ear-splitting and the drink remarkably expensive even for Paris. I sat in a corner with Byrd.

'Not my sort of place at all,' Byrd said. 'But in a curious way I like it.'

A girl in gold crochet pyjamas squeezed past our table, leaned over and kissed my ear. 'Chéri,' she said. 'Long time no see,' and thereby exhausted her entire English vocabulary.

'Dash me,' said Byrd. 'You can see right through it, dash me.'

The girl patted Byrd's shoulder affectionately and moved on.

'You do have some remarkable friends,' said Byrd. He had ceased to criticize me and begun to regard me as a social curiosity well worth observing.

'A journalist must have contacts,' I explained.

'My goodness yes,' said Byrd.

The music stopped suddenly. Byrd mopped his face with a red silk handkerchief. 'It's like a stokehold,' he said. The club was strangely silent.

'Were you an engineer officer?'

'I did gunnery school when I was on lieutenants' list. Finished a Commander; might have made Captain if there'd been a little war, Rear-Admiral if there'd been another big one. Didn't fancy waiting. Twenty-seven years of sea duty is enough. Right through the hostilities and out the other side, more ships than I care to remember.'

'You must miss it.'

'Never. Why should I? Running a ship is just like running a small factory; just as exciting at times and just as dull for the most part. Never miss it a bit. Never think about it, to tell you the truth.'

'Don't you miss the sea, or the movement, or the weather?'

'Good grief, laddie, you've got a nasty touch of the Joseph Conrads. Ships, especially cruisers, are large metal factories, rather prone to pitch in bad weather. Nothing good about that, old boy—damned inconvenient, that's the truth of it! The Navy was just a job of work for me, and it suited me fine. Nothing against the Navy mind, not at all, owe it an awful lot, no doubt of it, but it was just a job like any other; no magic to being a sailor.' There was a plonking sound as someone tapped the amplifier and put on another record. 'Painting is the only true magic,' said Byrd. 'Translating three dimensions into two—or if you are a master, four.' He nodded suddenly, the loud music started. The clientèle, who had been stiff and anxious during the silence, smiled and relaxed, for they no longer faced the strain of conversing together.

On a staircase a wedge of people were embracing and laughing like advertising photos. At the bar a couple of English photographers were talking in cockney and an English writer was explaining James Bond.

A waiter put four glasses full of ice cubes and a half-bottle of Johnnie Walker on the table before us. 'What's this?' I asked.

The waiter turned away without answering. Two Frenchmen at the bar began to argue with the English writer and a bar stool fell over. The noise wasn't loud enough for anyone to notice. On the dance floor a girl in a shiny plastic suit was swearing at a man who had burned a hole in it with his cigarette. I heard the English writer behind me say, 'But I have always immensely adored violence. His violence is his humanity. Unless you understand that you understand nothing.' He wrinkled his nose and smiled. One of the Frenchmen replied, 'He suffers in translation.' The photographer was clicking his fingers in time to the music.

'Don't we all?' said the English writer, and looked around.

Byrd said, 'Shocking noise.'

'Don't listen,' I said.

'What?' said Byrd.

The English writer was saying ' ... a violent Everyman in a violent but humdrum ... ' he paused, 'but humdrum world.' He nodded agreement to himself. 'Let me remind you of Baudelaire. There's a sonnet that begins ... '

'So this bird wants to get out of the car ... ' one of the photographers was saying.

'Speak a little more quietly,' said the English writer. 'I'm going to recite a sonnet.'

'Belt up,' said the photographer over his shoulder. 'This bird wanted to get out of the car ... '

'Baudelaire,' said the writer. 'Violent, macabre and symbolic.'

'You leave bollicks out of this,' said the photographer, and his friend laughed. The writer put a hand on his shoulder and said, 'Look my friend ... ' The photographer planted a right jab into his solar plexus without spilling the drink he was holding. The writer folded up like a deckchair and hit the floor. A waiter grabbed towards the photographer but stumbled over the English writer's inert body.

'Look here,' said Byrd, and a passing waiter turned so fast that the half-bottle of whisky and the four glasses of ice were knocked over. Someone aimed a blow at the photographer's head. Byrd got to his feet saying quietly and reasonably, 'You spilled the drink on the floor. Dash me, you'd better pay for it. Only thing to do. Damned rowdies.' The waiter pushed Byrd violently and he fell back and disappeared among the densely packed dancers. Two or three people began to punch each other. A wild blow took me in the small of the back, but the attacker had moved on. I got both shoulder-blades rested against the nearest piece of wall and braced the sole of my right foot for leverage. One of the photographers came my way, but he kept going and wound up grappling with a waiter. There was a scuffle going on at the top of the staircase, and then violence travelled through the place like a flash flood. Everyone was punching everyone, girls were screaming and the music seemed to be even louder than before. A man hurried a girl along the corridor past me. 'It's those English that make trouble,' he complained.

'Yes,' I said.

'You look English.'

'No, I'm Belgian,' I said. He hurried after the girl. When I got near the emergency exit a waiter was barring the way. Behind me the screaming, grunting and breaking noises continued unabated. Someone had switched the music to top volume.

'I'm coming through,' I said to the waiter.

'No,' he said. 'No one leaves.'

A small man moved quickly alongside me. I flinched away from what I expected would be a blow upon my shoulder but it was a pat of encouragement. The man stepped forward and felled the waiter with two nasty karate cuts. 'They are all damned rude,' he said, stepping over the prostrate waiter. 'Especially waiters. If they showed a little good manners their customers might behave better.'

'Yes,' I said.

'Come along,' said Byrd. 'Don't moon around. Stay close to the wall. Watch the rear. You!' he shouted to a man with a ripped evening suit who was trying to open the emergency door. 'Pull the top bolt, man, ease the mortice at the same time. Don't hang around, don't want to have to disable too many of them, this is my painting hand.'

We emerged into a dark side-street. Maria's car was drawn up close to the exit. 'Get in,' she called.

'Were you inside?' I asked her.

She nodded. 'I was waiting for Jean-Paul.'

'Well, you two get along,' said Byrd.

'What about Jean-Paul?' Maria said to me.

'You two get along,' said Byrd. 'He'll be quite safe.'

'Can't we give you a lift?' asked Maria.

'I'd better go back and see if Jean-Paul is all right,' said Byrd.

'You'll get killed,' said Maria.

'Can't leave Jean-Paul in there,' explained Byrd. 'Close ranks, Jean-Paul's got to stop hanging around in these sort of places and get to bed early. The morning light is the only light to paint in. I wish I could make him understand that.'

Byrd hurried back towards the club. 'He'll get killed,' said Maria.

'I don't think so,' I said. We got into Maria's E-type.

Hurrying along the street came two men in raincoats and felt hats.

'They are from the P.J. crime squad,' said Maria. One of the men signalled to her. She wound the window down. He leaned down and touched his hat in salute. 'I'm looking for Byrd,' he said to Maria.

'Why?' I asked, but Maria had already told them he was the man who had just left us.

'Police judiciaire. I'm arresting him for the murder of Annie Couzins,' he said. 'I've got sworn statements from witnesses.'

'Oh God,' said Maria. 'I'm sure he's not guilty, he's not the violent type.'

I looked back to the door but Byrd had disappeared inside. The two policemen followed. Maria revved the motor and we bumped off the pavement, skimmed past a *moto* and purred into the Boul. St Germain.

The sky was starry and the air was warm. The visitors had spread through Paris by now and they strolled around entranced, in love, jilted, gay, suicidal, inspired, bellicose, defeated; in clean cotton St Trop, wine-stained Shetland, bearded, bald, bespectacled, bronzed. Acned little girls in bumbag trousers, lithe Danes, fleshy Greeks, nouveau-riche communists, illiterate writers, would-be directors— Paris had them all that summer; and Paris can keep them.

'You didn't exactly inspire me with admiration,' said Maria.

'How was that?'

'You didn't exactly spring to the aid of the ladies.'

'I didn't exactly know which ones were ladies,' I said.

'All you did was to save your own skin.'

'It's the only one I've got left,' I explained. 'I used the others for lampshades.' The blow I'd had in my kidneys hurt like hell. I'm getting too old for that sort of thing.

'Your funny time is running out,' said Maria.

'Don't be aggressive,' I said. 'It's not the right mood for asking favours.'

'How did you know I was going to ask a favour?'

'I can read the entrails, Maria. When you mistranslated my reactions to the injections that Datt gave me you were saving me up for something.'

'Do you think I was?' she smiled. 'Perhaps I just salvaged you to take home to bed with me.'

'No, it was more than that. You are having some sort of trouble with Datt and you think—probably wrongly— that I can do something about it.'

128

'What makes you think so?' The streets were quieter at the other end of St Germain. We passed the bomb-scarred façade of the War Ministry and raced a cab over the river. The Place de la Concorde was a great concrete field, floodlit like a film set.

'There's something in the way you speak of him. Also that night when he injected me you always moved around to keep my body between you and him. I think you had already decided to use me as a bulwark against him.'

'Teach Yourself Psychiatry, volume three.'

'Volume five. The one with the Do-It-Yourself Brain Surgery Kit.'

'Loiseau wants to see you tonight. He said it's something you'll enjoy helping him with.'

'What's he doing—disembowelling himself?' I said.

She nodded. 'Avenue Foch. Meet him at the corner at midnight.' She pulled up outside the Café Blanc.

'Come and have coffee,' I suggested.

'No. I must get home,' she said. I got out of the car and she drove away. Jean-Paul was sitting on the terrace drinking a Coca-Cola. He waved and I walked over to him. 'Were you in Les Chiens this evening?' I asked.

'Haven't been there for a week,' he said. 'I was going tonight but I changed my mind.'

'There was a *bagarre*. Byrd was there.'

Jean-Paul pulled a face but didn't seem interested. I ordered a drink and sat down. Jean-Paul stared at me.

19

Jean-Paul stared at the Englishman and wondered why he had sought him out. It was more than a coincidence. Jean-Paul didn't trust him. He thought he had seen Maria's car in the traffic just before the Englishman sat down. What had they both been plotting? Jean-Paul knew that no woman could be trusted. They consumed one, devoured one, sapped one's strength and confidence and gave no reassurance in return. The very nature of women made them his ... was 'enemy' too strong a word? He decided that 'enemy' wasn't too strong a word. They took away his manhood and yet demanded more and more physical love. 'Insatiable' was the only word for them. The other conclusion was not worth considering—that his sexual prowess was under par. No. Women were hot and lustful and, if he was truthful with himself, evil. His life was an endless struggle to quench the lustful fires of the women he met. And if he ever failed they would mock him and humiliate him. Women were waiting to humiliate him.

'Have you seen Maria lately?' Jean-Paul asked.

'A moment ago. She gave me a lift here.'

Jean-Paul smiled but did not comment. So that was it. At least the Englishman had not dared to lie to him. He must have read his eyes. He was in no mood to be trifled with.

'How's the painting going?' I asked. 'Were the critics kind to your friend's show the other day?'

'Critics,' said Jean-Paul, 'find it quite impossible to separate modern painting from teenage pregnancy, juvenile delinquency and the increase in crimes of violence.

They think that by supporting the dull, repetitious, repre-
sentational type of painting that is out of date and
unoriginal, they are also supporting loyalty to the flag,
discipline, a sense of fair play and responsible use of world
supremacy.'

I grinned. 'And what about those people that like
modern painting?'

'People who buy modern paintings are very often interested only in gaining admittance to the world of the young
artists. They are often wealthy vulgarians who, terrified
of being thought old and square, prove that they are both
by falling prey to quick-witted opportunists who paint
modern—very modern—paintings. Provided that they
keep on buying pictures they will continue to be invited to
bohemian parties.'

'There are no genuine painters?'

'Not many,' said Jean-Paul. 'Tell me, are English and
American exactly the same language, exactly the same?'

'Yes,' I said. Jean-Paul looked at me. 'Maria is very
taken with you.' I said nothing. 'I despise all women.'

'Why?'

'Because they all despise each other. They treat each
other with a cruelty that no man would inflict upon
another man. They never have a woman friend who they
can be sure won't betray them.'

'That sounds like a good reason for men to be kind to
them,' I said.

Jean-Paul smiled. He felt sure it was not meant seriously.

'The police have arrested Byrd for murder,' I said.

Jean-Paul was not surprised. 'I have always thought of
him as a killer.'

I was shocked.

'They all are,' said Jean-Paul. 'They are all killers for
their work. Byrd, Loiseau, Datt, even you, my friend, are
killers if work demands.'

'What are you talking about? Whom did Loiseau kill?'

'He killed Maria. Or do you think she was always like she is now—treacherous and confused, and constantly in fear of all of you?'

'But you are not a killer?'

'No,' said Jean-Paul. 'Whatever faults I have I am not a killer, unless you mean ... ' He paused before carefully pronouncing the English word, 'a "lady-killer".'

Jean-Paul smiled and put on his dark glasses.

20

I got to the Avenue Foch at midnight.

At the corner of a narrow alley behind the houses were four shiny motor-cycles and four policemen in crash helmets, goggles and short black leather coats. They stood there impassively as only policemen stand, not waiting for anything to happen, not glancing at their watches or talking, just standing looking as though they were the only people with a right to be there. Beyond the policemen there was Loiseau's dark-green DS 19, and behind that red barriers and floodlights marked the section of the road that was being excavated. There were more policemen standing near the barriers. I noticed that they were not traffic policemen but young, tough-looking cops with fidgety hands that continually tapped pistol holsters, belts and batons to make sure that everything was ready.

Inside the barriers twenty thick-shouldered men were bent over road-rippers. The sound was deafening, like machine-guns firing long bursts. The generator trucks played a steady drone. Near to me the ripper operator lifted the handles and prised the point into a sunsoft area of tar. He fired a volley and the metal buried its point deep, and with a sigh a chunk of paving fell back into the excavated area. The operator ordered another man to take over, and turned towards us mopping his sweaty head with a blue handkerchief. Under the overalls he wore a clean shirt and a silk tie. It was Loiseau.

'Hard work,' he said.

'You are going into the cellars?'

'Not the cellars of Datt's place,' Loiseau said to me.

'We're punching a hole in these cellars two doors away, then we'll mousehole through into Datt's cellars.'

'Why didn't you ask these people?' I pointed at the house behind which the roadwork was going on. 'Why not just ask them to let you through?'

'I don't work that way. As soon as I ask a favour I show my hand. I hate the idea of *you* knowing what we are doing. I may want to deny it tomorrow.' He mopped his brow again. 'In fact I'm damned sure I will be denying it tomorrow.' Behind him the road-ripper exploded into action and the chiselled dust shone golden in the beams of the big lights, like illustrations for a fairy story, but from the damp soil came that sour aroma of death and bacteria that clings around a bombarded city.

'Come along,' said Loiseau. We passed three huge Berliot buses full of policemen. Most were dozing with their képis pulled forward over their eyes; a couple were eating crusty sandwiches and a few were smoking. They didn't look at us as we passed by. They sat muscles slack, eyes unseeing and minds unthinking, as experienced combat troops rest between battles.

Loiseau walked towards a fourth bus; the windows were of dark-blue glass and from its coachwork a thick cable curved towards the ground and snaked away into a manhole-cover in the road. He ushered me up the steps past a sentry. Inside the bus was a brightly lit command centre. Two policemen sat operating radio and teleprinter equipment. At the back of the bus a large rack of MAT 49 sub-machine guns was guarded by a man who kept his silver-braided cap on to prove he was an officer.

Loiseau sat down behind a desk, produced a bottle of Calvados and two glasses. He poured a generous measure and pushed one across the desk to me. Loiseau sniffed at his own drink and sipped it tentatively. He drank a mouthful and turned to me. 'We hit some old *pavé* just under the surface. The city engineer's department didn't know it was there. That's what slowed us down, otherwise we'd be into the cellars by now, all ready for you.'

'All ready for me,' I repeated.

'Yes,' said Loiseau. 'I want you to be the first into the house.'

'Why?'

'Lots of reasons. You know the layout there, you know what Datt looks like. You don't look too much like a cop—especially when you open your mouth—and you can look after yourself. And if something's going to happen to the first man in I'd rather it wasn't one of my boys. It takes a long time to train one of my boys.' He allowed himself a grim little smile.

'What's the real reason?'

Loiseau made a motion with the flattened hand. He dropped it between us like a shutter or screen. 'I want you to make a phone call from inside the house. A clear call for the police that the operator at the Prefecture will enter in the log. We'll be right behind you, of course, it's just a matter of keeping the record straight.'

'Crooked, you mean,' I said. 'It's just a matter of keeping the record crooked.'

'That depends where you are sitting,' said Loiseau.

'From where I'm sitting, I don't feel much inclined to upset the Prefecture. The *Renseignements généraux* are there in that building and they include dossiers on us foreigners. When I make that phone call it will be entered on to my file and next time I ask for my *carte de séjour* they will want to deport me for immoral acts and goodness knows what else. I'll never get another aliens permit.'

'Do what all other foreigners do,' said Loiseau. 'Take a second-class return ticket to Brussels every ninety days. There are foreigners who have lived here for twenty years who still do that rather than hang around for five hours at the Prefecture waiting for a *carte de séjour*.' He held his flat hand high as though shielding his eyes from the glare of the sun.

'Very funny,' I said.

'Don't worry,' Loiseau said. 'I couldn't risk your telling the whole Prefecture that the Sûreté had enlisted you for a job.' He smiled. 'Just do a good job for me and I'll make sure you have no trouble with the Prefecture.'

'Thanks,' I said. 'And what if there is someone waiting for me at the other side of the mousehole? What if I have one of Datt's guard dogs leap at my throat, jaws open wide? What happens then?'

Loiseau sucked his breath in mock terror. He paused. 'Then you get torn to pieces,' he said, and laughed, and dropped his hand down abruptly like a guillotine.

'What do you expect to find there?' I asked. 'Here you are with dozens of cops and noise and lights—do you think they won't get nervous in the house?'

'You think they will?' Loiseau asked seriously.

'Some will,' I told him. 'At least a few of the most sophisticated ones will suspect that something's happening.'

'Sophisticated ones?'

'Come along, Loiseau,' I said irritably. 'There must be quite a lot of people close enough to your department to know the danger signals.'

He nodded and stared at me.

'So that's it,' I said. 'You were ordered to do it like this. Your department couldn't issue a warning to its associates but it could at least warn them by handling things noisily.'

'Darwin called it natural selection,' said Loiseau. 'The brightest ones will get away. You can probably guess my reaction, but at least I shall have the place closed down and may catch a few of the less imaginative clients. A little more Calvados.' He poured it.

I didn't agree to go, but Loiseau knew I would. The wrong side of Loiseau could be a very uncomfortable place to reside in Paris.

It was another half-hour before they had broken into the cellars under the alley and then it took twenty minutes more to mousehole through into Datt's house. The final few demolitions had to be done brick by brick with a couple of men from a burglar-alarm company tapping around for wiring.

I had changed into police overalls before going through the final breakthrough. We were standing in the cellar of Datt's next-door neighbour under the temporary lights that Loiseau's men had slung out from the electric mains. The bare bulb was close to Loiseau's face, his skin was wrinkled and grey with brick dust through which little rivers of perspiration were shining bright pink.

'My assistant will be right behind you as far as you need cover. If the dogs go for you he will use the shotgun, but only if you are in real danger, for it will alert the whole house.'

Loiseau's assistant nodded at me. His circular spectacle lenses flashed in the light of the bare bulb and reflected in them I could see two tiny Loiseaus and a few hundred glinting bottles of wine that were stacked behind me. He broke the breech of the shotgun and checked the cartridges even though he had only loaded the gun five minutes before.

'Once you are into the house, give my assistant your overalls. Make sure you are unarmed and have no compromising papers on you, because once we come in you might well be taken into custody with the others and it's always possible that one of my more zealous officers might search you. So if there's anything in your pockets that would embarrass you ... '

'There's a miniaturized radio transmitter inside my denture.'

'Get rid of it.'

'It was a joke.'

Loiseau grunted and said, 'The switchboard at the Prefecture is being held open from now on' — he checked his watch to be sure he was telling the truth — 'so you'll get through very quickly.'

'You told the Prefecture?' I asked. I knew that there was bitter rivalry between the two departments. It seemed unlikely that Loiseau would have confided in them.

'Let's say I have friends in the Signals Division,' said Loiseau. 'Your call will be monitored by us here in the command vehicle on our loop line.'*

'I understand,' I said.

'Final wall going now,' a voice called softly from the next cellar. Loiseau smacked me lightly on the back and I climbed through the small hole that his men had made in the wall. 'Take this,' he said. It was a silver pen, thick and clumsily made. 'It's a gas gun,' explained Loiseau. 'Use it at four metres or less but not closer than one, or it might damage the eyes. Pull the bolt back like this and let it go. The recess is the locking slot; that puts it on safety. But I don't think you'd better keep it on safety.'

'No,' I said, 'I'd hate it to be on safety.' I stepped into the cellar and picked my way upstairs.

The door at the top of the service flight was disguised as a piece of panelling. Loiseau's assistant followed me. He was supposed to have remained behind in the cellars but it wasn't my job to reinforce Loiseau's discipline. And anyway I could use a man with a shotgun.

I stepped out through the door.

One of my childhood books had a photo of a fly's eye magnified fifteen thousand times. The enormous glass chandelier looked like that eye, glinting and clinking and unwinking above the great formal staircase. I walked

*Paris police have their own telephone system independent of the public one.

across the mirror-like wooden floor feeling that the chandelier was watching me. I opened the tall gilded door and peered in. The wrestling ring had disappeared and so had the metal chairs; the salon was like the carefully arranged rooms of a museum: perfect yet lifeless. Every light in the place was shining bright, the mirrors repeated the nudes and nymphs of the gilded stucco and the painted panels.

I guessed that Loiseau's men were moving up through the mouseholed cellars but I didn't use the phone that was in the alcove in the hall. Instead I walked across the hall and up the stairs. The rooms that M. Datt used as offices — where I had been injected — were locked. I walked down the corridor trying the doors. They were all bedrooms. Most of them were unlocked; all of them were unoccupied. Most of the rooms were lavishly rococo with huge four-poster beds under brilliant silk canopies and four or five angled mirrors.

'You'd better phone,' said Loiseau's assistant.

'Once I phone the Prefecture will have this raid on record. I think we should find out a little more first.'

'I think ... '

'Don't tell me what you think or I'll remind you that you're supposed to have stayed down behind the wainscoting.'

'Okay,' he said. We both tiptoed up the small staircase that joined the first floor to the second. Loiseau's men must be fretting by now. At the top of the flight of steps I put my head round the corner carefully. I put my head everywhere carefully, but I needn't have been so cautious, the house was empty. 'Get Loiseau up here,' I said.

Loiseau's men went all through the house, tapping panelling and trying to find secret doors. There were no documents or films. At first there seemed to be no secrets of any kind except that the whole place was a kind of secret: the strange cells with the awful torture instruments, rooms made like lush train compartments or Rolls Royce cars, and all kinds of bizarre environments for sexual intercourse, even beds.

The peep-holes and the closed-circuit TV were all designed for M. Datt and his 'scientific methods'. I wondered what strange records he had amassed and where he had taken them, for M. Datt was nowhere to be found. Loiseau swore horribly. 'Someone,' he said, 'must have told Monsieur Datt that we were coming.'

Loiseau had been in the house about ten minutes when he called his assistant. He called long and loud from two floors above. When we arrived he was crouched over a black metal device rather like an Egyptian mummy. It was the size and very roughly the shape of a human body. Loiseau had put cotton gloves on and he touched the object carefully.

'The diagram of the Couzins girl,' he demanded from his assistant.

It was obtained from somewhere, a paper pattern of Annie Couzins's body marked in neat red ink to show the stab wounds, with the dimensions and depth written near each in tiny careful handwriting.

Loiseau opened the black metal case. 'That's it,' he said. 'Just what I thought.' Inside the case, which was just large enough to hold a person, knife points were positioned exactly as indicated on the police diagram. Loiseau gave a lot of orders and suddenly the room was full of men with tape-measures, white powder and camera equipment. Loiseau stood back out of their way. 'Iron maidens I think they call them,' he said. 'I seem to have read about them in some old schoolboy magazines.'

'What made her get into the damn thing?' I said.

'You are naive,' said Loiseau. 'When I was a young officer we had so many deaths from knife wounds in
140

brothels that we put a policeman on the door in each one. Every customer was searched. Any weapons he carried were chalked for identity. When the men left they got them back. I'll guarantee that not one got by that cop on the door but still the girls got stabbed, fatally sometimes.'

'How did it happen?'

'The girls—the prostitutes—smuggled them in. You'll never understand women.'

'No,' I said.

'Nor shall I,' said Loiseau.

21

Saturday was sunny, the light bouncing and sparkling as it does only in impressionist paintings and Paris. The boulevard had been fitted with wall-to-wall sunshine and out of it came the smell of good bread and black tobacco. Even Loiseau was smiling. He came galloping up my stairs at 8.30 a.m. I was surprised; he had never visited me before, at least not when I was at home.

'Don't knock, come in.' The radio was playing classical music from one of the pirate radio ships. I turned it off.

'I'm sorry,' said Loiseau.

'Everyone's at home to a policeman,' I said, 'in this country.'

'Don't be angry,' said Loiseau. 'I didn't know you would be in a silk dressing-gown, feeding your canary. It's very Noël Coward. If I described this scene as typically English, people would accuse me of exaggerating. You were talking to that canary,' said Loiseau. 'You were *talking* to it.'

'I try out all my jokes on Joe,' I said. 'But don't stand on ceremony, carry on ripping the place apart. What are you looking for this time?'

'I've said I'm sorry. What more can I do?'

'You could get out of my decrepit but very expensive apartment and stay out of my life. And you could stop putting your stubby peasant finger into my supply of coffee beans.'

'I was hoping you'd offer me some. You have this very light roast that is very rare in France.'

'I have a lot of things that are very rare in France.'

142

'Like the freedom to tell a policeman to "scram"?'

'Like that.'

'Well, don't exercise that freedom until we have had coffee together, even if you let me buy some downstairs.'

'Oh boy! Now I know you are on the tap. A cop is really on the make when he wants to pick up the bill for a cup of coffee.'

'I've had good news this morning.'

'They are restoring public executions.'

'On the contrary,' said Loiseau, letting my remark roll off him. 'There has been a small power struggle among the people from whom I take my orders and at present Datt's friends are on the losing side. I have been authorized to find Datt and his film collection by any means I think fit.'

'When does the armoured column leave? What's the plan—helicopters and flame-throwers and the one that burns brightest must have been carrying a tin of film?'

'You are too hard on the police methods in France. You think we could work with bobbies in pointed helmets carrying a wooden stick, but let me tell you, my friend, we wouldn't last two minutes with such methods. I remember the gangs when I was just a child—my father was a policeman—and most of all I remember Corsica. There were bandits; organized, armed and almost in control of the island. They murdered gendarmes with impunity. They killed policemen and boasted of it openly in the bars. Finally we had to get rough; we sent in a few platoons of the Republican Guard and waged a minor war. Rough, perhaps, but there was no other way. The entire income from all the Paris brothels was at stake. They fought and used every dirty trick they knew. It was war.'

'But you won the war.'

'It was the very last war we won,' Loiseau said bitterly.

143

'Since then we've fought in Lebanon, Syria, Indo-China, Madagascar, Tunisia, Morocco, Suez and Algeria. Yes, that war in Corsica was the last one we won.'

'Okay. So much for your problems; how do I fit into your plans?'

'Just as I told you before; you are a foreigner and no one would think you were a policeman, you speak excellent French and you can look after yourself. What's more you would not be the sort of man who would reveal where your instructions came from, not even under pressure.'

'It sounds as though you think Datt still has a kick or two left in him.'

'They have a kick or two left in them even when they are suspended in space with a rope around the neck. I never underestimate the people I'm dealing with, because they are usually killers when it comes to the finale. Any time I overlook that, it will be one of my policemen who takes the bullet in the head, not me. So I don't overlook it, which means I have a tough, loyal, confident body of men under my command.'

'Okay,' I said. 'So I locate Datt. What then?'

'We can't have another fiasco like last time. Now Datt will be more than ever prepared. I want all his records. I want them because they are a constant threat to a lot of people, including stupid people in the Government of my country. I want that film because I loathe blackmail and I loathe blackmailers — they are the filthiest section of the criminal cesspit.'

'But so far there's been no blackmail, has there?'

'I'm not standing around waiting for the obvious to happen. I want that stuff destroyed. I don't want to hear that it was destroyed. I want to destroy it myself.'

'Suppose I don't want anything to do with it?'

Loiseau splayed out his hands. 'One,' he said, grabbing one pudgy finger, 'you are already involved. Two,' he grabbed the next finger, 'you are employed by some sort of British government department from what I can understand. They will be very angry if you turn down this chance of seeing the outcome of this affair.'

I suppose my expression changed.

'Oh, it's my business to know these things,' said Loiseau. 'Three. Maria has decided that you are trustworthy and in spite of her occasional lapses I have great regard for her judgment. She is, after all an employee of the Sûreté.'

Loiseau grabbed his fourth digit but said nothing. He smiled. In most people a smile or a laugh can be a sign of embarrassment, a plea to break the tension. Loiseau's smile was a calm, deliberate smile. 'You are waiting for me to threaten you with what will happen if you don't help me.' He shrugged and smiled again. 'Then you would turn my previous words about blackmail upon me and feel at ease in declining to help. But I won't. You are free to do as you wish in this matter. I am a very unthreatening type.'

'For a cop,' I said.

'Yes,' agreed Loiseau, 'a very unthreatening type for a cop.' It was true.

'Okay,' I said after a long pause. 'But don't mistake my motives. Just to keep the record straight, I'm very fond of Maria.'

'Can you really believe that would annoy me? You are so incredibly Victorian in these matters: so determined to play the game and keep a stiff upper lip and have the record straight. We do not do things that way in France; another man's wife is fair game for all. Smoothness of tongue and nimbleness of foot are the trump cards; nobleness of mind is the joker.'

'I prefer my way.'

Loiseau looked at me and smiled his slow, nerveless smile. 'So do I,' he said.

'Loiseau,' I said watching him carefully, 'this clinic of Datt's: is it run by your Ministry?'

'Don't *you* start that too. He's got half Paris thinking he's running that place for us.' The coffee was still hot. Loiseau got a bowl out of the cupboard and poured himself some. 'He's not connected with us,' said Loiseau. 'He's a criminal, a criminal with good connections but still just a criminal.'

'Loiseau,' I said, 'you can't hold Byrd for the murder of the girl.'

'Why not?'

'Because he didn't do it, that's why not. I was at the clinic that day. I stood in the hall and watched the girl run through and die. I heard Datt say, "Get Byrd here." It was a frame-up.'

Loiseau reached for his hat. 'Good coffee,' he said.

'It was a frame-up. Byrd is innocent.'

'So you say. But suppose Byrd had done the murder and Datt said that just for you to overhear? Suppose I told you that we know that Byrd was there? That would put this fellow Kuang in the clear, eh?'

'It might,' I said, 'if I heard Byrd admit it. Will you arrange for me to see Byrd? That's my condition for helping you.' I expected Loiseau to protest but he nodded. 'Agreed,' he said. 'I don't know why you worry about him. He's a criminal type if ever I saw one.' I didn't answer because I had a nasty idea that Loiseau was right.

'Very well,' said Loiseau. 'The bird market at eleven a.m. tomorrow.'

'It's Sunday tomorrow,' I said.

'All the better, the Palais de Justice is quieter on Sunday.' He smiled again. 'Good coffee.'

'That's what they all say,' I said.

22

A considerable portion of that large island in the Seine is occupied by the law in one shape or another. There's the Prefecture and the courts, Municipal and Judicial police offices, cells for remand prisoners and a police canteen. On a weekday the stairs are crammed with black-gowned lawyers clutching plastic briefcases and scurrying like disturbed cockroaches. But on Sunday the Palais de Justice is silent. The prisoners sleep late and the offices are empty. The only movement is the thin stream of tourists who respectfully peer at the high vaulting of the Sainte Chapelle, clicking and wondering at its unparalleled beauty. Outside in the Place Louis Lépine a few hundred caged birds twitter in the sunshine and in the trees are wild birds attracted by the spilled seed and commotion. There are sprigs of millet, cuttlebone and bright new wooden cages, bells to ring, swings to swing on and mirrors to peck at. Old men run their shrivelled hands through the seeds, sniff them, discuss them and hold them up to the light as though they were fine vintage Burgundies.

The bird market was busy by the time I got there to meet Loiseau. I parked the car opposite the gates of the Palais de Justice and strolled through the market. The clock was striking eleven with a dull dented sound. Loiseau was standing in front of some cages marked '*Caille reproductrice*'. He waved as he saw me, 'Just a moment,' he said. He picked up a box marked 'vitamine phosphate'. He read the label: '*Biscuits pour oiseaux*'. 'I'll have that too,' said Loiseau.

The woman behind the table said, 'The *mélange saxon* is very good, it's the most expensive, but it's the best.'

'Just half a litre,' said Loiseau.

She weighed the seed, wrapped it carefully and tied the package. Loiseau said, 'I didn't see him.'

'Why?' I walked with him through the market.

'He's been moved. I can't find out who authorized the move or where he's gone to. The clerk in the records office said Lyon but that can't be true.' Loiseau stopped in front of an old pram full of green millet.

'Why?'

Loiseau didn't answer immediately. He picked up a sprig of millet and sniffed at it. 'He's been moved. Some top-level instructions. Perhaps they intend to bring him before some *juge d'instruction* who will do as he's told. Or maybe they'll keep him out of the way while they finish the *enquêtes officieuses*.'*

'You don't think they've moved him away to get him quietly sentenced?'

Loiseau waved to the old woman behind the stall. She shuffled slowly towards us.

'I talk to you like an adult,' Loiseau said. 'You don't really expect me to answer that, do you? A sprig.' He turned and stared at me. 'Better make it two sprigs,' he

* Under French Law the Prefect of Paris Police can arrest, interrogate, inquire, search, confiscate letters in the post, without any other authority than his own. His only obligation is to inform the Public Prosecutor and bring the prisoner before a magistrate within twenty-four hours. Note that the magistrate is part of the law machine and not a separate functionary as he is in Britain.

When he is brought before the magistrate—*juge d'instruction*—the police explain that the man is *suspected* and the magistrate directs the building up of evidence. (In Britain, of course, the man is not brought before a magistrate until after the police have built up their case.)

Inquiries prior to the appearance before a *juge d'instruction* are called *enquêtes officieuses* (informal inquiries). In law the latter give no power to search or demand statements but in practice few citizens argue about this technicality when faced with the police.

said to the woman. 'My friend's canary wasn't looking so healthy last time I saw it.'

'Joe's all right,' I said. 'You leave him alone.'

'Suit yourself,' said Loiseau. 'But if he gets much thinner he'll be climbing out between the bars of that cage.'

I let him have the last word. He paid for the millet and walked between the cliffs of new empty cages, trying the bars and tapping the wooden panels. There were caged birds of all kinds in the market. They were given seed, millet, water and cuttlefish bone for their beaks. Their claws were kept trimmed and they were safe from birds of prey. But it was the birds in the trees that were singing.

23

I got back to my apartment about twelve o'clock. At twelve thirty-five the phone rang. It was Monique, Annie's neighbour. 'You'd better come quickly,' she said.

'Why?'

'I'm not allowed to say on the phone. There's a fellow sitting here. He won't tell me anything much. He was asking for Annie, he won't tell me anything. Will you come now?'

'Okay,' I said.

24

It was lunchtime. Monique was wearing an ostrich-feather-trimmed négligé when she opened the door. 'The English have got off the boat,' she said and giggled. 'You'd better come in, the old girl will be straining her earholes to hear, if we stand here talking.' She opened the door and showed me into the cramped room. There was bamboo furniture and tables, a plastic-topped dressing-table with four swivel mirrors and lots of perfume and cosmetic garnishes. The bed was unmade and a candle-wick bedspread had been rolled up under the pillows. A copy of *Salut les Copains* was in sections and arranged around the deep warm indentation. She went across to the windows and pushed the shutters. They opened with a loud clatter. The sunlight streamed into the room and made everything look dusty. On the table there was a piece of pink wrapping paper; she took a hard boiled egg from it, rapped the shell open and bit into it.

'I hate summer,' she said. 'Pimples and parks and open cars that make your hair tangled and rotten cold food that looks like left-overs. And the sun trying to make you feel guilty about being indoors. I like being indoors. I like being in bed; it's no sin, is it, being in bed?'

'Just give me the chance to find out. Where is he?'

'I hate summer.'

'So shake hands with Père Noël,' I offered. 'Where is he?'

'I'm taking a shower. You sit down and wait. You are all questions.'

'Yes,' I said. 'Questions.'

'I don't know how you think of all these questions. You must be clever.'

'I am,' I said.

'Honestly, I wouldn't know where to start. The only questions I ever ask are "Are you married?" and "What will you do if I get pregnant?" Even then I never get told the truth.'

'That's the trouble with questions. You'd better stick to answers.'

'Oh, I know all the answers.'

'Then you must have been asked all the questions.'

'I have,' she agreed.

She slipped out of the négligé and stood naked for one millionth of a second before disappearing into the bathroom. The look in her eyes was mocking and not a little cruel.

There was a lot of splashing and ohh-ing from the bathroom until she finally reappeared in a cotton dress and canvas tennis shoes, no stockings.

'Water was cold,' she said briefly. She walked right through the room and opened her front door. I watched her lean over the balustrade.

'The water's stone cold, you stupid old cow,' she shrieked down the stair-well. From somewhere below the voice of the old harridan said, 'It's not supposed to supply ten people for each apartment, you filthy little whore.'

'I have something men want, not like you, you old hag.'

'And you give it to them,' the harridan cackled back. 'The more the merrier.'

'Poof!' shouted Monique, and narrowing her eyes and aiming carefully she spat over the stair-well. The harridan must have anticipated it, for I heard her cackle triumphantly.

Monique returned to me. 'How am I expected to keep clean when the water is cold? Always cold.'

'Did Annie complain about the water?'

'Ceaselessly, but she didn't have the manner that brings results. I get angry. If she doesn't give me hot water I shall drive her into her grave, the dried-up old bitch. I'm leaving here anyway,' she said.

'Where are you going?' I asked.

'I'm moving in with my regular. Montmartre. It's an awful district, but it's larger than this, and anyway he wants me.'

'What's he do for a living?'

'He does the clubs, he's — don't laugh — he's a conjurer. It's a clever trick he does: he takes a singing canary in a large cage and makes it disappear. It looks fantastic. Do you know how he does it?'

'No.'

'The cage folds up. That's easy, it's a trick cage. But the bird gets crushed. Then when he makes it reappear it's just another canary that looks the same. It's an easy trick really, it's just that no one in the audience suspects that he would kill the bird each time in order to do the trick.'

'But you guessed.'

'Yes. I guessed the first time I saw it done. He thought I was clever to guess but as I said, "How much does a canary cost? Three francs, four at the very most." It's clever though, isn't it, you've got to admit it's clever.'

'It's clever,' I said, 'but I like canaries better than I like conjurers.'

'Silly,' Monique laughed disbelievingly. ' "The incredible Count Szell" he calls himself.'

'So you'll be a countess?'

'It's his stage name, silly.' She picked up a pot of face cream. 'I'll be just another stupid woman who lives with a married man.'

She rubbed cream into her face.

'Where is he?' I finally asked. 'Where's this fellow that

you said was sitting here?' I was prepared to hear that she'd invented the whole thing.

'In the café on the corner. He'll be all right there. He's reading his American newspapers. He's all right.'

'I'll go and talk to him.'

'Wait for me.' She wiped the cream away with a tissue and turned and smiled. 'Am I all right?'

'You're all right,' I told her.

25

The café was on the Boul. Mich., the very heart of the left bank. Outside in the bright sun sat the students; hirsute and earnest, they have come from Munich and Los Angeles sure that Hemingway and Lautrec are still alive and that some day in some left bank café they will find them. But all they ever find are other young men who look exactly like themselves, and it's with this sad discovery that they finally return to Bavaria or California and become salesmen or executives. Meanwhile here they sat in the hot seat of culture, where businessmen became poets, poets became alcoholics, alcoholics became philosophers and philosophers realized how much better it was to be businessmen.

Hudson. I've got a good memory for faces. I saw Hudson as soon as we turned the corner. He was sitting alone at a café table holding his paper in front of his face while studying the patrons with interest. I called to him.

'Jack Percival,' I called. 'What a great surprise.'

The American hydrogen research man looked surprised, but he played along very well for an amateur. We sat down with him. My back hurt from the rough-house in the discothèque. It took a long time to get served because the rear of the café was full of men with tightly wadded newspapers trying to pick themselves a winner instead of eating. Finally I got the waiter's attention. 'Three grands crèmes,' I said. Hudson said nothing else until the coffees arrived.

'What about this young lady?' Hudson asked. He

dropped sugar cubes into his coffee as though he was suffering from shock. 'Can I talk?'

'Sure,' I said. 'There are no secrets between Monique and me.' I leaned across to her and lowered my voice. 'This is very confidential, Monique,' I said. She nodded and looked pleased. 'There is a small plastic bead company with its offices in Grenoble. Some of the holders of ordinary shares have sold their holdings out to a company that this gentleman and I more or less control. Now at the next shareholders meeting we shall ... '

'Give over,' said Monique. 'I can't stand business talk.'

'Well run along then,' I said, granting her her freedom with an understanding smile.

'Could you buy me some cigarettes?' she asked.

I got two packets from the waiter and wrapped a hundred-franc note round them. She trotted off down the street with them like a dog with a juicy bone.

'It's not about your bead factory,' he said.

'There is no bead factory,' I explained.

'Oh!' He laughed nervously. 'I was supposed to have contacted Annie Couzins,' he said.

'She's dead.'

'I found that out for myself.'

'From Monique?'

'You are T. Davis?' he asked suddenly.

'With bells on,' I said and passed my resident's card to him.

An untidy man with a constantly smiling face walked from table to table winding up toys and putting them on the tables. He put them down everywhere until each table had its twitching mechanical figures bouncing through the knives, table mats and ashtrays. Hudson picked up the convulsive little violin player. 'What's this for?'

'It's on sale,' I said.

He nodded and put it down. 'Everything is,' he said.

He returned my resident's card to me.

'It looks all right,' he agreed. 'Anyway I can't go back to the Embassy, they told me that most expressly, so I'll have to put myself in your hands. I'm out of my depth to tell you the truth.'

'Go ahead.'

'I'm an authority on hydrogen bombs and I know quite a bit about all the work on the nuclear programme. My instructions are to put certain information about fall-out dangers at the disposal of a Monsieur Datt. I understand he is connected with the Red Chinese Government.'

'And why are you to do this?'

'I thought you'd know. It's such a mess. That poor girl being dead. Such a tragedy. I did meet her once. So young, such a tragic business. I thought they would have told you all about it. You were the only other name they gave me, apart from her I mean. I'm acting on U.S. Government orders, of course.'

'Why would the U.S. Government want you to give away fall-out data?' I asked him. He sat back in the cane chair till it creaked like elderly arthritic joints. He pulled an ashtray near him.

'It all began with the Bikini Atoll nuclear tests,' he began. 'The Atomic Energy Commission were taking a lot of criticism about the dangers of fall-out, the biological result upon wildlife and plants. The A.E.C. needed those tests and did a lot of follow-through testing on the sites, trying to prove that the dangers were not anything like as great as many alarmists were saying. I have to tell you that those alarmists were damn nearly right. A dirty bomb of about twenty-five megatons would put down about 15,000 square miles of lethal radio-activity. To survive that, you would have to stay underground for months, some say even a year or more.

'Now if we were involved in a war with Red China, and I dread the thought of such a thing, then we would have to use the nuclear fall-out as a weapon, because only ten per cent of the Chinese population live in large—quarter-million size—towns. In the U.S.A. more than half the population live in the large towns. China with its dispersed population can only be knocked out by fall-out … ' He paused. 'But knocked out it can be. Our experts say that about half a billion people live on one-fifth of China's land area. The prevailing wind is westerly. Four hundred bombs would kill fifty million by direct heat-blast effect, one hundred million would be seriously injured though they wouldn't need hospitalization, but three hundred and fifty million would die by windborne fall-out.

'The A.E.C. minimized the fall-out effects in their follow-through reports on the tests (Bikini, etc.). Now the more militant of the Chinese soldier-scientists are using the U.S. reports to prove that China can survive a nuclear war. We couldn't withdraw those reports, or say that they were untrue—not even slightly untrue—so I'm here to leak the correct information to the Chinese scientists. The whole operation began nearly eight months ago. It took a long time getting this girl Annie Couzins into position.'

'In the clinic near to Datt.'

'Exactly. The original idea was that she should introduce me to this man Datt and say I was an American scientist with a conscience.'

'That's a piece of C.I.A. thinking if ever I heard one?'

'You think it's an extinct species?'

'It doesn't matter what I think, but it's not a line that Datt will buy easily.'

'If you are going to start changing the plan now … '

'The plan changed when the girl was killed. It's a mess; the only way I can handle it is my way.'

'Very well,' said Hudson. He sat silent for a moment.

Behind me a man with a rucksack said, 'Florence. We hated Florence.'

'We hated Trieste,' said a girl.

'Yes,' said the man with the rucksack, 'my friend hated Trieste last year.'

'My contact here doesn't know why you are in Paris,' I said suddenly. I tried to throw Hudson, but he took it calmly.

'I hope he doesn't,' said Hudson. 'It's all supposed to be top secret. I hated to come to you about it but I've no other contact here.'

'You're at the Lotti Hotel.'

'How did you know?'

'It's stamped across your *Tribune* in big blue letters.'

He nodded. I said, 'You'll go to the Hotel Ministère right away. Don't get your baggage from the Lotti. Buy a toothbrush or whatever you want on the way back now.' I expected to encounter opposition to this idea but Hudson welcomed the game.

'I get you,' he said. 'What name shall I use?'

'Let's make it Potter,' I said. He nodded. 'Be ready to move out at a moment's notice. And Hudson, don't telephone or write any letters; you know what I mean. Because I could become awfully suspicious of you.'

'Yes,' he said.

'I'll put you in a cab,' I said, getting up to leave.

'Do that, their Métro drives me crazy.'

I walked up the street with him towards the cab-rank. Suddenly he dived into an optician's. I followed.

'Ask him if I can look at some spectacles,' he said.

'Show him some spectacles,' I told the optician. He put a case full of tortoiseshell frames on the counter.

'He'll need a test,' said the optician. 'Unless he has his prescription he'll need a test.'

'You'll need a test or a prescription,' I told Hudson.

He had sorted out a frame he liked. 'Plain glass,' he demanded.

'What would I keep plain glass around for?' said the optician.

'What would he keep plain glass for?' I said to Hudson.

'The weakest glass possible, then,' said Hudson.

'The weakest possible,' I said to the optician. He fixed the lenses in in a moment or so. Hudson put the glasses on and we resumed our walk towards the taxi. He peered around him myopically and was a little unsteady.

'Disguise,' said Hudson.

'I thought perhaps it was,' I said.

'I would have made a good spy,' said Hudson. 'I've often thought that.'

'Yes,' I said. 'Well, there's your cab. I'll be in touch. Check out of the Lotti into the Ministère. I've written the name down on my card, they know me there. Try not to attract attention. Stay inside.'

'Where's the cab?' said Hudson.

'If you'll take off those bloody glasses,' I said, 'you might be able to see.'

26

I went round to Maria's in a hurry. When she opened the door she was wearing riding breeches and a roll-neck pullover. 'I was about to go out,' she said.

'I need to see Datt,' I said.

'Why do you tell me that?'

I pushed past her and closed the door behind us. 'Where is he?'

She gave me a twitchy little ironical smile while she thought of something crushing to say. I grabbed her arm and let my fingertips bite. 'Don't fool about with me, Maria. I'm not in the mood. Believe me I would hit you.'

'I've no doubt about it.'

'You told Datt about Loiseau's raid on the place in the Avenue Foch. You have no loyalties, no allegiance, none to the Sûreté, none to Loiseau. You just give away information as though it was toys out of a bran tub.'

'I thought you were going to say I gave it away as I did my sexual favours,' she smiled again.

'Perhaps I was.'

'Did you remember that I kept your secret without giving it away? No one knows what you truly said when Datt gave you the injection.'

'No one knows yet. I suspect that you are saving it up for something special.'

She swung her hand at me but I moved out of range. She stood for a moment, her face twitching with fury.

'You ungrateful bastard,' she said. 'You're the first real bastard I've ever met.'

I nodded. 'There's not many of us around. Ungrateful

for what?' I asked her. 'Ungrateful for your loyalty? Was that what your motive was: loyalty?'

'Perhaps you're right,' she admitted quietly. 'I have no loyalty to anyone. A woman on her own becomes awfully hard. Datt is the only one who understands that. Somehow I didn't want Loiseau to arrest him.' She looked up. 'For that and many reasons.'

'Tell me one of the other reasons?'

'Datt is a senior man in the S.D.E.C.E., that's one reason. If Loiseau clashed with him, Loiseau could only lose.'

'Why do you think Datt is an S.D.E.C.E. man?'

'Many people know. Loiseau won't believe it but it's true.'

'Loiseau won't believe it because he has got too much sense. I've checked up on Datt. He's never had anything to do with any French intelligence unit. But he knew how useful it was to let people think so.'

She shrugged. 'I know it's true,' she said. 'Datt works for the S.D.E.C.E.'

I took her shoulders. 'Look, Maria. Can't you get it through your head that he's a phoney? He has no psychiatry diploma, has never been anything to do with the French Government except that he pulls strings among his friends and persuades even people like you who work for the Sûreté that he's a highly placed agent of S.D.E.C.E.'

'And what do you want?' she asked.

'I want you to help me find Datt.'

'Help,' she said. 'That's a new attitude. You come bursting in here making your demands. If you'd come in here asking for help I might have been more sympathetic. What is it you want with Datt?'

'I want Kuang; he killed the girl at the clinic that day. I want to find him.'

'It's not your job to find him.'

'You are right. It's Loiseau's job, but he is holding Byrd for it and he'll keep on holding him.'

'Loiseau wouldn't hold an innocent man. Poof, you don't know what a fuss he makes about the sanctity of the law and that sort of thing.'

'I am a British agent,' I said. 'You know that already so I'm not telling you anything new. Byrd is too.'

'Are you sure?'

'No, I'm not. I'd be the last person to be told anyway. He's not someone whom I would contact officially. It's just my guess. I think Loiseau has been instructed to hold Byrd for the murder—with or without evidence—so Byrd is doomed unless I push Kuang right into Loiseau's arms.'

Maria nodded.

'Your mother lives in Flanders. Datt will be at his house near by, right?' Maria nodded. 'I want you to take an American out to your mother's house and wait there till I phone.'

'She hasn't got a phone.'

'Now, now, Maria,' I said. 'I checked up your mother: she has a phone. Also I phoned my people here in Paris. They will be bringing some papers to your mother's house. They'll be needed for crossing the border. No matter what I say don't come over to Datt's without them.'

Maria nodded. 'I'll help. I'll help you pin that awful Kuang, I hate him.'

'And Datt, do you hate him too?'

She looked at me searchingly. 'Sometimes, but in a different sort of way,' she said. 'You see, I'm his illegitimate daughter. Perhaps you checked up on that too?'

27

The road was straight. It cared nothing for geography, geology or history. The oil-slicked highway dared children and divided neighbours. It speared small villages through their hearts and laid them open. It was logical that it should be so straight, and yet it was obsessive too. Carefully lettered signs—the names of villages and the times of Holy Mass—and then the dusty clutter of houses flicked past with seldom any sign of life. At Le Cateau I turned off the main road and picked my way through the small country roads. I saw the sign Plaisir ahead and slowed. This was the place I wanted.

The main street of the village was like something out of Zane Grey, heavy with the dust of passing vehicles. None of them stopped. The street was wide enough for four lanes of cars, but there was very little traffic. Plaisir was on the main road to nowhere. Perhaps a traveller who had taken the wrong road at St Quentin might pass through Plaisir trying to get back on to the Paris–Brussels road. Some years back when they were building the autoroute, heavy lorries had passed through, but none of them had stopped at Plaisir.

Today it was hot; scorching hot. Four mangy dogs had scavenged enough food and now were asleep in the centre of the roadway. Every house was shuttered tight, grey and dusty in the cruel biting midday light that gave them only a narrow rim of shadow.

I stopped the car near to a petrol pump, an ancient, handle-operated instrument bolted uncertainly on to a concrete pillar. I got out and thumped upon the garage doors, but there was no response. The only other vehicle in sight was an old tractor parked a few yards ahead. On the other side of the street a horse stood, tethered to a piece of rusty farm machinery, flicking its tail against the flies. I touched the engine of the tractor: it was still warm. I hammered the garage doors again, but the only movement was the horse's tail. I walked down the silent street, the stones hot against my shoes. One of the dogs, its left ear missing, scratched itself awake and crawled into the shade of the tractor. It growled dutifully at me as I passed, then subsided into sleep. A cat's eyes peered through a window full of aspidistra plants. Above the window, faintly discernible in the weathered woodwork, I read the word 'café'. The door was stiff and opened noisily. I went in.

There were half a dozen people standing at the bar. They weren't talking and I had the feeling that they had been watching me since I left the car. They stared at me.

'A red wine,' I said. The old woman behind the bar looked at me without blinking. She didn't move.

'And a cheese sandwich,' I added. She gave it another minute before slowly reaching for a wine bottle, rinsing a glass and pouring me a drink, all without moving her feet. I turned around to face the room. The men were mostly farm workers, their boots heavy with soil and their faces engraved with ancient dirt. In the corner a table was occupied by three men in suits and white shirts. Although it was long past lunchtime they had napkins tucked into their collars and were putting forkfuls of cheese into their pink mouths, honing their knives across the bread chunks and pouring draughts of red wine into their throats after it. They continued to eat. They were the only people in the room not looking at me except for a muscular man seated at the back of the room, his feet propped upon a chair, placing the cards of his patience game with quiet confidence. I watched him peel each card loose from the pack, stare at it with the superior impartiality of a computer and place it face up on the marble table-top. I watched him play for a minute or so, but he didn't look up.

It was a dark room; the only light entering it filtered through the jungle of plants in the window. On the marble-topped tables there were drip-mats advertising aperitifs; the mats had been used many times. The bar was brown with varnish and above the rows of bottles was an old clock that had ticked its last at 3.37 on some long-forgotten day. There were old calendars on the walls, a broken chair had been piled neatly under the window and the floor-boards squealed with each change of weight. In spite of the heat of the day three men had drawn their chairs close to a dead stove in the centre of the room. The body of the stove had cracked, and from it cold ash had spilled on to the floor. One of the men tapped his pipe against the stove. More ash poured out like the sands of time.

'I'm looking for Monsieur Datt,' I said to the whole room. 'Which is his house?'

There was not even a change of expression. Outside I heard the sudden yelp of a frightened dog. From the corner came the regular click of playing cards striking the marble. There was no other sound.

I said, 'I have important news for him. I know he lives somewhere in the village.' I moved my eyes from face to face searching for a flicker of comprehension; there was none. Outside the dogs began to fight. It was a ragged, vicious sound: low growls and sudden shrieks of pain.

'This is Plaisir?' I asked. There was no answer. I turned to the woman behind the bar. 'Is this the village of Plaisir?' She half smiled.

'Another carafe of red,' called one of the men in white shirts.

The woman behind the bar reached for a litre bottle of
166

wine, poured a carafe of it and pushed it down the counter. The man who had asked for it walked across to the counter, his napkin stuck in his collar, a fork still in his hand. He seized the carafe by the neck and returned to his seat. He poured a glass of wine for himself and took a large gulp. With the wine still in his mouth he leaned back in his chair, raised his eyes to mine and let the wine trickle into his throat. The dogs began fighting again.

'They are getting vicious,' said the man. 'Perhaps we should do away with one of them.'

'Do away with them all,' I said. He nodded.

I finished my drink. 'Three francs,' said the woman.

'What about a cheese sandwich?'

'We sell only wine.'

I put three new francs on the counter-top. The man finished his patience game and collected the dog-eared cards together. He drank his glass of red wine and carried the empty glass and the greasy pack of cards to the counter. He put them both down and laid two twenty old-franc pieces on top, then he wiped his hands on the front of his work jacket and stared at me for a moment. His eyes were quick and alert. He turned towards the door.

'Are you going to tell me how to get to Monsieur Datt's house?' I asked the woman again.

'We only sell wine,' she said, scooping up the coins. I walked out into the hot midday sun. The man who had been playing patience walked slowly across to the tractor. He was a tall man, better nourished and more alert than the local inhabitants, perhaps thirty years old, walking like a horseman. When he reached the petrol pump, he whistled softly. The door opened immediately and an attendant came out.

'Ten litres.'

The attendant nodded. He inserted the nozzle of the pump into the tank of the tractor, unlocked the handle and then rocked it to pump the spirit out. I watched them close to, but neither looked round. When the needle read ten litres, he stopped pumping and replaced the nozzle. 'See you tomorrow,' said the tall man. He did not pay. He threw a leg over the tractor seat and started the motor. There was an ear-splitting racket as it started. He let in the clutch too quickly and the big wheels slid in the dust for an instant before biting into the *pavé* and roaring away, leaving a trail of blue smoke. The one-eared dog awoke again as the sound and hot sun hit it and went bounding up the road barking and snapping at the tractor wheels. That awoke the other dogs and they, too, began to bark. The tall man leaned over his saddle like an apache scout and caught the dog under its only ear with a wooden stick. It sang a descant of pain and retired from the chase. The other dogs too lost heart, their energy sapped by the heat. The barking ended raggedly.

'I'm thinking of driving to the Datt house,' I said to the pump attendant. He stared after the tractor. 'He'll never learn,' he said. The dog limped back into the shade of the petrol pump. The attendant turned to face me. 'Some dogs are like that,' he said. 'They never learn.'

'If I drive to the Datt house I'll need twenty litres of the best.'

'Only one kind,' said the man.

'I'll need twenty litres *if* you'll be kind enough to direct me to the Datt place.'

'You'd better fill her up,' said the man. He raised his eyes to mine for the first time. 'You're going to need to come back, aren't you?'

'Right,' I said. 'And check the oil and water.' I took a ten-franc note from my pocket. 'That's for you,' I said. 'For your trouble.'

'I'll look at the battery too,' he said.

'I'll commend you to the tourist board,' I said. He

nodded. He took the pump nozzle and filled the tank, he opened up the rad cap with a cloth and then rubbed the battery. 'Everything's okay,' he said. I paid him for the petrol.

'Are you going to check the tyres?'

He kicked one of them. 'They'll do you. It's only down the road. Last house before the church. They are waiting for you.'

'Thanks,' I said, trying not to look surprised. Down the long straight road I watched the bus come, trailed by a cloud of dust. It stopped in the street outside the café. The customers came out to watch. The driver climbed on to the roof of the bus and got some boxes and cases down. One woman had a live chicken, another a birdcage. They straightened their clothes and stretched their limbs.

'More visitors,' I said.

He stared at me and we both looked towards the bus. The passengers finished stretching themselves and got back aboard again. The bus drove away, leaving just four boxes and a birdcage in the street. I glanced towards the café and there was a movement of eyes. It may have been the cat watching the fluttering of the caged bird; it was that sort of cat.

28

The house was the last one in the street, if you call endless high railings and walls a street. I stopped outside the gates; there was no name or bell pull. Beyond the house a small child attending two tethered goats stared at me for a moment and ran away. Near to the house was a copse and half concealed in it a large grey square concrete block: one of the Wehrmacht's indestructible contributions to European architecture.

A nimble little woman rushed to the gates and tugged them open. The house was tall and narrow and not particularly beautiful, but it was artfully placed in about twenty acres of ground. To the right, the kitchen garden sloped down to two large glasshouses. Beyond the house there was a tiny park where statues hid behind trees like grey stone children playing tag, and in between, there were orderly rows of fruit trees and an enclosure where laundry could just be glimpsed flapping in the breeze.

I drove slowly past a grimy swimming pool where a beach ball and some ice-cream wrappers floated. Tiny flies flickered close to the surface of the water. Around the rim of the pool there was some garden furniture: arm-chairs, stools and a table with a torn parasol. The woman puffed along with me. I recognized her now as the woman who had injected me. I parked in a paved yard, and she opened the side door of the house and ushered me through a large airy kitchen. She snapped a gas tap *en passant*, flipped open a drawer, dragged out a white apron and tied it around her without slowing her walk. The floor of the main hall was stone flags, the walls were white-washed and upon them were a few swords, shields and ancient banners. There was little furniture: an oak chest, some forbidding chairs, and tables bearing large vases full of freshly-cut flowers. Opening off the hall there was a billiard room. The lights were on and the brightly coloured balls lay transfixed upon the green baize like a pop-art tableau.

The little woman hurried ahead of me opening doors, waving me through, sorting amongst a bundle of large keys, locking each door and then darting around me and hurrying on ahead. Finally, she showed me into the lounge. It was soft and florid after the stark austerity of the rest of the house. There were four sofas with huge floral patterns, plants, knick-knacks, antique cases full of antique plates. Silver-framed photos, a couple of bizarre modern paintings in primary colours and a kidney-shaped bar trimmed in golden tin and plastic. Behind the bar were bottles of drink and arranged along the bar-top some bar-tender's implements: strainers, shakers and ice-buckets.

'I'm delighted to see you,' said Monsieur Datt.

'That's good.'

He smiled engagingly. 'How did you find me?'

'A little bird told me.'

'Damn those birds,' said Datt, still smiling. 'But no matter, the shooting season begins soon, doesn't it?'

'You could be right.'

'Why not sit down and let me get you a drink. It's damned hot, I've never known such weather.'

'Don't get ideas,' I said. 'My boys will come on in if I disappear for too long.'

'Such crude ideas you have. And yet I suppose the very vulgarity of your mind is its dynamic. But have no fear, you'll not have drugged food or any of that nonsense. On the contrary, I hope to prove to you how very wrong your whole notion of me is.' He reached towards a bevy of cut-glass decanters. 'What about Scotch whisky?'

'Nothing,' I said. 'Nothing at all.'

'You're right.' He walked across to the window. I followed him.

'Nothing,' he said. 'Nothing at all. We are both ascetics.'

'Speak for yourself,' I said. 'I like a bit of self-indulgence now and again.'

The windows overlooked a courtyard, its ivy-covered walls punctuated by the strict geometry of white shutters. There was a dovecote and white doves marched and counter-marched across the cobbles.

There was a hoot at the gate, then into the courtyard drove a large Citroën ambulance. 'Clinique de Paradis' it said along the side under the big red cross. It was very dusty as though it had made a long journey. Out of the driver's seat climbed Jean-Paul; he tooted the horn.

'It's my ambulance,' said Datt.

'Yes,' I said, 'Jean-Paul driving.'

'He's a good boy,' said Datt.

'Let me tell you what I want,' I said hurriedly.

Datt made a movement with his hand. 'I know why you are here. There is no need to explain anything.' He eased himself back into an armchair.

'How do you know I've not come to kill you?' I asked.

'My dear man. There is no question of violence, for many reasons.'

'For instance?'

'Firstly you are not a man to use gratuitous violence. You would only employ violent means when you could see the course of action that the violence made available to you. Secondly, we are evenly matched, you and I. Weight for weight we are evenly matched.'

172

'So are a swordfish and an angler, but one is sitting strapped into an armchair and the other is being dragged through the ocean with a hook in his mouth.'

'Which am I?'

'That's what I am here to discover.'

'Then begin, sir.'

'Get Kuang.'

'What do you mean?'

'I mean get Kuang, K.U.A.N.G. Get him here.'

Datt changed his mind about the drink; he poured himself a glass of wine and sipped it. 'I won't deny he's here,' he said finally.

'Then why not get him?'

He pressed a buzzer and the maid came in. 'Get Monsieur Kuang,' he said.

The old woman went away quietly and came back with Kuang. He was wearing grey flannel trousers, open-neck shirt and a pair of dirty white tennis shoes. He poured himself a large Perrier water from the bar and sat down in an armchair with his feet sprawled sideways over the arm. 'Well?' he said to me.

'I'm bringing you an American hydrogen expert to talk to.'

Kuang seemed unsurprised, 'Petty, Barnes, Bertram or Hudson?'

'Hudson.'

'Excellent, he's a top man.'

'I don't like it,' said Datt.

'You don't have to like it,' I said. 'If Kuang and Hudson want to talk a little it's nothing to do with you.' I turned to Kuang. 'How long will you want with him?'

'Two hours,' said Kuang. 'Three at the most, less if he has written stuff with him.'

'I believe he will have,' I said. 'He's all prepared.'

'I don't like it,' Datt complained.

'Be quiet,' said Kuang. He turned to me, 'Are you working for the Americans?'

'No,' I said. 'I'm acting for them, just this one operation.'

Kuang nodded. 'That makes sense; they wouldn't want to expose one of their regular men.'

I bit my lip in anger. Hudson had, of course, been acting on American instructions, not on his own initiative. It was a plan to expose me so that the C.I.A. could keep their own men covered. Clever bastards. Well, I'd grin and bear it and try to get something out of it.

'That's right,' I agreed.

'So you are not bargaining.'

'I'm not getting paid,' I said, 'if that's what you mean.'

'How much do you want?' asked Kuang wearily. 'But don't get big ideas.'

'We'll sort it out after you've seen Hudson.'

'A most remarkable display of faith,' said Kuang. 'Did Datt pay you for the incomplete set of documents you let us have?'

'No,' I said.

'Now that our cards are on the table I take it you don't really want payment.'

'That's right,' I said.

'Good,' said Kuang. He hooked his legs off the arm of the chair and reached for some ice from the silver bucket. Before pouring himself a whisky he pushed the telephone across to me.

Maria was waiting near the phone when I called her. 'Bring Hudson here,' I said. 'You know the way.'

'Yes,' said Maria. 'I know the way.'

29

Kuang went out to get ready for Hudson. I sat down again in a hard chair. Datt noticed me wince.

'You have a pain in the spine?'

'Yes,' I said. 'I did it in a discothèque.'

'Those modern dances are too strenuous for me,' said Datt.

'This one was too strenuous for me,' I said. 'My partner had brass knuckles.'

Datt knelt down at my feet, took off my shoe and probed at my heel with his powerful fingers. He felt my ankle bone and tut-tutted as though it had been designed all wrong. Suddenly he plunged his fingers hard into my heel. 'Ahh,' he said, but the word was drowned by my shout of pain. Kuang opened the door and looked at us.

'Are you all right?' Kuang asked.

'He's got a muscular contraction,' said Datt. 'It's acupuncture,' he explained to me. 'I'll soon get rid of that pain in your back.'

'Ouch,' I said. 'Don't do it if it's going to make me lame for life.'

Kuang retreated back to his room. Datt inspected my foot again and pronounced it ready.

'It should get rid of your pain,' he said. 'Rest for half an hour in the chair.'

'It is a bit better,' I admitted.

'Don't be surprised,' said Datt, 'the Chinese have practised these arts for centuries; it is a simple matter, a muscular pain.'

'You practise acupuncture?' I asked.

'Not really, but I have always been interested,' said Datt. 'The body and the mind. The interaction of two opposing forces: body and mind, emotion and reason, the duality of nature. My ambition has always been to discover something new about man himself.' He settled back into his chair. 'You are *simple*. I do not say that as a criticism but rather in admiration. Simplicity is the most sought-after quality in both art and nature, but your simplicity encourages you to see the world around you in black-and-white terms. You do not approve of my inquiry into human thoughts and actions. Your puritan origin, your Anglo-Saxon breeding make it sinful to inquire too deeply into ourselves.'

'But you don't inquire into yourself, you inquire into other people.'

He leaned back and smiled. 'My dear man, the reason that I collect information, compile dossiers and films and recordings and probe the personal secrets of a wide range of important men, is twofold. Primarily because important men control the fate of the world and I like to feel that in my small way I influence such men. Secondly, I have devoted my life to the study of mankind. I love people; I have no illusions about them, it's true, but that makes it much easier to love them. I am ceaselessly amazed and devoted to the strange convuluted workings of their devious minds, their rationalizations and the predictability of their weaknesses and failings. That's why I became so interested in the sexual aspect of my studies. At one time I thought I understood my friends best when I watched them gambling: their avarice, kindness, and fear were so much in evidence when they gambled. I was a young man at the time. I lived in Hanoi and I saw the same men every day in the same clubs. I liked them enormously. It's important that you believe that.' He looked up at me.

I shrugged. 'I believe it.'

'I liked them very much and I wished to understand them better. For me, gambling could never hold any fascination: dull, repetitive and trivial. But it did unleash the deepest emotions. I got more from seeing their re-actions to the game than from playing. So I began to keep dossiers on all my friends. There was no malign intent; on the contrary, it was expressly in order to understand and like them better that I did it.'

'And did you like them better?'

'In some ways. There were disillusions, of course, but a man's failings are so much more attractive than his successes — any woman will tell you that. Soon it occurred to me that alcohol was providing more information to the dossiers than gambling. Gambling showed me the hostili-ties and fears, but drink showed me the weaknesses. It was when a man felt sorry for himself that one saw the gaps in the armour. See how a man gets drunk and you will know him — I have told so many young girls that: see your man getting drunk and you will know him. Does he want to pull the blankets over his head or go out into the street and start a riot? Does he want to be caressed or to commit rape? Does he find everything humorous, or threatening? Does he feel the world is secretly mocking him, or does he throw his arms around a stranger's shoulders and shout that he loves everyone?'

'Yes. It's a good indication.'

'But there were even better ways to reach deep into the subconscious, and now I wanted not only to understand people but also to try planting ideas in their heads. If only I could have a man with the frailty and vulnerability of drunkenness but without the blurriness and loss of memory that drink brought, then I would have a chance of really improving my dossiers. How I envied the women who had access to my friends in their most vulnerable—post-coital *triste*—condition. Sex, I decided, was the key to man's drives and post-sex was his most vulnerable state. That's how my methods evolved.'

I relaxed now that Datt had become totally involved in his story. I suppose he had been sitting out here in this house, inactive and musing about his life and what had led to this moment of supreme power that he was now enjoying so much. He was unstoppable, as so many reserved men are once explanations start burbling out of them.

'Eight hundred dossiers I have now, and many of them are analyses that a psychiatrist would be proud of.'

'Are you qualified to practise psychiatry?' I asked.

'Is anyone qualified to practise it?'

'No,' I said.

'Precisely,' said Datt. 'Well, I am a little better able than most men. I know what can be done, because I have done it. Done it eight hundred times. Without a staff it would never have developed at the same rate. Perhaps the quality would have been even higher had I done it all myself, but the girls were a vital part of the operation.'

'The girls actually compiled the dossiers?'

'Maria might have been able to if she'd worked with me longer. The girl that died—Annie Couzins—was intelligent enough, but she was not temperamentally suited to the work. At one time I would work only with girls with qualifications in law or engineering or accountancy, but to find girls thus qualified and also sexually alluring is difficult. I wanted girls who would understand. With the more stupid girls I had to use recording machines, but the girls who understood produced the real results.'

'The girls didn't hide the fact that they understood?'

'At first. I thought—as you do now—that men would be afraid and suspicious of a woman who was clever, but they aren't, you see. On the contrary, men like clever women.

178

Why does a husband complain "my wife doesn't understand me" when he goes running off with another woman? Why, because what he needs isn't sex, it's someone to talk to.'

'Can't he talk to the people he works with?'

'He can, but he's frightened of them. The people he works with are after his job, on the watch for weakness.'

'Just as your girls are.'

'Exactly, but he does not understand that.'

'Eventually he does, surely?'

'By then he no longer cares—the therapeutic aspect of the relationship is clear to him.'

'You blackmail him into co-operating?'

Datt shrugged. 'I might have done had it ever proved necessary, but it never has. By the time a man has been studied by me and the girls for six months he needs us.'

'I don't understand.'

'You don't understand', said Datt patiently, 'because you persist in regarding me as some malign monster feeding on the blood of my victims.' Datt held up his hands. 'What I did for these men was helpful to them. I worked day and night, endless sessions to help them understand themselves: their motives, their aspirations, their weaknesses and strengths. The girls too were intelligent enough to be helpful, and reassuring. All the people that I have studied become better personalities.'

'Will become,' I corrected. 'That's the promise you hold out to them.'

'In some cases, not all.'

'But you have tried to increase their dependency upon you. You have used your skills to make these people *think* they need you.'

'You are splitting hairs. All psychiatrists must do that. That's what the word "transference" means.'

'But you have a hold over them. These films and re-cords: they demonstrate the type of power you want.'

'They demonstrate nothing. The films etc. are nothing to me. I am a scientist, not a blackmailer. I have merely used the sexual activities of my patients as a short cut to understanding the sort of disorders they are likely to have. A man reveals so much when he is in bed with a woman: it's this important element of *release*. It's common to all the activities of the subject. He finds release in talking to me, which gives him freedom in his sexual appetites. Greater and more varied sexual activity release in turn a need to talk at greater length.'

'So he talks to you.'

'Of course he does. He grows more and more free, and more and more confident.'

'But you are the only person he can boast to.'

'Not boast exactly, talk. He wishes to share this new, stronger, better life that he has created.'

'That you have created for him.'

'Some subjects have been kind enough to say that they lived at only ten per cent of their potential until they came to my clinic.' M. Datt smiled complacently. 'It's vital and important work showing men the power they have within their own minds if they merely take courage enough to use it.'

'You sound like one of those small ads from the back pages of skin magazines. The sort that's sandwiched between acne cream and peeping-tom binoculars.'

'*Honi soit qui mal y pense*. I know what I am doing.'

I said, 'I really believe you do, but I don't *like* it.'

'Mind you,' he said urgently, 'don't think for one moment I'm a Freudian. I'm not. Everyone thinks I'm a Freudian because of this emphasis on sex. I'm not.'

'You'll publish your results?' I asked.

'The conclusions possibly, but not the case histories.'

180

'It's the case histories that are the important factor,' I said.

'To some people,' said Datt. 'That's why I have to guard them so carefully!'

'Loiseau tried to get them.'

'But he was a few minutes too late.' Datt poured himself another small glass of wine, measured its clarity and drank a little. 'Many men covet my dossiers but I guard them carefully. This whole neighbourhood is under surveillance. I knew about you as soon as you stopped for fuel in the village.'

The old woman knocked discreetly and entered, 'A car with Paris plates—it sounds like Madame Loiseau—coming through the village.'

Datt nodded. 'Tell Robert I want the Belgian plates on the ambulance and the documents must be ready. Jean-Paul can help him. No, on second thoughts don't tell Jean-Paul to help him. I believe they don't get along too well.' The old woman said nothing. 'Yes, well that's all.'

Datt walked across to the window and as he did so there was the sound of tyres crunching on gravel.

'It's Maria's car,' said Datt.

'And your backyard Mafia didn't stop it?'

'They are not there to stop people,' explained Datt. 'They are not collecting entrance money, they are there for my protection.'

'Did Kuang tell you that?' I said. 'Perhaps those guards are there to stop you getting out?'

'Poof,' said Datt, but I knew I had planted a seed in his mind. 'I wish she'd brought the boy with her.'

I said, 'It's Kuang who's in charge. He didn't ask you before agreeing to my bringing Hudson here.'

'We have our areas of authority,' said Datt. 'Everything concerning data of a technical kind—of the kind that Hudson can provide—is Kuang's province.' Suddenly he flushed with anger. 'Why should I explain such things to you?'

'I thought you were explaining them to yourself,' I said.

Datt changed the subject abruptly. 'Do you think Maria told Loiseau where I am?'

'I'm sure she didn't,' I said. 'She has a lot of explaining to do the next time she sees Loiseau. She has to explain why she warned you about his raid on the clinic.'

'That's true,' said Datt. 'A clever man, Loiseau. At one time I thought you were his assistant.'

'And now?'

'Now I think you are his victim, or soon will be.'

I said nothing. Datt said, 'Whoever you work for, you run alone. Loiseau has no reason to like you. He's jealous of your success with Maria—she adores you, of course. Loiseau pretends he's after me, but you are his real enemy. Loiseau is in trouble with his department, he might have decided that you could be the scapegoat. He visited me a couple of weeks ago, wanted me to sign a document concerning you. A tissue of lies, but cleverly riddled with half-truth that could prove bad for you. It needed only my signature. I refused.'

'Why didn't you sign?'

M. Datt sat down opposite me and looked me straight in the eye. 'Not because I like you particularly. I hardly know you. It was because I had given you that injection when I first suspected that you were an agent provocateur sent by Loiseau. If I treat a person he becomes my patient. I become responsible for him. It is my proud boast that if one of my patients committed even a murder he could come to me and tell me; in confidence. That's my relationship with Kuang. I must have that sort of relationship with my patients—Loiseau refuses to understand that. I must have it.' He stood up suddenly and said, 'A drink—and now I insist. What shall it be?'

The door opened and Maria came in, followed by Hudson and Jean-Paul. Maria was smiling, but her eyes were narrow and tense. Her old roll-neck pullover and riding breeches were stained with mud and wine. She looked tough and elegant and rich. She came into the room quietly and aware, like a cat sniffing, and moving stealthily, on the watch for the slightest sign of things hostile or alien. She handed me the packet of documents: three passports, one for me, one for Hudson, one for Kuang. There were some other papers inside, money and some cards and envelopes that would prove I was someone else. I put them in my pocket without looking at them.

'I wish you'd brought the boy,' said M. Datt to Maria. She didn't answer. 'What will you drink, my good friends? An aperitif perhaps?' He called to the woman in the white apron, 'We shall be seven to dinner but Mr Hudson and Mr Kuang will dine separately in the library. And take Mr Hudson into the library now,' he added. 'Mr Kuang is waiting there.'

'And leave the door ajar,' I said affably.

'And leave the door ajar,' said M. Datt.

Hudson smiled and gripped his briefcase tight under his arm. He looked at Maria and Jean-Paul, nodded and withdrew without answering. I got up and walked across to the window, wondering if the woman in the white apron was sitting in at dinner with us, but then I saw the dented tractor parked close behind Maria's car. The tractor driver was here. With all that room to spare the tractor needn't have boxed both cars tight against the wall.

30

'Read the greatest thinkers of the eighteenth century', M.
Datt was saying, 'and you'll understand what the Frenchman still thinks about women.' The soup course was
finished and the little woman — dressed now in a maid's
formal uniform — collected the dishes. 'Don't stack them,'
M. Datt whispered loudly to her. 'That's how they get
broken. Make two journeys; a well-trained maid never
stacks plates.' He poured a glass of white wine for each of
us. 'Diderot thought they were merely courtesans,
Montesquieu said they were pretty children. For Rousseau
they existed only as an adjunct to man's pleasure and for
Voltaire they didn't exist at all.' He pulled the side of
smoked salmon towards him and sharpened the long
knife.

Jean-Paul smiled knowingly. He was more nervous than
usual. He patted the white starched cuff that artfully
revealed the Cartier watch and fingered the small disc of
adhesive plaster that covered a razor nick on his chin.

Maria said, 'France is a land where men command and
women obey. "Elle me plaît" is the greatest compliment a
woman can expect from men; they mean she obeys. How
can anyone call Paris a woman's city? Only a prostitute
can have a serious career there. It took two world wars to
give Frenchwomen the vote.'

Datt nodded. He removed the bones and the salmon's
smoke-hard surface with two long sweeps of the knife. He
brushed oil over the fish and began to slice it, serving
Maria first. Maria smiled at him.

Just as an expensive suit wrinkles in a different way

from a cheap one, so did the wrinkles in Maria's face add to her beauty rather than detract from it. I stared at her, trying to understand her better. Was she treacherous, or was she exploited, or was she, like most of us, both?

'It's all very well for you, Maria,' said Jean-Paul. 'You are a woman with wealth, position, intelligence,' he paused, 'and beauty … '

'I'm glad you added beauty,' she said still smiling.

Jean-Paul looked towards M. Datt and me. 'That illustrates my point. Even Maria would sooner have beauty than brains. When I was eighteen—ten years ago—I wanted to give the women I loved the things I wanted for myself: respect, admiration, good food, conversation, wit and even knowledge. But women despise those things. Passion is what they want, intensity of emotion. The same trite words of admiration repeated over and over again. They don't want good food—women have poor palates—and witty conversation worries them. What's worse it diverts attention away from them. Women want men who are masterful enough to give them confidence, but not cunning enough to outwit them. They want men with plenty of faults so that they can forgive them. They want men who have trouble with the little things in life; women excel at little things. They remember little things too; there is no occasion in their lives, from confirmation to eightieth birthday, when they can't recall every stitch they wore.' He looked accusingly at Maria.

Maria laughed. 'That part of your tirade at least is true.'

M. Datt said, 'What did you wear at your confirmation?'

'White silk, high-waisted dress, plain-front white silk shoes and cotton gloves that I hated.' She reeled it off.

'Very good,' said M. Datt and laughed. 'Although I must say, Jean-Paul, you are far too hard on women. Take that girl Annie who worked for me. Her academic standards were tremendous … '

185

'Of course,' said Maria, 'women leaving university have such trouble getting a job that anyone enlightened enough to employ them is able to demand very high qualifications.'

'Exactly,' said M. Datt. 'Most of the girls I've ever used in my research were brilliant. What's more they were deeply involved in the research tasks. Just imagine that the situation had required men employees to involve themselves sexually with patients. In spite of paying lip-service to promiscuity men would have given me all sorts of puritanical reasons why they couldn't do it. These girls understood that it was a vital part of their relationship with patients. One girl was a mathematical genius and yet such beauty. Truly remarkable.'

Jean-Paul said, 'Where is this mathematical genius now? I would dearly appreciate her advice. Perhaps I could improve my technique with women.'

'You couldn't,' said Maria. She spoke clinically, with no emotion showing. 'Your technique is all too perfect. You flatter women to saturation point when you first meet them. Then, when you decide the time is right, you begin to undermine their confidence in themselves. You point out their shortcomings rather cleverly and sympathetically until they think that you must be the only man who would deign to be with them. You destroy women by erosion because you hate them.'

'No,' Jean-Paul said. 'I love women. I love all women too much to reject so many by marrying one.' He laughed.

'Jean-Paul feels it is his duty to make himself available to every girl from fifteen to fifty,' said Maria quietly.

'Then you'll soon be outside my range of activity,' said Jean-Paul.

The candles had burned low and now their light came through the straw-coloured wine and shone golden on face and ceiling.

Maria sipped at her wine. No one spoke. She placed the glass on the table and then brought her eyes up to Jean-Paul's. 'I'm sorry for you, Jean-Paul,' she said.

The maid brought the fish course to the table and served it: *sole Dieppoise*, the sauce dense with shrimps and speckled with parsley and mushroom, the bland smell of the fish echoed by the hot butter. The maid retired, conscious that her presence had interrupted the conversation. Maria drank a little more wine and as she put the glass down she looked at Jean-Paul.

He didn't smile. When she spoke her voice was mellow and any trace of bitterness had been removed by the pause.

'When I say I'm sorry for you, Jean-Paul, with your endless succession of lovers, you may laugh at me. But let me tell you this: the shortness of your relationships with women is due to a lack of flexibility in you. You are not able to adapt, change, improve, enjoy new things each day. Your demands are constant and growing narrower. Everyone else must adapt to you, never the other way about.

'Marriages break up for this same reason — my marriage did and it was at least half my fault: two people become so set in their ways that they become vegetables. The antithesis of this feeling is to be in love. I fell in love with you, Jean-Paul. Being in love is to drink in new ideas, new feelings, smells, tastes, new dances — even the air seems to be different in flavour. That's why infidelity is such a shock. A wife set in the dull, lifeless pattern of marriage is suddenly liberated by love, and her husband is terrified to see the change take place, for just as I felt ten years younger, so I saw my husband as ten years older.'

Jean-Paul said, 'And that's how you now see me?'

'Exactly. It's laughable how I once worried that you were younger than me. You're not younger than me at all. You are an old fogey. Now I no longer love you I can see that. You are an old fogey of twenty-eight and I am a young girl of thirty-two.'

'You bitch.'

'My poor little one. Don't be angry. Think of what I tell you. Open your mind. Open your mind and you will discover what you want so much: how to be eternally a young man.'

Jean-Paul looked at her. He wasn't as angry as I would have expected. 'Perhaps I am a shallow and vain fool,' he said. 'But when I met you, Maria, I truly loved you. It didn't last more than a week, but for me it was real. It was the only time in my life that I truly believed myself capable of something worthwhile. You were older than me but I liked that. I wanted you to show me the way out of the stupid labyrinth life I led. You are highly intelligent **and** you, I thought, could show me the solid good reasons for living. But you failed me, Maria. Like all women you are weak-willed and indecisive. You can be loyal only for a moment to whoever is near to you. You have never made one objective decision in your life. You have never really wanted to be strong and free. You have never done one decisive thing that you truly believed in. You are a puppet, Maria, with many puppeteers, and they quarrel over who shall operate you.' His final words were sharp and bitter and he stared hard at Datt.

'Children,' Datt admonished. 'Just as we were all getting along so well together.'

Jean-Paul smile a tight, film-star smile. 'Turn off your charm,' he said to Datt. 'You always patronize me.'

'If I've done something to give offence … ' said Datt. He didn't finish the sentence but looked around at his guests, raising his eyebrows to show how difficult it was to even imagine such a possibility.

'You think you can switch me on and off as you please,' said Jean-Paul. 'You think you can treat me like a child;

well you can't. Without me you would be in big trouble now. If I had not brought you the information about Loiseau's raid upon your clinic you would be in prison now.'

'Perhaps,' said Datt, 'and perhaps not.'

'Oh I know what you want people to believe,' said Jean-Paul. 'I know you like people to think you are mixed up with the S.D.E.C.E. and secret departments of the Government, but we know better. I saved you. Twice. Once with Annie, once with Maria.'

'Maria saved me,' said Datt, 'if anyone did.'

'Your precious daughter', said Jean-Paul, 'is good for only one thing.' He smiled. 'And what's more she hates you. She said you were foul and evil; that's how much she wanted to save you before I persuaded her to help.'

'Did you say that about me?' Datt asked Maria, and even as she was about to reply he held up his hand. 'No, don't answer. I have no right to ask you such a question. We all say things in anger that later we regret.' He smiled at Jean-Paul. 'Relax, my good friend, and have another glass of wine.'

Datt filled Jean-Paul's glass but Jean-Paul didn't pick it up. Datt pointed the neck of the bottle at it. 'Drink.' He picked up the glass and held it to Jean-Paul. 'Drink and say that these black thoughts are not your truly considered opinion of old Datt who has done so much for you.'

Jean-Paul brought the flat of his hand round in an angry sweeping gesture. Perhaps he didn't like to be told that he owed Datt anything. He sent the full glass flying across the room and swept the bottle out of Datt's hands. It slid across the table, felling the glasses like ninepins and flooding the cold blond liquid across the linen and cutlery. Datt stood up, awkwardly dabbing at his waistcoat with a table napkin. Jean-Paul stood up too. The only sound was of the wine, still chug-chugging out of the bottle.

'*Salaud!*' said Datt. 'You attack me in my own home! You *casse-pieds*! You insult me in front of my guests and assault me when I offer you wine!' He dabbed at himself and threw the wet napkin across the table as a sign that the meal would not continue. The cutlery jangled mournfully. 'You will learn,' said Datt. 'You will learn here and now.'

Jean-Paul finally understood the hornet's nest he had aroused in Datt's brain. His face was set and defiant, but you didn't have to be an amateur psychologist to know that if he could set the clock back ten minutes he'd rewrite his script.

'Don't touch me,' Jean-Paul said. 'I have villainous friends just as you do, and my friends and I can destroy you, Datt. I know all about you, the girl Annie Couzins and why she had to be killed. There are a few things you don't know about that story. There are a few more things that the police would like to know too. Touch me, you fat old swine, and you'll die as surely as the girl did.' He looked around at us all. His forehead was moist with exertion and anxiety. He managed a grim smile. 'Just touch me, just you try ... !'

Datt said nothing, nor did any one of us. Jean-Paul gabbled on until his steam ran out. 'You need me,' he finally said to Datt, but Datt didn't need him any more and there was no one in the room who didn't know it.

'Robert!' shouted Datt. I don't know if Robert was standing in the sideboard or in a crack in the floor, but he certainly came in fast. Robert was the tractor-driver who had slapped the one-eared dog. He was as tall and broad as Jean-Paul but there the resemblance ended: Robert was teak against Jean-Paul's papier-mâché.

Right behind Robert was the woman in the white apron. Now that they were standing side by side you could see a family resemblance: Robert was clearly the woman's son. He walked forward and stood before Datt like a man waiting to be given a medal. The old woman stood in the doorway with a 12-bore shotgun held steady in her fists. It was a battered old relic, the butt was scorched and stained and there was a patch of rust around the muzzle as though it had been propped in a puddle. It was just the sort of thing that might be kept around the hall of a country house for dealing with rats and rabbits: an ill-finished, mass-production job without styling or finish. It wasn't at all the sort of gun I'd want to be shot with. That's why I remained very, very still.

Datt nodded towards me, and Robert moved in and brushed me lightly but efficiently. 'Nothing,' he said. Robert walked over to Jean-Paul. In Jean-Paul's suit he found a 6·35 Mauser automatic. He sniffed it and opened it, spilled the bullets out into his hand and passed the gun, magazine and bullets to Datt. Datt handled them as though they were some kind of virus. He reluctantly dropped them into his pocket.

'Take him away, Robert,' said Datt. 'He makes too much noise in here. I can't bear people shouting.' Robert nodded and turned upon Jean-Paul. He made a movement of his chin and a clicking noise of the sort that encourages horses. Jean-Paul buttoned his jacket carefully and walked to the door.

'We'll have the meat course now,' Datt said to the woman. She smiled with more deference than humour and withdrew backwards, muzzle last.

'Take him out, Robert,' repeated Datt.

'Maybe you think you don't,' said Jean-Paul earnestly, 'but you'll find … ' His words were lost as Robert pulled him gently through the door and closed it.

'What are you going to do to him?' asked Maria.

'Nothing, my dear,' said Datt. 'But he's become more and more tiresome. He must be taught a lesson. We must frighten him, it's for the good of all of us.'

'You're going to kill him,' said Maria.

'No, my dear.' He stood near the fireplace, and smiled reassuringly.

'You are, I can feel it in the atmosphere.'

Datt turned his back on us. He toyed with the clock on the mantelpiece. He found the key for it and began to wind it up. It was a noisy ratchet.

Maria turned to me. 'Are they going to kill him?' she asked.

'I think they are,' I said.

She went across to Datt and grabbed his arm. 'You mustn't,' she said. 'It's too horrible. Please don't. Please father, please don't, if you love me.' Datt put his arm around her paternally but said nothing.

'He's a wonderful person,' Maria said. She was speaking of Jean-Paul. 'He would never betray you. Tell him,' she asked me, 'he must not kill Jean-Paul.'

'You mustn't kill him,' I said.

'You must make it more convincing than that,' said Datt. He patted Maria. 'If our friend here can tell us a way to guarantee his silence, some other way, then perhaps I'll agree.'

He waited but I said nothing. 'Exactly,' said Datt.

'But I love him,' said Maria.

'That can make no difference,' said Datt. 'I'm not a plenipotentiary from God. I've got no halos or citations to distribute. He stands in the way—not of me but of what I believe in; he stands in the way because he is spiteful and stupid. I do believe, Maria, that even if it were you I'd still do the same.'

Maria stopped being a suppliant. She had that icy calm that women take on just before using their nails.

'I love him,' said Maria. That meant that he should never be punished for anything except infidelity. She looked at me. 'It's your fault for bringing me here.'

Datt heaved a sigh and left the room.

'And your fault that he's in danger,' she said.

'Okay,' I said, 'blame me if you want to. On my colour soul the stains don't show.'

'Can't you stop them?' she said.

'No,' I told her, 'it's not that sort of film.'

Her face contorted as though cigar smoke was getting in her eyes. It went squashy and she began to sob. She didn't cry. She didn't do that mascara-respecting display of grief that winkles tear-drops out of the eyes with the corner of a tiny lace handkerchief while watching the whole thing in a well-placed mirror. She sobbed and her face collapsed. The mouth sagged, and the flesh puckered and wrinkled like blow-torched paintwork. Ugly sight, and ugly sound.

'He'll die,' she said in a strange little voice.

I don't know what happened next. I don't know whether Maria began to move before the sound of the shot or after. Just as I don't know whether Jean-Paul had really lunged at Robert, as Robert later told us. But I was right behind Maria as she opened the door. A ·45 is a big pistol. The first shot had hit the dresser, ripping a hole in the carpentry and smashing half a dozen plates. They were still falling as the second shot fired. I heard Datt shouting about his plates and saw Jean-Paul spinning drunkenly like an exhausted whipping top. He fell against the dresser, supporting himself on his hand, and stared at me pop-eyed with hate and grimacing with pain, his cheeks bulging as though he was looking for a place to vomit. He grabbed at his white shirt and tugged it out of his trousers. He wrenched it so hard that the buttons popped and pinged away across the room. He had a great bundle of shirt in his hand now and he stuffed it into his mouth like a conjurer doing a trick called 'how to swallow my white shirt'. Or how to swallow my pink-dotted shirt. How to swallow my pink shirt, my red, and finally dark-red shirt. But he never did the trick. The cloth fell away from his mouth and his blood poured over his chin, painting his teeth pink and dribbling down his neck and ruining his shirt. He knelt upon the ground as if to pray but his face sank to the floor and he died without a word, his ear flat against the ground, as if listening for hoof-beats pursuing him to another world.

He was dead. It's difficult to wound a man with a ·45. You either miss them or you blow them in half.

The legacy the dead leave us are life-size effigies that only slightly resemble their former owners. Jean-Paul's bloody body only slightly resembled him: its thin lips pressed together and the small circular plaster just visible on his chin.

Robert was stupefied. He was staring at the gun in horror. I stepped over to him and grabbed the gun away from him. I said 'You should be ashamed,' and Datt repeated that.

The door opened suddenly and Hudson and Kuang stepped into the kitchen. They looked down at the body of Jean-Paul. He was a mess of blood and guts. No one spoke, they were waiting for me. I remembered that I was the one holding the gun. 'I'm taking Kuang and Hudson and I'm leaving,' I said. Through the open door to the hall I could see into the library, its table covered with their scientific documents: photos, maps and withered plants with large labels on them.

'Oh no you don't,' said Datt.

'I have to return Hudson intact because that's my part of the deal. The information he's given Kuang has to be got back to the Chinese Government or else it wasn't much good delivering it. So I must take Kuang too.'

'I think he's right,' said Kuang. 'It makes sense, what he says.'

'How do you know what makes sense?' said Datt. 'I'm

arranging your movements, not this fool; how can we trust him? He admits this task is for the Americans.'

'It makes sense,' said Kuang again. 'Hudson's information is genuine, I can tell: it fills out what I learnt from that incomplete set of papers you passed to me last week. If the Americans want me to have the information, then they must want it to be taken back home.'

'Can't you see that they might want to capture you for interrogation?' said Datt.

'Rubbish!' I interrupted. 'I could have arranged that at any time in Paris without risking Hudson out here in the middle of nowhere.'

'They are probably waiting down the road,' said Datt. 'You could be dead and buried in five minutes. Out here in the middle of the country no one would hear, no one would see the diggings.'

'I'll take that chance,' said Kuang. 'If he can get Hudson into France on false papers, he can get me out.'

I watched Hudson, fearful that he would say I'd done no such thing for him, but he nodded sagely and Kuang seemed reassured.

'Come with us,' said Hudson, and Kuang nodded agreement. The two scientists seemed to be the only ones in the room with any mutual trust.

I was reluctant to leave Maria but she just waved her hand and said she'd be all right. She couldn't take her eyes off Jean-Paul's body.

'Cover him, Robert,' said Datt.

Robert took a table-cloth from a drawer and covered the body. 'Go,' Maria called again to me, and then she began to sob. Datt put his arm around her and pulled her close. Hudson and Kuang collected their data together and then, still waving the gun around, I showed them out and followed.

As we went across the hall the old woman emerged carrying a heavily laden tray. She said, 'There's still the *poulet sauté chasseur.*'

'Vive le sport,' I said.

31

From the garage we took the camionette—a tiny grey corrugated-metal van—because the roads of France are full of them. I had to change gear constantly for the small motor, and the tiny headlights did no more than probe the hedgerows. It was a cold night and I envied the warm grim-faced occupants of the big Mercs and Citroëns that roared past us with just a tiny peep of the horn, to tell us they had done so.

Kuang seemed perfectly content to rely upon my skill to get him out of France. He leaned well back in the hard upright seat, folded his arms and closed his eyes as though performing some oriental contemplative ritual. Now and again he spoke. Usually it was a request for a cigarette.

The frontier was little more than a formality. The Paris office had done us proud: three good British passports—although the photo of Hudson was a bit dodgy—over twenty-five pounds in small notes (Belgian and French), and some bills and receipts to correspond to each passport. I breathed more easily after we were through. I'd done a deal with Loiseau so he'd guaranteed no trouble, but I still breathed more easily after we'd gone through.

Hudson lay flat upon some old blankets in the rear. Soon he began to snore. Kuang spoke.

'Are we going to an hotel or are you going to blow one of your agents to shelter me?'

'This is Belgium,' I said. 'Going to an hotel is like going to a police station.'

'What will happen to him?'

'The agent?' I hesitated. 'He'll be pensioned off. It's bad luck but he was the next due to be blown.'

'Age?'

'Yes,' I said.

'And you have someone better in the area?'

'You know we can't talk about that,' I said.

'I'm not interested professionally,' said Kuang. 'I'm a scientist. What the British do in France or Belgium is nothing to do with me, but if we are blowing this man I owe him his job.'

'You owe him nothing,' I said. 'What the hell do you think this is? He'll be blown because it's his job. Just as I'm conducting you because that's my job. I'm not doing it as a favour. You owe no one anything, so forget it. As far as I'm concerned you are a parcel.'

Kuang inhaled deeply on his cigarette, then removed it from his mouth with his long delicate fingers and stubbed it into the ashtray. I imagined him killing Annie Couzins. Passion or politics? He rubbed the tobacco shreds from his fingertips like a pianist practising trills.

As we passed through the tightly shuttered villages the rough *pavé* hammered the suspension and bright-eyed cats glared into our lights and fled. One a little slower than the others had been squashed as flat as an ink blot. Each successive set of wheels contributed a new pattern to the little tragedy that morning would reveal.

I had the camionette going at its top speed. The needles were still and the loud noise of the motor held a constant note. Everything was unchanging except a brief fusillade of loose gravel or the sudden smell of tar or the beep of a faster car.

'We are near to Ypres,' said Kuang.

'This was the Ypres salient,' I said. Hudson asked for a cigarette. He must have been awake for some time.

'Ypres,' said Hudson as he lit the cigarette, 'was that the site of a World War One battle?'

'One of the biggest,' I said. 'There's scarcely an Englishman that didn't have a relative die here. Perhaps a piece of Britain died here too.'

Hudson looked out of the rear windows of the van. 'It's quite a place to die,' he said.

32

Across the Ypres salient the dawn sky was black and getting lower and blacker like a Bulldog Drummond ceiling. It's a grim region, like a vast ill-lit military depot that goes on for miles. Across country go the roads: narrow slabs of concrete not much wider than a garden path, and you have the feeling that to go off the edge is to go into bottomless mud. It's easy to go around in circles and even easier to imagine that you are. Every few yards there are the beady-eyed green-and-white notices that point the way to military cemeteries where regiments of Blanco-white headstones parade. Death pervades the topsoil but untidy little farms go on operating, planting their cabbages right up to 'Private of the West Riding — Known only to God'. The living cows and dead soldiers share the land and there are no quarrels. Now in the hedges evergreen plants were laden with tiny red berries as though the ground was sweating blood. I stopped the car. Ahead was Passchendaele, a gentle upward slope.

'Which way were your soldiers facing?' Kuang said.

'Up the slope,' I said. 'They advanced up the slope, sixty pounds on their backs and machine guns down their throats.'

Kuang opened the window and threw his cigarette butt on to the road. There was an icy gust of wind.

'It's cold,' said Kuang. 'When the wind drops it will rain.'

Hudson leaned close to the window again. 'Oh boy,' he said, 'trench warfare here,' and shook his head when no word came. 'For them it must have seemed like for ever.'

'For a lot of them it was for ever,' I said. 'They are still here.'

'In Hiroshima even more died,' said Kuang.

'I don't measure death by numbers,' I said.

'Then it's a pity you were so careful not to use your atom bomb on the Germans or Italians,' said Kuang.

I started the motor again to get some heat in the car, but Kuang got out and stamped around on the concrete roadway. He did not seem to mind the cold wind and rain. He picked up a chunk of the shiny, clay-heavy soil peculiar to this region, studied it and then broke it up and threw it aimlessly across the field of cabbages.

'Are we expecting to rendezvous with another car?' he asked.

'Yes,' I said.

'You must have been very confident that I would come with you.'

'Yes,' I said. 'I was. It was logical.'

Kuang nodded. 'Can I have another cigarette?' I gave him one.

'We're early,' complained Hudson. 'That's a sure way to attract attention.'

'Hudson fancies his chances as a secret agent,' I said to Kuang.

'I don't take to your sarcasm,' said Hudson.

'Well that's real old-fashioned bad luck, Hudson,' I said, 'because you are stuck with it.'

Grey clouds rushed across the salient. Here and there old windmills—static in spite of the wind—stood across the skyline, like crosses waiting for someone to be nailed upon them. Over the hill came a car with its headlights on.

They were thirty minutes late. Two men in a Renault 16, a man and his son. They didn't introduce themselves, in fact they didn't seem keen to show their faces at all. The older man got out of the car and came across to me. He spat upon the road and cleared his throat.

'You two get into the other car. The American stays in this one. Don't speak to the boy.' He smiled and gave a short, croaky, mirthless laugh. 'In fact don't speak to me even. There's a large-scale map in the dashboard. Make sure that's what you want.' He gripped my arm as he said it. 'The boy will take the camionette and dump it somewhere near the Dutch border. The American stays in this car. Someone will meet them at the other end. It's all arranged.'

Hudson said to me, 'Going with you is one thing, but taking off into the blue with this kid is another. I think I can find my own way ... '

'Don't think about it,' I told him. 'We just follow the directions on the label. Hold your nose and swallow.' Hudson nodded.

We got out of the car and the boy came across, slowly detouring around us as though his father had told him to keep his face averted. The Renault was nice and warm inside. I felt in the glove compartment and found not only a map but a pistol.

'No prints,' I called to the Fleming. 'Make sure there's nothing else, no sweet wrappers or handkerchiefs.'

'Yes,' said the man. 'And none of those special cigarettes that are made specially for me in one of those exclusive shops in Jermyn Street.' He smiled sarcastically. 'He knows all that.' His accent was so thick as to be almost unintelligible. I guessed that normally he spoke Flemish and the French was not natural to him. The man spat again in the roadway before climbing into the driver's seat alongside us. 'He's a good boy,' the man said. 'He knows what to do.' By the time he got the Renault started the camionette was out of sight.

I'd reached the worrying stage of the journey. 'Did you

take notes?' I asked Kuang suddenly. He looked at me without answering. 'Be sensible,' I said. 'I must know if you are carrying anything that would need to be destroyed. I know there's the box of stuff Hudson gave you.' I drummed upon it. 'Is there anything else?'

'A small notebook taped to my leg. It's a thin book. I could be searched and they would not find it.'

I nodded. It was something more to worry about.

The car moved at high speed over the narrow concrete lanes. Soon we turned on to the wider main road that led north to Ostend. We had left the over-fertilized salient behind us. The fearful names: Tyne Cot, St Julien, Poelcapelle, Westerhoek and Pilckem faded behind us as they had faded from memory, for fifty years had passed and the women who had wept for the countless dead were also dead. Time and TV, frozen food and transistor radios had healed the wounds and filled the places that once seemed unfillable.

'What's happening?' I said to the driver. He was the sort of man who had to be questioned or else he would offer no information.

'His people,' he jerked his head towards Kuang, 'want him in Ostend. Twenty-three hundred hours tonight at the harbour. I'll show you on the city plan.'

'Harbour? What's happening? Is he going aboard a boat tonight?'

'They don't tell me things like that,' said the man. 'I'm just conducting you to my place to see your case officer, then on to Ostend to see his case officer. It's all so bloody boring. My wife thinks I get paid because it's dangerous but I'm always telling her: I get paid because it's so bloody boring. Tired?' I nodded. 'We'll make good time, that's one advantage, there's not much traffic about at this time of morning. There's not much commercial traffic if you avoid the inter-city routes.'

'It's quiet,' I said. Now and again small flocks of birds darted across the sky, their eyes seeking food in the hard morning light, their bodies weakened by the cold night air.

'Very few police,' said the man. 'The cars keep to the main roads. It will rain soon and the cyclists don't move much when it's raining. It'll be the first rain for two weeks.'

'Stop worrying,' I said. 'Your boy will be all right.'

'He knows what to do,' the man agreed.

33

The Fleming owned an hotel not far from Ostend. The car turned into a covered alley that led to a cobbled courtyard. A couple of hens squawked as we parked and a dog howled. 'It's difficult,' said the man, 'to do anything clandestine around here.'

He was a small broad man with a sallow skin that would always look dirty no matter what he did to it. The bridge of his nose was large and formed a straight line with his forehead, like the nose metal of a medieval helmet. His mouth was small and he held his lips tight to conceal his bad teeth. Around his mouth were scars of the sort that you get when thrown through a windscreen. He smiled to show me it was a joke rather than an apology, and the scars made a pattern round his mouth like a tightened hairnet.

The door from the side entrance of the hotel opened and a woman in a black dress and white apron stared at us.

'They have come,' said the man.

'So I see,' she said. 'No luggage?'

'No luggage,' said the man. She seemed to need some explanation, as though we were a man and girl trying to book a double room.

'They need to rest, *ma jolie môme*,' said the man. She was no one's pretty child, but the compliment appeased her for a moment.

'Room four,' she said.

'The police have been?'

'Yes,' she said.

'They won't be back until night,' said the man to us.

'Perhaps not then even. They check the book. It's for the taxes more than to find criminals.'

'Don't use all the hot water,' said the woman. We followed her through the yellow peeling side door into the hotel entrance hall. There was a counter made of carelessly painted hardboard and a rack with eight keys hanging from it. The lino had the large square pattern that's supposed to look like inlaid marble; it curled at the edges and something hot had indented a perfect circle near the door.

'Name?' said the woman grimly as though she was about to enter us in the register.

'Don't ask,' said the man. 'And they won't ask our name.' He smiled as though he had made a joke and looked anxiously at his wife, hoping that she would join in. She shrugged and reached behind her for the key. She put it down on the counter very gently so she could not be accused of anger.

'They'll need two keys, Sybil.'

She scowled at him. 'They'll pay for the rooms,' he said.

'We'll pay,' I said. Outside the rain began. It bombarded the window and rattled the door as though anxious to get in.

She slammed the second key down upon the counter. '*You* should have taken it and dumped it,' said the woman angrily. 'Rik could have driven these two back here.'

'This is the important stage,' said the man.

'You lazy pig,' said the woman. 'If the alarm is out for the car and Rik gets stopped driving it, then we'll see which is the important stage.'

The man didn't answer, nor did he look at me. He picked up the keys and led the way up the creaky staircase. 'Mind the handrail,' he said. 'It's not fixed properly yet.'

'Nothing is,' called the woman after us. 'The whole place is only half-built.'

He showed us into our rooms. They were cramped and rather sad, shining with yellow plastic and smelling of quick-drying paint. Through the wall I heard Kuang swish back the curtain, put his jacket on a hanger and hang it up. There was the sudden chug-chug of the water pipe as he filled the wash-basin. The man was still behind me, hanging on as if waiting for something. I put my finger to my eye and then pointed towards Kuang's room; the man nodded. 'I'll have the car ready by twenty-two hundred hours. Ostend isn't far from here.'

'Good,' I said. I hoped he would go but he stayed there. 'We used to live in Ostend,' he said. 'My wife would like to go back there. There was life there. The country is too quiet for her.' He fiddled with the broken bolt on the door. It had been painted over but not repaired. He held the pieces together, then let them swing apart.

I stared out of the window; it faced south-west, the way we had come. The rain continued and there were puddles in the roadway and the fields were muddy and windswept. Sudden gusts had knocked over the pots of flowers under the crucifix and the water running down the gutters was bright red with the soil it had carried from somewhere out of sight.

'I couldn't let the boy bring you,' the man said. 'I'm conducting you. I couldn't let someone else do that, not even family.' He rubbed his face hard as if he hoped to stimulate his thought. 'The other was less important to the success of the job. This part is vital.' He looked out of the window. 'We needed this rain,' he said, anxious to have my agreement.

'You did right,' I said.

He nodded obsequiously, as if I'd given him a ten-pound tip, then smiled and backed towards the door. 'I know I did,' he said.

34

My case officer arrived about 11 a.m.; there were cooking smells. A large black Humber pulled into the courtyard and stopped. Byrd got out. 'Wait,' he said to the driver. Byrd was wearing a short Harris tweed overcoat and a matching cap. His boots were muddy and his trouser-bottoms tucked up to avoid being soiled. He clumped up-stairs to my room, dismissing the Fleming with only a grunt.

'You're my case officer?'

'That's the ticket.' He took off his cap and put it on the bed. His hair stood up in a point. He lit his pipe. 'Damned good to see you,' he said. His eyes were bright and his mouth firm, like a brush salesman sizing up a prospect.

'You've been making a fool of me,' I complained.

'Come, come, trim your yards, old boy. No question of that. No question of that at all. Thought you did well actually. Loiseau said you put in quite a plea for me.' He smiled again briefly, caught sight of himself in the mirror over the wash-basin and pushed his disarranged hair into place.

'I told him you didn't kill the girl, if that's what you mean.'

'Ah well,' he looked embarrassed. 'Damned nice of you.' He took the pipe from his mouth and searched around his teeth with his tongue. 'Damned nice, but to tell you the truth, old boy, I did.'

I must have looked surprised.

'Shocking business of course, but she'd opened us right up. Every damned one of us. They got to her.'

'With money?'

'No, not money; a man.' He put the pipe in to the ashtray. 'She was vulnerable to men. Jean-Paul had her eating out of his hand. That's why they aren't suited to this sort of work, bless them. Men were deceivers ever, eh? Gels get themselves involved, what? Still, who are we to complain about that, wouldn't want them any other way myself.'

I didn't speak, so Byrd went on.

'At first the whole plan was to frame Kuang as some sort of oriental Jack-the-Ripper. To give us a chance to hold him, talk to him, sentence him if necessary. But the plans changed. Plans often do, that's what gives us so much trouble, eh?'

'Jean-Paul won't give you any more trouble; he's dead.'

'So I hear.'

'Did you arrange that too?' I asked.

'Come, come, don't be bitter. Still, I know just how you feel. I muffed it, I'll admit. I intended it to be quick and clean and painless, but it's too late now to be sentimental or bitter.'

'Bitter,' I said. 'If you really killed the girl, how come you got out of prison?'

'Set-up job. French police. Gave me a chance to disappear, talk to the Belgians. Very co-operative. So they should be, with this damned boat these Chinese chappies have got anchored three miles out. Can't touch them legally, you see. Pirate radio station; think what it could do if the balloon went up. Doesn't bear thinking of.'

'No. I see. What will happen?'

'Government level now, old chap. Out of the hands of blokes like you and me.'

He went to the window and stared across the mud and cabbage stumps. White mist was rolling across the flat ground like a gas attack.

'Look at that light,' said Byrd. 'Look at it. It's positively ethereal and yet you could pick it up and rap it. Doesn't it make you ache to pick up a paint brush?'

'No,' I said.

'Well it does me. First of all a painter is interested in form, that's all they talk about at first. But everything is the light falling on it—no light and there's no form, as I'm always saying; light's the only thing a painter should worry about. All the great painters knew that; Francesca, El Greco, Van Gogh.' He stopped looking at the mist and turned back towards me glowing with pleasure. 'Or Turner. Turner most of all, take Turner any day ... ' He stopped talking but he didn't stop looking at me. I asked him no question but he heard it just the same. 'Painting is my life,' he said. 'I'd do anything just to have enough money to go on painting. It consumes me. Perhaps you wouldn't understand what art can do to a person.'

'I think I'm just beginning to,' I said.

Byrd stared me out. 'Glad to hear it, old boy.' He took a brown envelope out of his case and put it on the table.

'You want me to take Kuang up to the ship?'

'Yes, stick to the plan. Kuang is here and we'd like him out on the boat. Datt will try to get on the boat, we'd like him here, but that's less important. Get Kuang to Ostend. Rendezvous with his case chappie—Major Chan—hand him over.'

'And the girl, Maria?'

'Datt's daughter—illegitimate—divided loyalties. Obsessed about these films of her and Jean-Paul. Do anything to get them back. Datt will use that factor, mark my words. He'll use her to transport the rest of his stuff.' He ripped open the brown envelope.

'And you'll try to stop her?'

'Not me, old boy. Not my part of the ship those dossiers, not yours either. Kuang to Ostend, forget everything else.

Kuang out to the ship, then we'll give you a spot of leave'. He counted out some Belgian money and gave me a Belgian press card, an identity card, a letter of credit and two phone numbers to ring in case of trouble. 'Sign here,' he said. I signed the receipts.

'Loiseau's pigeon, those dossiers,' he said. 'Leave all that to him. Good fellow, Loiseau.'

Byrd kept moving like a flyweight in the first round. He picked up the receipts, blew on them and waved them to dry the ink.

'You used me, Byrd,' I said. 'You sent Hudson to me, complete with prefabricated hard-luck story. You didn't care about blowing a hole in me as long as the overall plan was okay.'

'London decided,' Byrd corrected me gently.

'All eight million of 'em?'

'Our department heads,' he said patiently. 'I personally opposed it.'

'All over the world people are personally opposing things they think are bad, but they do them anyway because a corporate decision can take the blame.'

Byrd had half turned towards the window to see the mist.

I said, 'The Nuremberg trials were held to decide that whether you work for Coco-Cola, Murder Inc. or the Wehrmacht General Staff, you remain responsible for your own actions.'

'I must have missed that part of the Nuremberg trials,' said Byrd unconcernedly. He put the receipts away in his wallet, picked up his hat and pipe and walked past me towards the door.

'Well let me jog your memory,' I said as he came level and I grabbed at his chest and tapped him gently with my right. It didn't hurt him but it spoiled his dignity and he backed away from me, smoothing his coat and pulling at the knot of his tie which had disappeared under his shirt collar.

Byrd had killed, perhaps many times. It leaves a blemish in the eyeballs and Byrd had it. He passed his right hand round the back of his collar. I expected a throwing knife or a cheesewire to come out, but he was merely straightening his shirt.

'You were too cynical,' said Byrd. 'I should have expected you to crack.' He stared at me. 'Cynics are disappointed romantics; they keep looking for someone to admire and can never find anyone. You'll grow out of it.'

'I don't want to grow out of it,' I said.

Byrd smiled grimly. He explored the skin where my hand had struck him. When he spoke it was through his fingers. 'Nor did any of us,' he said. He nodded and left.

35

I found it difficult to get to sleep after Byrd had gone and yet I was too comfortable to make a move. I listened to the articulated trucks speeding through the village: a crunch of changing gears as they reached the corner, a hiss of brakes at the crossroads, and an ascending note as they saw the road clear and accelerated. Lastly, there was the splash as they hit the puddle near the 'Drive carefully because of our children' sign. Every few minutes another came down the highway, a sinister alien force that never stopped and seemed not friendly towards the inhabitants. I looked at my watch. Five thirty. The hotel was still but the rain hit the window lightly. The wind seemed to have dropped but the fine rain continued relentlessly, like a long-distance runner just getting his second breath. I stayed awake for a long time thinking about them all. Suddenly I heard a soft footstep in the corridor. There was a pause and then I saw the door knob revolve silently. 'Are you asleep?' Kuang called softly. I wondered if my conversation with Byrd had awakened him, the walls were so thin. He came in.

'I would like a cigarette. I can't sleep. I have been downstairs but no one is about. There is no machine either.' I gave him a pack of Players. He opened it and lit one. He seemed in no hurry to go. 'I can't sleep,' he said. He sat down in the plastic-covered easy chair and watched the rain on the window. Across the shiny landscape nothing moved. We sat silent a long time, then I said, 'How did you first meet Datt?'

He seemed glad to talk. 'Vietnam, 1954. Vietnam was a

mess in those days. The French *colons* were still there but they'd begun to realize the inevitability of losing. No matter how much practice they get the French are not good at losing. You British are skilled at losing. In India you showed that you knew a thing or two about the realities of compromise that the French will never learn. They knew they were going and they got more and more vicious, more and more demented. They were determined to leave nothing; not a hospital blanket nor a kind word.

'By the early 'fifties Vietnam was China's Spain. The issues were clear, and for us party members it was an honour to go there. It meant that the party thought highly of us. I had grown up in Paris. I speak perfect French. I could move about freely. I was working for an old man named de Bois. He was pure Vietnamese. Most party members had acquired Vietnamese names no matter what their origins, but de Bois couldn't bother with such niceties. That's the sort of man he was. A member since he was a child. Communist party adviser; purely political, nothing to do with the military. I was his secretary—it was something of an honour; he used me as a messenger boy. I'm a scientist, I haven't got the right sort of mind for soldiering, but it was an honour.

'Datt was living in a small town. I was told to contact him. We wanted to make contact with the Buddhists in that region. They were well organized and we were told at that time that they were sympathetic to us. Later the war became more defined (the Vietcong versus the Americans' puppets), but then the whole country was a mess of different factions, and we were trying to organize them. The only thing that they had in common was that they were anti-colonial—anti-French-colonial, that is: the French had done our work for us. Datt was a sort of soft-minded liberal, but he had influence with the Buddhists— he was something of a Buddhist scholar and they respected

214

him for his learning—and more important, as far as we were concerned, he wasn't a Catholic.

'So I took my bicycle and cycled sixty kilometres to see Datt, but in the town it was not good to be seen with a rifle, so two miles from the town where Datt was to be found I stopped in a small village. It was so small, that village, that it had no name. Isn't it extraordinary that a village can be so small as to be without a name? I stopped and deposited my rifle with one of the young men of the village. He was one of us: a Communist, in so far as a man who lives in a village without a name can be a Communist. His sister was with him. A short girl—her skin bronze, almost red—she smiled constantly and hid behind her brother, peering out from behind him to study my features. Han Chinese* faces were uncommon around there then. I gave him the rifle—an old one left over from the Japanese invasion; I never did fire a shot from it. They both waved as I cycled away.

'I found Datt.

'He gave me cheroots and brandy and a long lecture on the history of democratic government. Then we found that we used to live near each other in Paris and we talked about that for a while. I wanted him to come back and see de Bois. It had been a long journey for me, but I knew Datt had an old car and that meant that if I could get him to return with me I'd get a ride back too. Besides I was tired of arguing with him. I wanted to let old de Bois have a go, they were more evenly matched. My training had been scientific, I wasn't much good at the sort of arguing that Datt was offering me.

'He came. We put the cycle in the back of his old Packard and drove west. It was a clear moonlit night and

* A Chinese description to differentiate pure Chinese from various minority groups in China or even Vietnamese etc. Ninety-five per cent of China's population are Han Chinese.

soon we came to the village that was too small even to have a name.

' "I know this village," said Datt. "Sometimes I walk out as far as this. There are pheasants."

'I told him that walking this far from the town was dangerous. He smiled and said there could be no danger to a man of goodwill.

'I knew that something was wrong as soon as we stopped, for usually someone will run out and stare, if not smile. There was no sound. There was the usual smell of sour garbage and woodsmoke that all the villages have, but no sound. Even the stream was silent, and beyond the village the rice paddy shone in the moonlight like spilled milk. Not a dog, not a hen. Everyone had gone. There were only men from the Sûreté there. The rifle had been found; an informer, an enemy, the chief—who knows who found it. The smiling girl was there, dead, her nude body covered with the tiny burns that a lighted cigarette end can inflict. Two men beckoned Datt. He got out of the car. They didn't worry very much about me; they knocked me about with a pistol, but they kicked Datt. They kicked him and kicked him and kicked him. Then they rested and smoked Gauloises, and then they kicked him some more. They were both French, neither was more than twenty years old, and even then Datt wasn't young; but they kicked him mercilessly. He was screaming. I don't think they thought that either of us was Viet Minh. They'd waited for a few hours for someone to claim that rifle, and when we stopped near by they grabbed us. They didn't even want to know whether we'd come for the rifle. They kicked him and then they urinated over him and then they laughed and they lit more cigarettes and got in their Citroën car and drove away.

'I wasn't hurt much. I'd lived all my life with the wrong-coloured skin. I knew a few things about how to be

216

kicked without getting hurt, but Datt hadn't. I got him back in the car—he'd lost a lot of blood and he was a heavy man, even then he was heavy. "Which way do you want me to drive?" I said. There was a hospital back in the town and I would have taken him to it. Datt said, "Take me to Comrade de Bois." I'd said "comrade" all the time I'd spoken with Datt, but that was perhaps the first time Datt had used the word. A kick in the belly can show a man where his comrades are. Datt was badly hurt.'

'He seems to have recovered now,' I said, 'apart from the limp.'

'He's recovered now, apart from the limp,' said Kuang. 'And apart from the fact that he can have no relationships with women.'

Kuang examined me carefully and waited for me to answer.

'It explains a lot,' I said.

'Does it?' said Kuang mockingly.

'No,' I said. 'What right does he have to identify thuggery with capitalism?' Kuang didn't answer. The ash was long on his cigarette and he walked across the room to tap it into the wash-basin. I said, 'Why should he feel free to probe and pry into the lives of people and put the results at your disposal?'

'You fool,' said Kuang. He leaned against the wash-basin smiling at me. 'My grandfather was born in 1878. In that year thirteen million Chinese died in the famine. My second brother was born in 1928. In that year five million Chinese people died in the famine. We lost twenty million dead in the Sino-Japanese war and the Long March meant the Nationalists killed two and a half million. But we are well over seven hundred million and increasing at the rate of fourteen or fifteen million a year. We are not a country or a party, we are a whole civilization, unified and moving forward at a speed that has never

217

before been equalled in world history. Compare our industrial growth rate with India's. We are unstoppable.' I waited for him to go on, but he didn't.

'So what?' I said.

'So we don't need to set up clinics to study your foolishness and frailty. We are not interested in your minor psychological failings. Datt's amusing pastime is of no interest to my people.'

'Then why did you encourage him?'

'We have done no such thing. He financed the whole business himself. We have never aided him, or ordered him, nor have we taken from him any of his records. It doesn't interest us. He has been a good friend to us but no European can be very close to our problems.'

'You just used him to make trouble for us.'

'That I will admit. We didn't stop him making trouble. Why should we? Perhaps we have used him rather heartlessly, but a revolution must use everyone so.' He returned my pack of cigarettes.

'Keep the pack,' I said.

'You are very kind,' he said. 'There are ten left in it.'

'They won't go far among seven hundred million of you,' I said.

'That's true,' he said, and lit another.

36

I was awakened at nine thirty. It was *la patronne*. 'There is time for a bath and a meal,' she said. 'My husband prefers to leave early, sometimes the policeman calls in for a drink. It would be best if you were not here then.'

I suppose she noticed me look towards the other room. 'Your colleague is awake,' she said. 'The bathroom is at the end of the corridor. I have put soap there and there is plenty of hot water at this time of night.'

'Thanks,' I said. She went out without answering.

We ate most of the meal in silence. There was a plate of smoked ham, trout *meunière* and an open tart filled with rice pudding. The Fleming sat across the table and munched bread and drank a glass of wine to keep us company through the meal.

'I'm conducting tonight.'

'Good,' I said. Kuang nodded.

'You've no objection?' he asked me. He didn't want to show Kuang that I was senior man, so he put it as though it was a choice between friends.

'It will suit me,' I said. 'Me too,' said Kuang.

'I've got a couple of scarves for you, and two heavy woollen sweaters. We are meeting his case officer right on the quayside. You are probably going out by boat.'

'Not me,' I said. 'I'll be coming straight back.'

'No,' said the man. 'Operations were quite clear about that.' He rubbed his face in order to remember more clearly. 'You will come under his case officer, Major Chan, just as he takes orders from me at this moment.'

Kuang stared impassively. The man said, 'I suppose

they'll need you if they run into a coastguard or fisheries protection vessel or something unexpected. It's just for territorial waters. You'll soon know if their case officer tries something.'

'That sounds like going into a refrigerator to check that the light goes out,' I said.

'They must have worked something out,' said the man. 'London must … ' He stopped and rubbed his face again.

'It's okay,' I said. 'He knows we are London.'

'London seemed to think it's okay.'

'That's really put my mind at rest,' I said.

The man chuckled. 'Yes,' he said, 'yes,' and rubbed his face until his eye watered. 'I suppose I'm blown now,' he said.

'I'm afraid so,' I agreed. 'This will be the last job you'll do for us.'

He nodded. 'I'll miss the money,' he said sadly. 'Just when we could most do with it too.'

37

Maria kept thinking about Jean-Paul's death. It had thrown her off balance, and now she had to think lop-sidedly, like a man carrying a heavy suitcase; she had to compensate constantly for the distress in her head.

'What a terrible waste,' she said loudly.

Ever since she was a little girl Maria had had the habit of speaking to herself. Many times she had been embarrassed by someone coming close to her and hearing her babbling on about her trivial troubles and wishes. Her mother had never minded. It doesn't matter, she had said, if you speak to yourself, it's what you say that matters. She tried to stand back and see herself in the present dilemma. Ridiculous, she pronounced, all her life had been something of a pantomime but driving a loaded ambulance across northern France was more than she could have bargained for even in her most imaginative moments. An ambulance loaded with eight hundred dossiers and sex films; it made her want to laugh, almost. Almost.

The road curved and she felt the wheels start to slide and corrected for it, but one of the boxes tumbled and brought another box down with it. She reached behind her and steadied the pile of tins. The metal boxes that were stacked along the neatly made bed jangled gently together, but none of them fell. She enjoyed driving, but there was no fun in thrashing this heavy old blood-wagon over the ill-kept back roads of northern France. She must avoid the main roads; she knew—almost instinctively— which ones would be patrolled. She knew the way the road patrols would obey Loiseau's order to intercept Datt,

Datt's dossiers, tapes and films, Maria, Kuang or the Englishman, or any permutation of those that they might come across. Her fingers groped along the dashboard for the third time. She switched on the wipers, cursed, switched them off, touched the choke and then the lighter. Somewhere there must be a switch that would extinguish that damned orange light that was reflecting the piled-up cases, boxes and tins in her windscreen. It was dangerous to drive with that reflection in the screen but she didn't want to stop. She could spare the time easily but she didn't want to stop. Didn't want to stop until she had completed the whole business. Then she could stop, then she could rest, then perhaps she could be reunited with Loiseau again. She shook her head. She wasn't at all sure she wanted to be reunited with Loiseau again. It was all very well thinking of him now in the abstract like this. Thinking of him surrounded by dirty dishes and with holes in his socks, thinking of him sad and lonely. But if she faced the grim truth he wasn't sad or lonely; he was self-contained, relentless and distressingly complacent about being alone. It was unnatural, but then so was being a policeman unnatural.

She remembered the first time she'd met Loiseau. A village in Périgord. She was wearing a terrible pink cotton dress that a friend had sold her. She went back there again years later. You hope that the ghost of him will accompany you there and that some witchcraft will reach out to him and he will come back to you and you will be madly in love, each with the other, as you were once before. But when you get there you are a stranger; the people, the waitress, the music, the dances, all of them are new and you are unremembered.

Heavy damned car; the suspension and steering were coarse like a lorry's. It had been ill treated, she imagined, the tyres were balding. When she entered the tiny villages the ambulance slid on the *pavé* stones. The villages were old and grey with just one or two brightly painted signs advertising beer or *friture*. In one village there were bright flashes of a welding torch as the village smith worked late into the night. Behind her, Maria heard the toot, toot, toot of a fast car. She pulled over to the right and a blue Land-Rover roared past, flashing its headlights and tooting imperious thanks. The blue rooftop light flashed spookily over the dark landscape, then disappeared. Maria slowed down; she hadn't expected any police patrols on this road and she was suddenly aware of the beating of her heart. She reached for a cigarette in the deep soft pockets of her suede coat, but as she brought the packet up to her face they spilled across her lap. She rescued one and put it in her mouth. She was going slowly now, and only half her attention was on the road. The lighter flared and trembled, and as she doused the flame, more flames grew across the horizon. There were six or seven of them, small flaring pots like something marking an unknown warrior's tomb. The surface of the road was black and shiny like a deep lake, and yet it couldn't be water, for it hadn't rained for a week. She fancied that the water would swallow the ambulance up if she didn't stop. But she didn't stop. Her front wheels splashed. She imagined the black water closing above her, and shivered. It made her feel claustrophobic. She lowered the window and recoiled at the overwhelming smell of *vin rouge*. Beyond the flares there were lamps flaring and a line of headlights. Farther still were men around a small building that had been built across the road. She thought at first that it was a customs control hut, but then she saw that it wasn't a building at all. It was a huge wine tanker tipped on to its side and askew across the road, the wine gushing from the split seams. The front part of the vehicle hung over the ditch. Lights flashed behind shattered glass as men tried to extricate the driver. She slowed up. A policeman beckoned her into the side of the road, nodding frantically.

'You made good time,' the policeman said. 'There's four dead and one injured. He's complaining, but I think he's only scratched.'

Another policeman hurried over. 'Back up against the car and we'll lift him in.'

At first Maria was going to drive off but she managed to calm down a little. She took a drag on the cigarette. 'There'll be another ambulance,' she said. She wanted to get that in before the real ambulance appeared.

'Why's that?' said the policeman. 'How many casualties did they say on the phone?'

'Six,' lied Maria.

'No,' said the policeman. 'Just one injured, four dead. The car driver injured, the four in the tanker died instantly. Two truck-drivers and two hitch-hikers.'

Alongside the road the policemen were placing shoes, a broken radio, maps, clothes and a canvas bag, all in an impeccably straight line.

Maria got out of the car. 'Let me see the hitch-hikers,' she said.

'Dead,' said the policeman. 'I know a dead 'un, believe me.'

'Let me see them,' said Maria. She looked up the dark road, fearful that the lights of an ambulance would appear.

The policeman walked over to a heap in the centre of the road. There from under a tarpaulin that police patrols carry especially for this purpose stuck four sets of feet. He lifted the edge of the tarpaulin. Maria stared down, ready to see the mangled remains of the Englishman and Kuang, but they were youths in beards and denim. One of them had a fixed grin across his face. She drew on the cigarette fiercely. 'I told you,' said the policeman. 'Dead.'

'I'll leave the injured man for the second ambulance,' said Maria.

'And have him ride with four stiffs? Not on your life,' said the policeman. 'You take him.' The red wine was still gurgling into the roadway and there was a sound of tearing metal as the hydraulic jacks tore the cab open to release the driver's body.

'Look,' said Maria desperately. 'It's my early shift. I can get away if I don't have to book a casualty in. The other ambulance won't mind.'

'You're a nice little darling,' said the policeman. 'You don't believe in work at all.'

'Please.' Maria fluttered her eyelids at him.

'No I wouldn't darling and that's a fact,' said the policeman. 'You are taking the injured one with you. The stiffs I won't insist upon and if you say there's another ambulance coming then I'll wait here. But not with the injured one I won't.' He handed her a little bundle. 'His personal effects. His passport's in there, don't lose it now.'

'No, I don't parle,' said a loud English voice. 'And let me down, I can toddle myself, thanks.'

The policeman who had tried to carry the boy released him and watched as he climbed carefully through the ambulance rear doors. The other policeman had entered the ambulance before him and cleared the tins off the bed. 'Full of junk,' said the policeman. He picked up a film tin and looked at it.

'It's hospital records,' said Maria. 'Patients transferred. Documents on film. I'm taking them to the other hospitals in the morning.'

The English tourist—a tall boy in a black woollen shirt and pink linen trousers—stretched full length on the bed. 'That's just the job,' he said appreciatively. The policeman locked the rear doors carefully. Maria heard him say, 'We'll leave the stiffs where they are. The other ambulance will find them. We'll get up to the road blocks. Everything is happening tonight. Accident, road blocks, contraband search and the next thing you know we'll be asked to do a couple of hours' extra duty.'

'Let the ambulance get away,' said the second policeman. 'We don't want her to report us leaving the scene before the second ambulance arrived.'

'That lazy bitch,' said the first policeman. He slammed his fist against the roof of the ambulance and called loudly, 'Right, off you go.'

Maria turned around in her seat and looked for the switch for the interior light. She found it and switched off the orange lamp. The policeman leered in through the window. 'Don't work too hard,' he said.

'Policeman,' said Maria. She said it as if it was a dirty word and the policeman flinched. He was surprised at the depth of her hatred.

He spoke softly and angrily, 'The trouble with you people from hospitals,' he said, 'you think you're the only normal people left alive.'

Maria could think of no answer. She drove forward. From behind her the voice of the Englishman said, 'I'm sorry to be causing you all this trouble.' He said it in English hoping that the tone of his voice would convey his meaning.

'It's all right,' said Maria.

'You speak English!' said the man. 'That's wonderful.'

'Is your leg hurting you?' She tried to make it as professional and clinical as she knew how.

'It's nothing. I did it running down the road to find a telephone. It's hilarious really: those four dead and me unscratched except for a strained knee running down the road.'

'Your car?'

'That's done for. Cheap car, Ford Anglia. Crankcase

sticking through the rear axle the last I saw of it. Done for. It wasn't the lorry driver's fault. Poor sod. It wasn't my fault either, except that I was going too fast. I always drive too fast, everyone tells me that. But I couldn't have avoided this lot. He was right in the centre of the road. You do that in a heavy truck on these high camber roads. I don't blame him. I hope he doesn't blame me too much either.'

Maria didn't answer; she hoped he'd go to sleep so she could think about this new situation.

'Can you close the window?' he asked. She rolled it up a little, but kept it a trifle open. The tension of her claustrophobia returned and she knocked the window handle with her elbow, hoping to open it a little more without the boy's noticing.

'You were a bit sharp with the policeman,' said the boy. Maria grunted an affirmative.

'Why?' asked the boy. 'Don't you like policemen?'

'I married one.'

'Go on,' said the boy. He thought about it. 'I never got married. I lived with a girl for a couple of years ... ' He stopped.

'What happened?' said Maria. She didn't care. Her worries were all upon the road ahead. How many road blocks were out tonight? How thoroughly would they examine papers and cargo?

'She chucked me,' said the boy.

'Chucked?'

'Rejected me. What about you?'

'I suppose mine chucked me,' said Maria.

'And you became an ambulance driver,' said the boy with the terrible simplicity of youth.

'Yes,' said Maria and laughed aloud.

'You all right?' asked the boy anxiously.

'I'm all right,' said Maria. 'But the nearest hospital

that's any good is across the border in Belgium. You lie back and groan and behave like an emergency when we get to the frontier. Understand?'

Maria deliberately drove eastward, cutting around the Forêt de St Michel through Watigny and Signy-le-Petit. She'd cross the border at Riezes.

'Suppose they are all closed down at the frontier?' asked the boy.

'Leave it with me,' said Maria. She cut back through a narrow lane, offering thanks that it hadn't begun to rain. In this part of the world the mud could be impassable after half an hour's rain.

'You certainly know your way around,' said the boy. 'Do you live near here?'

'My mother still does.'

'Not your father?'

'Yes, he does too,' said Maria. She laughed.

'Are you all right?' the boy asked again.

'You're the casualty,' said Maria. 'Lie down and sleep.'

'I'm sorry to be a bother,' said the boy.

Pardon me for breathing, thought Maria; the English were always apologizing.

38

Already the brief butterfly summer of the big hotels is almost gone. Some of the shutters are locked and the waiters are scanning the ads for winter resort jobs. The road snakes past the golf club and military hospital. Huge white dunes, shining in the moonlight like alabaster temples, lean against the grey Wehrmacht gun emplacements. Between the points of sand and the cubes of concrete nightjars swoop open-mouthed upon the moths and insects. The red glow of Ostend is nearer now and yellow trams rattle alongside the motor road and over the bridge by the Royal Yacht Club where white yachts—sails neatly rolled and tied—sleep bobbing on the grey water like seagulls.

'I'm sorry,' I said. 'I thought they would be earlier than this.'

'A policeman gets used to standing around,' Loiseau answered. He moved back across the cobbles and scrubby grass, stepping carefully over the rusty railway lines and around the shapeless debris and abandoned cables. When I was sure he was out of sight I walked back along the *quai*. Below me the sea made soft noises like a bathful of serpents, and the joints of four ancient fishing boats creaked. I walked over to Kuang. 'He's late,' I said. Kuang said nothing. Behind him, farther along the *quai*, a freighter was being loaded by a huge travelling crane. Light spilled across the waterfront from the spotlights on the cranes. Could their man have caught sight of Loiseau and been frightened away? It was fifteen minutes later than rendezvous. The standard control procedure was to wait only four minutes, then come back twenty-four hours later; but I hung on. Control procedures were invented by diligent men in clean shirts and warm offices. I stayed. Kuang seemed not to notice the passage of time — or more accurately perhaps he revelled in it. He stood patiently. He hadn't stamped his feet, breathed into his hands or smoked a cigarette. When I neared him he didn't raise a quizzical eyebrow, remark about the cold or even look at his watch. He stared across the water, glanced at me to be sure I was not about to speak again, and then resumed his pose.

'We'll give him ten more minutes,' I said. Kuang looked at me. I walked back down the quayside.

The yellow headlight turned off the main road a trifle too fast and there was a crunch as the edge of an offside wing touched one of the oil drums piled outside the Fina station. The lights kept coming, main beams. Kuang was illuminated as bright as a snowman and there was only a couple of foot of space between him and the wire fence around the sand heap. Kuang leapt across the path of the car. His coat flapped across the headlight, momentarily eclipsing its beam. There was a scream as the brakes slammed on and the engine stalled. Suddenly it was quiet. The sea splashed greedily against the jetty. Kuang was sucking his thumb as I got down from the oil drum. It was an ambulance that had so nearly run us down.

Out of the ambulance stepped Maria.

'What's going on?' I said.

'I'm Major Chan,' said Maria.

'You are?' Kuang said. He obviously didn't believe her.

'You're Major Chan, case officer for Kuang here?' I said.

'For the purposes that we are all interested in, I am,' she said.

'What sort of answer is that?' I asked.

'Whatever sort of answer it is,' said Maria, 'it's going to have to do.'

'Very well,' I said. 'He's all yours.'

'I won't go with her,' said Kuang. 'She tried to run me down. You saw her.'

'I know her well enough to know that she could have tried a lot harder,' I said.

'You didn't show that sort of confidence a couple of minutes ago,' Maria said. 'Scrambling out of the way when you thought I was going to run *you* down.'

'What's confidence?' I said. 'Smiling as you fall off a cliff to prove that you've jumped?'

'That's what it is,' said Maria and she leaned forward and gave me a tiny kiss, but I refused to be placated. 'Where's your contact?'

'This is it,' said Maria, playing for time. I grabbed her arm and clutched it tight. 'Don't play for time,' I told her. 'You said you're the case officer. So take Kuang and start to run him.' She looked at me blankly. I shook her.

'They should be here,' she said. 'A boat.' She pointed along the jetty. We stared into the darkness. A small boat moved into the pool of light cast by the loading freighter. It turned towards us.

'They will want to load the boxes from the ambulance.'

'Hold it,' I told her. 'Take your payment first.'

'How did you know?'

'It's obvious, isn't it?' I said. 'You bring Datt's dossiers as far as this, using your ingenuity, your knowledge of police methods and routes, and if the worst comes to the worst you use your influence with your ex-husband. For what? In return Datt will give you your own dossier and film, etc. Am I right?'

'Yes,' she said.

'Then let them worry about loading.' The motor boat

231

was closer now. It was a high-speed launch; four men in pea-jackets stood in the stern. They stared towards us but didn't wave or call. As the boat got to the stone steps, one man jumped ashore. He took the rope and made it fast to a jetty ring. 'The boxes,' I called to them. 'Your papers are here.'

'Load first,' said the sailor who had jumped ashore.

'Give me the boxes,' I said. The sailors looked at me and at Kuang. One of the men in the boat made a motion with his hand and the others took two tin boxes, adorned with red seals, from the bottom of the boat and passed them to the first man, who carried them up the steps to us.

'Help me with the boxes,' said Maria to the Chinese sailor.

I still had hold of her arm. 'Get back into the ambulance and lock the doors from inside,' I said.

'You said I should start ... '

I pushed her roughly towards the driver's door.

I didn't take my eyes off Maria but on the periphery of my vision to the right I could see a man edging along the side of the ambulance towards me. He kept one hand flat against the side of the vehicle, dabbing at the large scarlet cross as if testing to see if the paint was wet. I let him come to within arm's length and still without swivelling my head I flicked out my hand so that my fingertips lashed his face, causing him to blink and pull back. I leaned a few inches towards him while sweeping my hand back the way it had come, slapping him not very hard across the side of the cheek.

'Give over,' he shouted in English. 'What the hell are you on?'

'Get back in the ambulance,' Maria called to him. 'He's harmless,' she said. 'A motor accident on the road. That's how I got through the blocks so easily.'

'You said Ostend hospital,' said the boy.

'Stay out of this, sonny,' I said. 'You are in danger even if you keep your mouth shut. Open it and you're dead.'

'I'm the case officer,' she insisted.

'You are what?' I said. I smiled one of my reassuring smiles, but I see now that to Maria it must have seemed like mockery. 'You are a child, Maria, you've no idea of what this is all about. Get into the ambulance,' I told her. 'Your ex-husband is waiting down the jetty. If you have this cartload of documents with you when he arrests you things might go easier for you.'

'Did you hear him?' Maria said to the sailor and Kuang. 'Take the documents, and take me with you—he's betrayed us all to the police.' Her voice was quiet but the note of hysteria was only one modulation away.

The sailor remained impassive and Kuang didn't even look towards her.

'Did you hear him?' she said desperately. No one spoke. A rowboat was moving out around the far side of the Yacht Club. The flutter of dripping blades skidding upon the surface and the gasp of oars biting into the water was a lonely rhythm, like a woman's sobs, each followed by the sharp intake of breath.

I said, 'You don't know what it's all about. This man's job is to bring Kuang back to their ship. He's also instructed to take me. As well as that he'll try to take the documents. But he doesn't change plans because you shout news about Loiseau waiting to arrest you. In fact, that's a good reason for leaving right away because their big command is to stay out of trouble. This business doesn't work like that.'

I signalled Kuang to go down to the motor boat and the sailor steadied him on the slimy metal ladder. I punched Maria lightly on the arm. 'I'll knock you unconscious, Maria, if that's the way you insist I do it.' I smiled but I meant it.

'I can't face Loiseau. Not with that case I can't face him.' She opened the driver's door and got into the seat. She would rather face Datt than Loiseau. She shivered. The boy said, 'I feel I'm making a lot of trouble for you. I'm sorry.'

'Just don't say you're sorry once again,' I heard Maria say.

'Get,' I called to the sailor. 'The police will be here any moment. There's no time to load boxes.' He was at the foot of the ladder and I had my heavy shoes on. He shrugged and stepped into the boat. I untied the rope and someone started the motor. There was a bright flurry of water and the boat moved quickly, zigzagging through the water as the helmsman got the feel of the rudder.

At the end of the bridge there was a flashlight moving. I wondered if the whistles were going. I couldn't hear anything above the sound of the outboard motor. The flashlight was reflected suddenly in the driver's door of the ambulance. The boat lurched violently as we left the harbour and entered the open sea. I looked at the Chinese sailor at the helm. He didn't seem frightened, but then how would he look if he did? I looked back. The figures on the quay were tiny and indistinct. I looked at my watch: it was 2.10 a.m. The Incredible Count Szell had just killed another canary, they cost only three francs, four at the very most.

39

Three miles out from Ostend the water was still and a layer of mist hugged it; a bleak bottomless cauldron of broth cooling in the cold morning air. Out of the mist appeared M. Datt's ship. It was a scruffy vessel of about 10,000 tons, an old cargo boat, its rear derrick broken. One of the bridge wings had been mangled in some long-forgotten mishap and the grey hull, scabby and peeling, had long brown rusty stains dribbling from the hawse pipes down the anchor fleets. It had been at anchor a long time out here in the Straits of Dover. The most unusual feature of the ship was a mainmast about three times taller than usual and the words 'Radio Janine' newly painted in ten-foot-high white letters along the hull.

The engines were silent, the ship still, but the current sucked around the draught figures on the stem and the anchor chain groaned as the ship tugged like a bored child upon its mother's hand. There was no movement on deck, but I saw a flash of glass from the wheelhouse as we came close. Bolted to the hull-side there was an ugly metal accommodation ladder, rather like a fire-escape. At water level the steps ended in a wide platform complete with stanchion and guest warp to which we made fast. M. Datt waved us aboard.

As we went up the metal stairs Datt called to us, 'Where are they?' No one answered, no one even looked up at him. 'Where are the packets of documents—my work? Where is it?'

'There's just me,' I said.

'I told you ... ' Datt shouted to one of the sailors.

'It was not possible,' Kuang told him. 'The police were right behind us. We were lucky to get away.'

'The dossiers were the important thing,' said Datt. 'Didn't you even wait for the girl?' No one spoke. 'Well didn't you?'

'The police almost certainly got her,' Kuang said. 'It was a close thing.'

'And my documents?' said Datt.

'These things happen,' said Kuang, showing little or no concern.

'Poor Maria,' said Datt. 'My daughter.'

'You care only about your dossiers,' said Kuang calmly. 'You do not care for the girl.'

'I care for you all,' said Datt. 'I care even for the Englishman here. I care for you all.'

'You are a fool,' said Kuang.

'I will report this when we are in Peking.'

'How can you?' asked Kuang. 'You will tell them that you gave the documents to the girl and put my safety into her hands because you were not brave enough to perform your duties as conducting officer. You let the girl masquerade as Major Chan while you made a quick getaway, alone and unencumbered. You gave her access to the code greeting and I can only guess what other secrets, and then you have the effrontery to complain that your stupid researches are not delivered safely to you aboard the ship here.' Kuang smiled.

Datt turned away from us and walked forward. Inside, the ship was in better condition and well lit. There was the constant hum of the generators and from some far part of the ship came the sound of a metal door slamming. He kicked a vent and smacked a deck light which miraculously lit. A man leaned over the bridge wing and looked down on us, but Datt waved him back to work. He walked up the lower bridge ladder and I followed him, but Kuang remained at the foot of it. 'I am hungry,' Kuang said. 'I have heard enough. I'm going below to eat.'

'Very well,' said Datt without looking back. He opened the door of what had once been the captain's cabin and waved me to precede him. His cabin was warm and comfortable. The small bed was dented where someone had been lying. On the writing table there were a heap of papers, some envelopes, a tall pile of gramophone records and a vacuum flask. Datt opened a cupboard above the desk and reached down two cups. He poured hot coffee from the flask and then two brandies into tulip glasses. I put two heaps of sugar into my coffee and poured the brandy after it, then I downed the hot mixture and felt it doing wonders for my arteries.

Datt offered me his cigarettes. He said, 'A mistake. A silly mistake. Do you ever make silly mistakes?'

I said, 'It's one of my very few creative activities.' I waved away his cigarettes.

'Droll,' said Datt. 'I felt sure that Loiseau would not act against me. I had influence and a hold on his wife. I felt sure he wouldn't act against me.'

'Was that your sole reason for involving Maria?'

'To tell you the truth: yes.'

'Then I'm sorry you guessed wrong. It would have been better to have left Maria out of this.'

'My work was almost done. These things don't last for ever.' He brightened. 'But within a year we'll do the same operation again.'

I said, 'Another psychological investigation with hidden cameras and recorders, and available women for influential Western men? Another large house with all the trimmings in a fashionable part of Paris?'

Datt nodded, 'Or a fashionable part of Buenos Aires, or Tokyo, or Washington, or London.'

'I don't think you are a true Marxist at all,' I said. 'You

merely relish the downfall of the West. A Marxist at least comforts himself with the idea of the proletariat joining hands across national frontiers, but you Chinese Communists relish aggressive nationalism just at a time when the world was becoming mature enough to reject it.'

'I relish nothing. I just record,' said Datt. 'But it could be said that the things of Western Europe that you are most anxious to preserve are better served by supporting the real, uncompromising power of Chinese communism than by allowing the West to splinter into internecine warrior states. France, for example, is travelling very nicely down that path; what will she preserve in the West if her atom bombs are launched? We will conquer, we will preserve. Only we can create a truly world order based upon seven hundred million true believers.'

'That's really 1984,' I said. 'Your whole set-up is Orwellian.'

'Orwell,' said Datt, 'was a naive simpleton. A middle-class weakling terrified by the realities of social revolution. He was a man of little talent and would have remained unknown had the reactionary press not seen in him a powerful weapon of propaganda. They made him a *guru*, a pundit, a seer. But their efforts will rebound upon them, for Orwell in the long run will be the greatest ally the Communist movement ever had. He warned the bourgeoisie to watch for militancy, organization, fanaticism and thought-planning, while all the time the seeds of their destruction are being sown by their own inadequacy, apathy, aimless violence and trivial titillation. Their destruction is in good hands: their own. The rebuilding will be ours. My own writings will be the basis of our control of Europe and America. Our control will rest upon the satisfaction of their own basest appetites. Eventually a new sort of European man will evolve.'

'History,' I said. 'That's always the alibi.'

238

'Progress is only possible if we learn from history.'

'Don't believe it. Progress is man's indifference to the lessons of history.'

'You are cynical as well as ignorant,' said Datt as though making a discovery. 'Get to know yourself, that's my advice. Get to know yourself.'

'I know enough awful people already,' I said.

'You feel sorry for the people who came to my clinic. That's because you really feel sorry for yourself. But these people do not deserve your sympathy. Rationalization is their destruction. Rationalization is the aspirin of mental health and, as with aspirin, an overdose can be fatal.

'They enslave themselves by dipping deeper and deeper into the tube of taboos. And yet each stage of their journey is described as greater freedom.' He laughed grimly. 'Permissiveness is slavery. But so has history always been. Your jaded, overfed section of the world is comparable to the ancient city states of the Middle East. Outside the gates the hard nomads waited their chance to plunder the rich, decadent city-dwellers. And in their turn the nomads would conquer, settle into the newly-conquered city and grow soft, and new hard eyes watched from the barren stony desert until their time was ripe. So the hard, strong, ambitious, idealistic peoples of China see the over-ripe condition of Europe and the U.S.A. They sniff the air and upon it floats the aroma of garbage cans overfilled, idle hands and warped minds seeking diversions bizarre and perverted, they smell violence, stemming not from hunger, but from boredom, they smell the corruption of government and the acrid flash of fascism. They sniff, my friend: you!'

I said nothing, and waited while Datt sipped at his coffee and brandy. He looked up, 'Take off your coat.'

'I'm not staying.'

'Not staying?' He chuckled. 'Where are you going?'

'Back to Ostend,' I said. 'And you are going with me.'

'More violence?' He raised his hands in mock surrender.

I shook my head. 'You know you've got to go back,' I said. 'Or are you going to leave all your dossiers back there on the quayside less than four miles away?'

'You'll give them to me?'

'I'm promising nothing,' I told him, 'but I know that you have to go back there. There is no alternative.' I poured myself more coffee and gestured to him with the pot. 'Yes,' he said absent-mindedly. 'More.'

'You are not the sort of man that leaves a part of himself behind. I know you, Monsieur Datt. You could bear to have your documents on the way to China and yourself in the hands of Loiseau, but the converse you cannot bear.'

'You expect me to go back there and give myself up to Loiseau?'

'I know you will,' I said. 'Or live the rest of your life regretting it. You will recall all your work and records and you will relive this moment a million times. Of course you must return with me. Loiseau is a human being and human activities are your speciality. You have friends in high places, it will be hard to convict you of any crime on the statute book ... '

'That is very little protection in France.'

'Ostend is in Belgium,' I said. 'Belgium doesn't recognize Peking, Loiseau operates there only on sufferance. Loiseau too will be amenable to any debating skill you can muster. Loiseau fears a political scandal that would involve taking a man forcibly from a foreign country ... '

'You are glib. Too glib,' said Datt. 'The risk remains too great.'

'Just as you wish,' I said. I drank the rest of my coffee and turned away from him.

'I'd be a fool to go back for the documents. Loiseau
240

can't touch me here.' He walked across to the barometer and tapped it. 'It's going up.' I said nothing.

He said, 'It was my idea to make my control centre a pirate radio boat. We are not open to inspection nor even under the jurisdiction of any government in the world. We are, in effect, a nation unto ourselves on this boat, just as all the other pirate radio ships are.'

'That's right,' I said. 'You're safe here.' I stood up. 'I should have said nothing,' I said. 'It is not my concern. My job is done.' I buttoned my coat tight and blessed the man from Ostend for providing the thick extra sweater.

'You despise me?' said Datt. There was an angry note in his voice.

I stepped towards him and took his hand in mine. 'I don't,' I said anxiously. 'Your judgment is as valid as mine. Better, for only you are in a position to evaluate your work and your freedom.' I gripped his hand tight in a stereotyped gesture of reassurance.

He said, 'My work is of immense value. A breakthrough you might almost say. Some of the studies seemed to have … ' Now he was anxious to convince me of the importance of his work.

But I released his hand carefully. I nodded, smiled and turned away. 'I must go. I have brought Kuang here, my job is done. Perhaps one of your sailors would take me back to Ostend.'

Datt nodded. I turned away, tired of my game and wondering whether I really wanted to take this sick old man and deliver him to the mercies of the French Government. They say a man's resolution shows in the set of his shoulders. Perhaps Datt saw my indifference in mine. 'Wait,' he called. 'I will take you.'

'Good,' I said. 'It will give you time to think.'

Datt looked around the cabin feverishly. He wet his lips and smoothed his hair with the flat of his hand. He

241

flicked through a bundle of papers, stuffed two of them in his pocket, and gathered up a few possessions.

They were strange things that Datt took with him: an engraved paper-weight, a half-bottle of brandy, a cheap notebook and finally an old fountain pen which he inspected, wiped and carefully capped before pushing it into his waistcoat pocket. 'I'll take you back,' he said. 'Do you think Loiseau will let me just look through my stuff?'

'I can't answer for Loiseau,' I said. 'But I know he fought for months to get permission to raid your house on the Avenue Foch. He submitted report after report proving beyond all normal need that you were a threat to the security of France. Do you know what answer he got? They told him that you were an X., an *ancien X*. You were a Polytechnic man, one of the ruling class, the elite of France. You could *tutoyer* his Minister, call half the Cabinet *cher camarade*. You were a privileged person, inviolate and arrogant with him and his men. But he persisted, he showed them finally what you were, Monsieur Datt. And now perhaps he'll want them to pay their bill. I'd say Loiseau might see the advantage in letting a little of your poison into their bloodstream. He might decide to give them something to remember the next time they are about to obstruct him and lecture him, and ask him for the fiftieth time if he isn't mistaken. Permit you to retain the dossiers and tapes?' I smiled. 'He might well insist upon it.'

Datt nodded, cranked the handle of an ancient wall phone and spoke some rapid Chinese dialect into it. I noticed his large white fingers, like the roots of some plant that had never been exposed to sunlight.

He said, 'You are right, no doubt about it. I must be where my research is. I should never have parted company from it.'

He pottered about absent-mindedly. He picked up his

Monopoly board. 'You must reassure me on one thing,' he said. He put the board down again. 'The girl. You'll see that the girl's all right?'

'She'll be all right.'

'You'll attend to it? I've treated her badly.'

'Yes,' I said.

'I threatened her, you know. I threatened her about her file. About her pictures. I shouldn't have done that really but I cared for my work. It's not a crime, is it, caring about your work?'

'Depends upon the work.'

'Mind you,' said Datt, 'I have given her money. I gave her the car too.'

'It's easy to give away things you don't need,' I said. 'And rich people who give away money need to be quite sure they're not trying to buy something.'

'I've treated her badly.' He nodded to himself. 'And there's the boy, my grandson.'

I hurried down the iron steps. I wanted to get away from the boat before Kuang saw what was happening, and yet I doubt if Kuang would have stopped us; with Datt out of the way the only report going back would be Kuang's.

'You've done me a favour,' Datt pronounced as he started up the outboard motor.

'That's right,' I said.

40

The Englishman had told her to lock the ambulance door. She tried to, but as her finger hovered over the catch, the nausea of fear broke over her. She imagined just for a moment the agony of being imprisoned. She shuddered and pushed the thought aside. She tried again, but it was no use, and while she was still trying to push the lock the English boy with the injured knee leaned across her and locked the door. She wound the window down, urgently trying to still the claustrophobia. She leaned forward with her eyes closed and pressed her head against the cold windscreen. What had she done? It had seemed so right when Datt had put it to her: if she took the main bulk of the documents and tapes up to the rendezvous for him, then he would be waiting there with her own film and dossier. A fair exchange, he had said. She touched the locks of the case that had come from the boat. She supposed that her documents were inside, but suddenly she didn't care. Fine rain beaded the windscreen with little lenses. The motor boat was repeated a thousand times upside down.

'Are you all right?' the boy asked. 'You don't look well.'

She didn't answer.

'Look here,' he said, 'I wish you'd tell me what all this is about. I know I've given you a lot of trouble and all that, you see ... '

'Stay here in the car,' Maria said. 'Don't touch anything and don't let anyone else touch anything. Promise?'

'Very well. I promise.'

She unlocked the door with a sigh of relief and got out

into the cold salty air. The car was on the very brink of the waterside and she stepped carefully across the worn stones. Along the whole quayside men were appearing out of doorways and warehouse entrances. Not ordinary men but men in berets and anklets. They moved quietly and most of them were carrying automatic rifles. A group of them near to her stepped under the wharfside lights and she saw the glitter of the paratroop badges. Maria was frightened of the men. She stopped near the rear doors of the ambulance and looked back; the boy stared at her across the metal boxes and film tins. He smiled and nodded to reassure her that he wouldn't touch anything. Why did she care whether he touched anything? One man broke away from the group of paratroops near her. He was in civlian clothes, a thigh-length black leather coat and an old-fashioned trilby hat. He had taken only one step when she recognized Loiseau.

'Maria, is it you?'

'Yes, it's me.'

He hurried towards her, but when he was a pace away stopped. She had expected him to embrace her. She wanted to hang on to him and feel his hand slapping her awkwardly on the back, which was his inadequate attempt to staunch miseries of various kinds.

'There are a lot of people here,' she said. '*Bif?*'

'Yes, the army,' said Loiseau. 'A paratroop battalion. The Belgians gave me full co-operation.'

Maria resented that. It was his way of saying that she had never given him full co-operation. 'Just to take me into custody,' she said, 'a whole battalion of Belgian paratroops? You must have exaggerated.'

'There is a ship out there. There is no telling how many men are aboard. Datt might have decided to take the documents by force.'

He was anxious to justify himself, like a little boy seeking an advance on his pocket money. She smiled and repeated, 'You must have exaggerated.'

'I did,' said Loiseau. He did not smile, for distorting truth was nothing to be proud of. But in this case he was anxious that there should be no mistakes. He would rather look a fool for over-preparation than be found inadequate. They stood there staring at each other for several minutes.

'The documents are in the ambulance?' Loiseau asked.

'Yes,' she said. 'The film of me is there too.'

'What about the tape of the Englishman? The questioning that you translated when he was drugged?'

'That's there too, it's a green tin; number B fourteen.' She touched his arm. 'What will you do with the Englishman's tape?' She could not ask about her own.

'Destroy it,' said Loiseau. 'Nothing has come of it, and I've no reason to harm him.'

'And that's part of your agreement with him,' she accused.

Loiseau nodded.

'And my tape?'

'I will destroy that too.'

'Doesn't that go against your principles? Isn't destruction of evidence the cardinal sin for a policeman?'

'There is no rule book that can be consulted in these matters whatever the Church and the politicians and the lawyers tell us. Police forces, governments and armies are just groups of men. Each man must do as his conscience dictates. A man doesn't obey without question or he's not a man any more.'

Maria gripped his arm with both hands, and pretended just for a moment that she would never have to let go.

'Lieutenant,' Loiseau called along the wharf. One of the paratroops slammed to attention and doubled along the waterfront. 'I'll have to take you into custody,' Loiseau said quietly to Maria.

'My documents are on the front seat of the ambulance,' she told him hurriedly before the lieutenant reached them.

'Lieutenant,' Loiseau said, 'I want you to take the boxes out of the ambulance and bring them along to the shed. By the way, you had better take an inventory of the tins and boxes; mark them with chalk. Keep an armed guard on the whole operation. There might be an attempt to recover them.'

The lieutenant saluted Loiseau warmly and gave Maria a passing glance of curiosity.

'Come along, Maria,' said Loiseau. He turned and walked towards the shed.

Maria patted her hair and followed him.

*   *   *

It was a wooden hut that had been put up for the duration of World War Two. A long, badly-lit corridor ran the whole length of the hut, and the rest was divided into four small, uncomfortable offices. Maria repaired her make-up for the third time. She decided to do one eye at a time and get them really right.

'How much longer?' she asked. Her voice was distorted as she held her face taut to paint the line over her right eye.

'Another hour,' said Loiseau. There was a knock at the door and the paratroop lieutenant came in. He looked briefly at Maria and then saluted Loiseau.

'We're having a little trouble, sir, getting the boxes out of the ambulance.'

'Trouble?' said Loiseau.

'There's some madman with an injured leg. He's roaring and raging and punching the soldiers who are trying to unload the vehicle.'

'Can't you deal with it?'

'Of course I can deal with it,' said the paratroop officer. Loiseau detected a note of irritation in his voice. 'It's just that I don't know who the little squirt is.'

'I picked him up on the road,' said Maria. 'He was injured in a road crash. I told him to look after the documents when I got out of the car. I didn't mean ... he's nothing to do with ... he's just a casualty.'

'Just a casualty,' Loiseau repeated to the lieutenant. The lieutenant smiled. 'Get him along to the hospital,' said Loiseau.

'The hospital,' repeated Maria. 'Everything in its proper place.'

'Very good sir,' said the lieutenant. He saluted with an extra display of energy to show that he disregarded the sarcasm of the woman. He gave the woman a disapproving look as he turned about and left.

'You have another convert,' said Maria. She chuckled as she surveyed her painted eye, twisting her face slightly so that the unpainted eye was not visible in the mirror. She tilted her head high to keep her chin line. She heard the soldiers piling the boxes in the corridor. 'I'm hungry,' she said after a while.

'I can send out,' said Loiseau. 'The soldiers have a lorry full of coffee and sausage and some awful fried things.'

'Coffee and sausage.'

'Go and get two sweet coffees and some sausage sandwiches,' Loiseau said to the young sentry.

'The corporal has gone for his coffee,' said the soldier.

'That's all right,' said Loiseau. 'I'll look after the boxes.'

'He'll look after the boxes,' Maria said flatly to the mirror.

The soldier looked at her, but Loiseau nodded and the soldier turned to get the coffee. 'You can leave your gun with me,' Loiseau said. 'You'll not be able to carry the coffee with that slung round your neck and I don't want guns left lying around in the corridor.'

'I'll manage the coffee and the gun,' said the soldier. He said it defiantly, then he slung the strap of the gun around his neck to prove it was possible. 'You're a good soldier,' said Loiseau.

'It won't take a moment,' said the soldier.

Loiseau swung around in the swivel chair, drummed his fingers on the rickety desk and then swivelled back the other way. He leaned close to the window. The condensation was heavy on it and he wiped a peephole clear so that he could see the waterfront. He had promised the Englishman that he would wait. He wished he hadn't: it spoiled his schedule and also it gave this awkward time of hanging about here with Maria. He couldn't have her held in the local police station, obviously she had to wait here with him; it was unavoidable, and yet it was a bad situation. He had been in no position to argue with the Englishman. The Englishman had offered him all the documents as well as the Red Chinese conducting officer. What's more, he had said that if Loiseau would wait here he would bring Datt off the ship and deliver him to the quayside. Loiseau snorted. There was no good reason for Datt to leave the pirate radio ship. He was safe out there beyond the three-mile limit and he knew it. All the other pirate radio ships were out there and safe. Datt had only to tune in to the other ships to confirm it.

'Have you got a cold?' Maria asked him, still inspecting her painted eye.

'No.'

'It sounds like it. Your nose is stuffed up. You know that's always the first sign with those colds you get. It's having the bedroom window open, I've told you about that hundreds of times.'

'And I wish you'd stop telling me.'

'Just as you like.' She scrubbed around in the tin of eye

black and spat into it. She had smudged the left eye and now she wiped it clean so that she looked curiously lop-sided: one eye dramatically painted and the other white and naked. 'I'm sorry,' she said. 'Really sorry.'

'It will be all right,' said Loiseau. 'Somehow I will find a way.'

'I love you,' she said.

'Perhaps.' His face was grey and his eyes deep sunk the way they always were when he had missed a lot of sleep.

They had occupied the same place in her mind, Loiseau and her father, but now she suddenly saw Loiseau as he really was. He was no superman, he was middle-aged and fallible and unrelaxingly hard upon himself. Maria put the eye-black tin down and walked across to the window near Loiseau.

'I love you,' she said again.

'I know you do,' said Loiseau. 'And I am a lucky man.'

'Please help me,' said Maria, and Loiseau was amazed, for he could never have imagined her asking for help, and Maria was amazed, for she could not imagine herself asking for help.

Loiseau put his nose close to the window. It was hard to see through it because of the reflections and condensation. Again he rubbed a clear place to look through.

'I will help you,' said Loiseau.

She cleared her own little portion of glass and peered along the waterfront. 'He's a damn long time with that coffee,' said Loiseau.

'There's the Englishman,' said Maria, 'and Datt.'

'Well I'm damned,' said Loiseau. 'He's brought him.'

Datt's voice echoed down the corridor as the hut door swung open. 'This is it,' he said excitedly. 'All my documents. Colour seals denote year, index letters code names.' He tapped the boxes proudly. 'Where is Loiseau?' he asked the Englishman as he walked slowly down the rank

250

of stacked tins and boxes, stroking them as he read the code letters.

'The second door,' said the Englishman, easing his way past the boxes.

Maria knew exactly what she had to do. Jean-Paul said she'd never made one real decision in her life. It was not hysteria, nor heightened emotion. Her father stood in the doorway, tins of documents in his arms, nursing them as though they were a newly-born child. He smiled the smile she remembered from her childhood. His body was poised like that of a tightrope walker about to step off the platform. This time his powers of persuasion and manipulation were about to be tried to the utmost, but she had no doubt that he would succeed. Not even Loiseau was proof against the smooth cool method of Datt, her puppet-master. She knew Datt's mind and could predict the weapons he would use: he would use the fact that he was her father and the grandfather of Loiseau's child. He would use the hold he had over so many important people. He would use everything he had and he would win.

Datt smiled and extended a hand. 'Chief Inspector Loiseau,' he said. 'I think I can be of immeasurable help to you—and to France.'

She had her handbag open now. No one looked at her.

Loiseau motioned towards a chair. The Englishman moved aside and glanced quickly around the room. Her hand was around the butt by now, the safety catch slid down noiselessly. She let go of the handbag and it sat upon the gun like a tea cosy.

'The ship's position,' said Datt, 'is clearly marked upon this chart. It seemed my duty to pretend to help them.'

'Just a moment,' said Loiseau wearily.

The Englishman saw what was happening. He punched towards the handbag. And then Datt realized, just as the pistol went off. She pulled the trigger again as fast as she

could. Loiseau grabbed her by the neck and the Englishman punched her arm. She dropped the bag. Datt was
through the door and fumbling with the lock to prevent
them chasing him. He couldn't operate the lock and ran
down the corridor. There was the sound of the outer door
opening. Maria wrenched herself free and ran after Datt,
the gun still in her hand. Everyone was shouting. Behind
her she heard Loiseau call, 'Lieutenant, stop that man.'

The soldier with the tray of coffee may have heard
Loiseau's shout or he may have seen Maria or the
Englishman brandishing a pistol. Whatever it was that
prompted him, he threw the tray of coffee aside. He
swung the rifle around his neck like a hula-hoop. The
stock slammed into his hand and a burst of fire echoed
across the waterfront almost simultaneously with the
sound of the coffee cups smashing. From all over the
waterfront shots were fired; Maria's bullets must have
made very little difference.

*   *   *

You can recognize a head shot by a high-velocity weapon;
a cloud of blood particles appeared like vapour in the air
above him as Datt and his armful of tapes, film and papers
was punched off the waterfront like a golf ball.

'There,' called Loiseau. The high-power lamps operated
by the soldiers probed the spreading tangle of recording
tapes and films that covered the water like a Sargasso Sea.
A great bubble of air rose to the surface and a cluster of
pornographic photos slid apart and drifted away. Datt
was in there amongst it and for a moment it looked as
though he was still alive as he turned in the water very
slowly and laboriously, his stiff arm clawing out through
the air like a swimmer doing the crawl. For a moment it
seemed as if he stared at us. The tapes caught in his
252

fingers and the soldiers flinched. 'He's turning over, that's all,' said Loiseau. 'Men float face down, women face up. Get the hook under his collar. He's not a ghost man, just a corpse, a criminal corpse.'

A soldier tried to reach him with a fixed bayonet, but the lieutenant stopped him. 'They'll say we did it, if the body is full of bayonet wounds. They'll say we tortured him.' Loiseau turned to me and passed me a small reel of tape in a tin. 'This is yours,' he said. 'Your confession, I believe, although I haven't played it.'

'Thanks,' I said.

'That was the agreement,' said Loiseau.

'Yes,' I said, 'that was the agreement.'

Datt's body floated deeper now, even more entangled in the endless tape and film.

Maria had hidden the gun, or perhaps she'd thrown it away. Loiseau didn't look at her. He was concerned with the body of Datt—too concerned with it, in fact, to be convincing.

I said, 'Is that your ambulance, Maria?' She nodded; Loiseau was listening but he didn't turn round.

'That's a silly place to leave it. It's a terrible obstruction; you'll have to move.' I turned to the Belgian para officer. 'Let her move it,' I said.

Loiseau nodded.

'How far?' said the officer. He had a mind like Loiseau's. Perhaps Loiseau read my thoughts. He grinned.

'It's all right,' said Loiseau. 'The woman can go.' The lieutenant was relieved to get a direct order. 'Yes sir,' he said and saluted Loiseau gravely. He walked towards the ambulance.

Maria touched Loiseau's arm. 'I'll go to my mother's. I'll go to the boy,' she said. He nodded. Her face looked strange, for only one eye was made up. She smiled and followed the officer.

'Why did you do that?' Loiseau asked.

'I couldn't risk you doing it,' I said. 'You'd never forgive yourself.'

It was light now. The sea had taken on a dawn-fresh sparkle and the birds began to think about food. Along the shore herring gulls probed for tiny shellfish left by the tide. They carried them high above the dunes and dropped them upon the concrete blockhouses. Some fell to safety in the sand, some hit the ancient gun emplacements and cracked open, some fell on to the concrete but did not crack; these last were retrieved by the herring gulls and then dropped again and again. The tops of the blockhouses were covered in tiny fragments of shell, for eventually each shell cracked. Very high, one bird flew purposefully and alone on a course as straight as a light beam. Farther along the shore, in and out of the dunes, a hedgehog wandered, aimlessly sniffing and scratching at the colourless grass and watching the gulls at their game. The hedgehog would fly higher and stronger than any of the birds, if only he knew how.